MW00477144

SHELTER FOR ELIZABETH

BADGE OF HONOR, BOOK 5

SUSAN STOKER

CHAPTER 1

BETH WATCHED with a mixture of disbelief, horror, and fascination when the flames hissed and spit as they climbed higher and higher out of the pan on her stove. As soon as the oil caught fire she'd thrown water on it, but of course, that had only made it worse. She'd called nine-one-one, as she was taught when she was five years old, but instead of getting out of the apartment, as the operator ordered, all Beth could do was back out of the kitchen and watch as the fire spread.

The truth was, she wouldn't have been able to go outside even if the entire apartment was on fire. Her body wanted to do it, but her brain held her captive. Being agoraphobic was a pain in the ass most days, but especially right this second. Even thinking about going out of the apartment caused a panic attack, which usually took at least a day to get over and feel normal again.

She hadn't always been afraid, but being kidnapped

and tortured had thrown everything she'd ever known for a loop. She'd been to therapy—was still *in* therapy, albeit remotely—but one of the only things that helped was simply avoiding unknown situations altogether.

Beth heard the frantic knocking on the door, but couldn't make herself walk the ten or so feet to open it. She couldn't even get enough air in her lungs to call out to the firefighters who were desperately trying to get inside.

Eventually the door was thrust open with the help of a battering ram, a three-foot-long piece of steel about five inches in diameter with a blunt front end, and three firefighters, dressed from head to toe in their fire-retardant uniforms, burst in. Without sparing a glance at her, the one with the large fire extinguisher rushed into her small kitchen and let loose a burst of dry chemicals on the flames.

Beth watched as they crackled but eventually sputtered and died when the chemicals did their job.

The entire experience was fascinating.

Beth supposed she should've been freaking out— hell, she was afraid of just about everything these days —but there was something mesmerizing about the fire that had fascinated her. From the way the flames had so quickly gathered strength and gotten out of control to how they'd immediately died away with one spurt from the extinguisher. It was as if they could be commanded to rise or fall at the whim of humans.

Beth was brought out of her semi-trance by a man standing in front of her. He was looking at her expectantly. She'd obviously missed whatever it was that he'd said.

"I'm sorry, what?"

"I asked if you were all right? Were you burned?"

Beth shook her head. "No, I'm okay."

"Come on, let's clear out of here and get you some fresh air. The medics will be here any second, they can check you out." He reached out his hand as if to take her elbow and lead her out of the apartment.

Before the man was finished speaking, Beth was shaking her head. "No, I'm fine. I don't need anything." Her words weren't as forceful as she'd have liked them to be, since she finished with a hacking cough as the smoke in the air drifted over to their corner of the room.

"You don't sound fine. What was your name again?"

Beth knew she hadn't given it to the firefighter in the first place, but she told him what he wanted to know anyway. "It's Beth, and seriously, I'm okay. I'm not going outside."

The man had the nerve to reach out and grab her biceps and start pulling her toward her front door as he informed her, "You can sign the 'Against Medical Advice' form outside once you're checked out."

The thought of stepping foot outside her safe apartment, where there were probably hordes of people standing around gawking at the fire engines and the ambulance, was more than Beth could handle. She felt her heartbeat speed up and the dizziness that usually accompanied it flooded her. She wrenched her

3

arm out of the man's hold and quickly backed away from him.

She saw him talking to her again, but couldn't hear his words...only the frantic beating of her heart. Sweat broke out on her forehead and she swayed. Beth knew if she didn't sit down, she was going to fall down. And if she passed out, they would surely take her outside and she'd be completely vulnerable.

"Here, sit."

The words barely made it through her consciousness, but she obeyed them without thinking. She felt the cushion of her couch give under her and a gentle hand landed on the back of her neck and pushed her head between her knees.

"Deep breaths...that's it. Relax. You're okay, just sit here and get your bearings."

Beth did as the deep voice asked, and concentrated on taking huge gulps of air into her lungs. As she got control over the panic attack, she heard the two men talking about her.

"...dumbass. Didn't you see she was panicking? You can't force people to do what you want. You should know better."

"I was trying to get her to the medics."

"I get that, but you have to be more aware of the headspace of your victim."

Beth raised her head. The hell with that. She might be afraid to step outside of her apartment, but she'd be damned if she'd be labeled a victim ever again. She'd had enough of that to last her a lifetime. She tried to shrug away from the hand at her neck, but was only partially successful. The man only moved it to her shoulder as she sat up.

"You have a bit of color back…do you still feel dizzy? Do you want some water?" he asked in a calm voice, the ire that had filled it when he'd spoken to the other firefighter now absent.

Beth croaked out, "Yes, please."

The man who had first approached her walked off, she supposed to find her something to drink, but the second man stayed by her side.

"You really should get checked out."

Beth knew he was right, but also knew it wasn't going to happen. When she'd first been diagnosed, she promised herself she wasn't going to be embarrassed about it. What happened to her three years ago wasn't *her* fault; she wasn't going to take that on as well as everything else. "I can't…at least not without losing it. I'm agoraphobic. Please don't force me to go outside."

She watched as the firefighter thought about what she said. She expected him to ask what agoraphobia was or to dismiss her words, but her opinion of him climbed a notch when he merely nodded. He'd removed his helmet and was crouching on the floor at her feet. He was wearing the typical yellow and black turnout gear that most firefighters wore. He was perspiring a bit, but the short strands of his dark hair sticking to his forehead were anything but a turnoff. His gray eyes were fixed on her, assessing but, amazingly, not judging.

5

"Okay. We can work around it, I think. Would it be all right if the medic came inside to look at you? You sound okay, you're not coughing, and once we open up the windows and the front door, the rest of this smoke should dissipate quickly. If you're given the all clear, you'll have to sign the AMA form."

Beth almost cried. She hadn't met anyone recently, other than the people in her therapy group, who'd been as understanding as this man. She almost sobbed the words in relief. "Yes, they can come inside."

"Great. I'll just go and get them."

The words popped out before Beth could call them back. "Will you come back with them?"

The firefighter had stood up, but he paused and looked down at her. "If you want me to."

"Please."

"Then I'll be right back. Hang tight. Stay there, your color might be better but you're still too pale for my liking."

Beth watched as the man headed out of her apartment with long, confident strides and she took a deep breath. She wished she'd asked the man what his name was, but he'd promised to come back. She'd ask him in a bit. There was just something about him that made her feel...safe. From his strong, square jawline and the scruff on his face, to the fact that he seemed to be a couple inches taller than her five-eight. Beth imagined that he was probably very strong under the turnout gear he was wearing. It made her want to bury herself against his chest and have him put his arms around her and hold on tight and keep her safe from the world.

Leaning down and resting her forehead on her knees, she tried to get herself together. She couldn't rely on anyone to help her...she had to help herself. She could get through this. She could. One minute at a time. As long as no one made her leave her apartment, she was golden.

* * *

Cade "Sledge" Turner, so named because he'd once taken a sledgehammer and beaten his way inside a mangled car at a wreck when it was obvious they only had seconds before it burst into flames, watched as the medics looked over Beth. She seemed to be okay, other than being nervous. He felt bad for her. Apparently, she'd been trying out a new recipe for fried chicken, but had put too much oil in the pan with the heat too high, and the entire thing had gone up in flames.

He knew about agoraphobia. His sister had a good friend in her therapy group who had it. They'd had a long conversation one night about what it might be like to be afraid to go outside. Cade couldn't imagine it. He loved camping, fishing, sports...generally anything that had to do with the great outdoors. To be trapped inside was akin to being stuck in a horror movie for him.

Cade worked with some great firefighters, but the

man who'd almost forced Beth to go outside was one of the newer guys at the station. He'd transferred from somewhere up north. He'd made some minor mistakes in the past, enough to make Cade wary of the man, but this one was almost unforgivable. Thinking about the angst he could've caused Beth, when all it would've taken was a few questions to find out why she was resistant to seeing a medic, made Cade see red. He'd definitely be talking to their captain about him the first chance he had.

When Beth had asked hesitantly if Cade would mind coming back in while the medic looked her over, something in her voice struck a chord. He wasn't a ladies' man, never had been. He'd had girlfriends, even a few serious ones, but at thirty-four, had never found the right partner.

But this woman…there was something about her, and it wasn't just that she was feeling vulnerable at the moment. He'd treated hundreds of female patients throughout his career. He'd seen single mothers with kids, hot college girls, even women fifteen years older than him—all who had been in similar situations as Beth—but not one had ever made him feel the way he did right now. A lightning bolt hadn't come down from the heavens and struck, letting him know the woman was "his," but he *was* attracted to her.

Cade knew in his bones he had what many considered to be a character flaw. He enjoyed being a knight in shining armor. It probably wasn't healthy and so far hadn't been good for a long-term relationship, but it was a part of who he was. There was just something that made him feel complete when he had someone to look after. He'd been called overprotective more than once in the past, but Cade knew he wasn't going to change anytime soon.

But he had a feeling trying to get to know Beth better would be a waste of time. No matter how much he had the urge to fight her demons for her, they were just too different. He loved being outdoors, she couldn't handle it. He worked long hours, and the last thing he wanted to do was come home and hole up inside on his time off. He wondered if she even had friends. How could she have friends if she never left her house?

"Oh my God! Beth? Are you all right?"

Cade turned to the door in surprise and saw Penelope, his sister and fellow firefighter, burst into the room. Beth looked up.

"Hey, Pen. Yeah, I managed to screw up my mom's recipe big time and almost burned the place down." Her voice was laced with humor and self-depreciation.

Penelope gave Beth a huge hug and sat next to her, holding her hand. "I was at home and heard your address come across the scanner and about had a heart attack! I got here as fast as I could. I was hoping the call wasn't about you, but then I heard your apartment number on the scanner and that you were refusing to go outside."

Beth cocked her head and gestured sheepishly with her free hand. "It's me."

"Well shit, woman. If you wanted some fried chicken, you should've just called me! I would've brought some over."

They both laughed and Cade cleared his throat, trying to get Penelope's attention. It worked.

"Oh, Beth, this is Cade...otherwise known as Sledge. We not only work at Station 7 together, but he has the lucky job of being my brother as well."

"We met earlier, but I didn't catch his name." Beth smiled shyly at him. "I knew Pen had a brother, but I didn't know you guys worked together too."

Cade noted absently that she seemed calmer somehow. He wasn't sure if it was the fact that she wasn't going to have to go outside or that Penelope was now with her. Whatever it was, he liked it. Her eyes were sparkling with humor and intelligence and the smile she aimed at him lit up her face. He liked this non-timid version of her.

"It's nice to officially meet you, Beth. I didn't know you were the 'Beth' Penelope is always talking about either...all good things, of course."

"Suuuure." Beth laughed. She looked at her friend. "Just remember, Pen, I know as many secrets about you as you do about me."

Penelope threw her head back and laughed uproariously. "I seriously doubt that, my friend. Cade, Beth is the smartest person I know. She might only be twenty-five, but I swear she knows more about computers, Internet, and code than anyone I've ever met. I bet if you put Garcia from *Criminal Minds* and her in a room together, Beth would wipe the floor with her."

"You do know that Penelope Garcia is a made-up TV character, don't you?" Beth intoned before Cade could respond, as if she'd told her friend the same thing a thousand times before.

Penelope chuckled and shook her head, answering her friend as if her brother wasn't in the room. "I know but the shit you do is *real*." Her voice dropped. "I've lived it, and you know it."

Beth put her arm around Penelope's shoulders and hugged her. "I know. I wish I'd known you before you went overseas. I would've done whatever I needed to in order to help. Those asshats wouldn't have had a chance."

Cade watched his sister and Beth in fascination. Since Penelope had gotten back from overseas, she'd seemed withdrawn and less like the bubbly, never-let-anything-get-her-down sister he knew. It frustrated the hell out of him because there was absolutely nothing he could do about it but be there for his sister, no matter what she needed. Being kidnapped by the terrorist group ISIS had definitely changed Penelope's personality, and Cade was thrilled to see a glimpse of the old Penelope he knew and loved.

"I know," Penelope sighed, "and I appreciate it. It's enough that you get my pizza order moved to the top of the line nowadays."

The two women shared a laugh again before they were interrupted by the medic. He held out a clipboard with a piece of paper on it. "I hate to interrupt, but we've got to get going. I still do highly recommend you being checked out by your doctor. Since you've told us you don't want to be transported, please sign this form saying that you won't hold the ambulance company responsible for any repercussions of not being taken to the hospital."

Beth reached out, took the clipboard and balanced it on her knees, without letting go of Penelope's hand. She signed the form and handed it back to the medic. "Thanks. I appreciate your help. I promise if I start feeling bad, I'll get in touch with my doctor."

The man left and Penelope turned to Beth. "If you need to go, just call me. You know I'll go with you."

"I know you will, and I appreciate it."

"You're okay for now? You don't need anything? You been to the store lately?"

Cade was riveted by the back and forth between his sister and Beth. There used to be a time when Penelope told him everything going on in her life. While she'd mentioned her friend with agoraphobia, she'd never said anything about visiting her, or otherwise helping her in any way.

"There's this thing called the Internet, Pen...you might have heard of it?"

Penelope laughed. "Okay, but I know it's hard to get fresh fruit and stuff on Amazon. I know you've done the delivery thing a few times from the grocery store, but most of the fruit was on the verge of going bad. Just call me and we'll go one night when I get off shift."

"I appreciate it. Thanks."

"No problem."

Penelope stood up after hugging her friend, and headed for the door. "Come on, bro, get the lead out...I think it's your turn to make lunch."

Cade hesitated before following his sister. He looked at Beth. She was still standing by her couch. She was looking uneasy and nervous again, and he hated that. This was a woman who he could easily see laughing and smiling. Who *should* be laughing and smiling. He'd gotten a glimpse of it with her interaction with Penelope—and he liked what he'd seen.

He took a step toward her, unconsciously wanting to be closer. "You're sure you're all right? Can I do anything for you?"

Beth studied him for a moment, then glanced over to her kitchen and gestured toward it with her head. "Is there an easy way to clean that up?"

Glad she hadn't immediately blown him off, Cade smiled. "Well, you can probably do an Internet search and get your answer before I can fully explain it, but generally you'll want to vacuum up as much of the powder as you can. Make sure you clean the metal surfaces first—those chemicals can be corrosive."

"Do I need special things to clean it with?"

Cade shrugged. "Probably, if you want to do it right."

Her shoulders slumped just a bit, but she recovered quickly. "Okay, I'll see what I can find online and I'll order whatever I need. Thanks."

"I can come back later, help repair your door, and bring you some special stuff we've got at the station…if you want." Cade hadn't known he was going to offer until the words had left his mouth. But he wasn't sorry.

Beth fidgeted and bit her lip. Finally, she agreed shyly. "Okay, if you're sure. I'd appreciate it. It'll take a few days for the stuff I need to get here if I order it. But only if you don't mind."

"I don't mind." Cade wasn't sure why he was so pleased. He'd pretty much talked himself out of even thinking about Beth as someone he should be interested in before his sister came into the room. Now here he was, inviting himself over and feeling happy she'd accepted. He mentally shrugged. Oh well, if nothing else he was doing his sister's friend a favor. It was the humane thing to do.

"Then thank you. Whenever you get here is fine."

"I'm off around nine, is that too late?"

"No. I don't sleep much and get most of my work done at night anyway, so that's perfect."

Not commenting on her not sleeping well, but for some reason wanting to, Cade agreed. "Great. I can see if Penelope can come too, if you'd feel more comfortable."

"No," Beth refused immediately. "She doesn't like going out at night. But if you're Pen's brother, then you get a free pass on the trust front."

Cade had forgotten that about his sister. Penelope always put on a brave face, but she'd told him once that because of everything that had happened to her in the

Middle East, she'd started sleeping with a light on. He should've put two and two together, but hadn't.

He smiled. "Okay, I'll see you later then."

"Bye."

Cade shut the door behind him and jogged to the fire truck and his friends, who were waiting for him. For the first time in a long time, something other than work was heavy on his mind.

After taking his turn making lunch, he would get online and research agoraphobia. If he was going to spend time with Beth, he didn't want to do or say anything that would make her feel uncomfortable.

CHAPTER 2

"TELL ME ABOUT BETH," Cade ordered his sister as they settled in the breakroom after lunch. The other crew members had scattered across the fire station. Crash and Squirrel were throwing a football out in front of the station. Chief and Taco were working out in the weight room, and Driftwood and Moose were in the kitchen getting dinner prepped and arguing about who was a better cook.

He couldn't help but be fascinated by his sister's friend. He'd heard about her, but when he'd looked into her frightened eyes he'd been struck by how pretty she was. It wasn't as if Pen would wax poetic about her friend's looks, but he'd been surprised all the same. She was fairly tall, only a few inches shorter than he was. He liked that. He also liked her long hair. It was probably hard, if not impossible, for her to get to a salon, but he was grateful she hadn't cut it. The long brown strands hung down her chest, hiding the curves of her breasts while at the same time highlighting them. Her big brown eyes looked at him as if they held deep dark secrets, and only made Cade want to slay all her dragons for her.

Her nose had a slight bump in the middle, as if it'd been broken at some point. She'd worn small hoops in her pierced ears and her lips were full and lush. She'd bitten her lip when she'd talked to him and he imagined taking it between his own lips and caressing away any small hurt she gave herself. She had straight white teeth and a tendency to shift nervously in front of him as she spoke to him.

All in all, she was a mixture of bravado and vulnerability, and totally his type.

Penelope looked at her brother with sad eyes. "She's amazing. I have no idea how she's been able to cope with everything she's gone through and still be as sweet and as put-together as she is. Before I started helping her, she was living through the Internet. By that I mean, everything she ate, wore, or needed to live, she got through ordering it online."

There was a lot there that Cade wanted more information about, but he concentrated on the thing that was bothering him the most. "Everything she went through?"

His sister's voice softened. "Yeah. What happened to me was tough...but what *she* experienced made my three months in captivity look like a walk in the park."

Cade ran his hand over his short brown hair in agitation. He knew he didn't want to hear it, but he also *needed* to hear it. "She was raped." It wasn't a question.

"Yeah. And choked. And burned with cigarettes. And stabbed."

"Jesus."

Penelope went on as if Cade hadn't spoken. "She was kidnapped by a serial killer out in California a few years ago. She was minding her own business, going back to her car after shopping at Walmart. He nabbed her and brought her to a cabin in the woods."

"What did he want?"

"Besides the obvious? From what she told our therapy group, strangely enough, he didn't care about *her*, per se. He just needed a warm body. He was torturing *another* woman who he'd already snatched away from her workplace. He didn't even really look at Beth while he was hurting her...he was watching this other woman, telling her that everything he was doing to Beth, he was going to do to her next."

Cade couldn't sit anymore. He got to his feet and paced in front of Penelope, trying to control the anger and frustration that were coursing through his veins. "She got away, obviously. How?"

Penelope shrugged. "Beth said the boyfriend of the other woman and his SEAL team arrived and killed the guy."

"Good. And the agoraphobia?"

"Cade, this really isn't my story to tell," Penelope protested, a bit too late. "I know I've already told you too much."

He'd been expecting that, but was pleasantly surprised at how much Penelope *had* shared before she'd balked, and didn't give her too much shit. "Just one more question, and I'll stop. You go over and help her? How?"

Penelope was silent for a moment, obviously thinking through what she wanted to say. Finally, she told him, "She's scared to be outside, but she doesn't have a typical case of agoraphobia...I don't think. I admit I don't know a whole lot about it; just what she's shared with me and the group. I don't know how she was before we met, but she *can* go places and do stuff, at least now, but she has to be with someone she trusts. She just can't do it on her own. I go with her. We go to the grocery store, the mall, things like that. *Never* Walmart, that's a big trigger for her. She has to have physical contact with me while we're out. But she *can* do it. She acts like it's no big deal...but it's obvious it's tough for her."

"The hand-holding," Cade said in understanding.

"Yeah. She was self-conscious at first, but I don't give a shit, and I told her so. I think she's embarrassed about holding hands but she was taken so randomly before. She figures if it happened to her once, completely out of the blue, it could happen again, even if statistically it's practically impossible."

"So there's safety in numbers."

Penelope nodded. "Something like that, I think."

Cade sat back down next to his sister and angled his body on the couch so he was facing her. He didn't want to pry into Beth's background too much; for some reason, he wanted her to open up and talk to him herself. He was interested. Way interested. It was too much too soon, but the little voice inside wouldn't let him blow off the strong woman he'd met that day.

At the moment, however, Cade had something else to address before the others interrupted them. "So... how are *you* holding up?"

"I'm good." Penelope's answer was immediate—and expected. Except Cade didn't believe it for a second.

"The lights?"

Penelope swore under her breath. "I guess if I'm telling *her* secrets, it's only fair if mine come up too, huh?"

"I told her I'd come over tonight and help her clean up the mess we made. I asked if she'd rather have you come with me to make her feel more comfortable, and she said you preferred not to go out at night."

"It's fine, Cade. I'm handling it."

"Handling what?" Moose asked as he strode into the room.

"Nothing," Penelope insisted quickly, not looking at either of the men. She got up and headed into the kitchen.

"What'd I miss?" the other firefighter asked.

Cade shook his head and shrugged.

"If there's anything I can do for your sister, you'd tell me, right? I worry about her."

Cade looked at Tucker "Moose" Jacobs. He knew a lot of guys worried about their friends dating their sister, but Cade didn't give a shit about that. He'd love it if Penelope fell in love with one of the guys at the station. He knew his close circle of friends as if they'd grown up together, trusted them all, and they were all absolutely stand-up men. He could see her with someone like Taco or Driftwood, because they were as intense as she was and loved their job almost as much as Penelope did.

But now that he thought about it...Moose was perfect for his sister. He was a big man, almost a foot taller than Penelope, and he watched over her on calls almost as much as Cade did. He thought there might be something between them, but he wasn't going to play matchmaker. Moose was on his own.

"I think we all just have to be patient with her. She's doing great at dealing with what happened to her, but it's going to take time."

"You'd tell me though? If there's anything she needs?"

"I'd tell you."

"Thanks. I...she means a lot to me."

Cade opened his mouth to say something, but the tones of dispatch rang loudly through the room and both men were moving before the dispatcher started reading off the address of the person needing assistance. All thoughts of Beth and Penelope dealing with the shit life had thrown their way were sidelined as the men headed to the locker room to put on their bunker gear and head out to the fire truck.

* * *

"Hey, Mom, I wanted to call and let you know that I screwed up your fried chicken recipe big time today."

"What happened?" Mary Parkins asked in a tone that never failed to soothe Beth. She missed her mom so much.

"I think I let the oil sit on the burner too long."

"Ouch. Let me guess...you saw flames?"

Beth shivered, remembering how fascinating the fire had been as it exploded upward, looking for something to feed it.

"Yeah, that's an understatement. I had to call the fire department."

"Bethy...and did you have an...episode?"

"No, Mom. Luckily they arrived quickly and put it out so I didn't have to leave the apartment."

"I worry about you."

"I know. And I appreciate it. But I'm working on it. I like my therapy group, and it's great that they let me telecommute via computer. Oh! And one of the firefighters was Penelope from my group."

"The Army Princess?"

Beth rolled her eyes in solidarity for her friend. Penelope hated that nickname and it didn't fit the woman Beth had come to know at all. She might look like a princess...she was tiny and beautiful with her blonde hair and thin stature, but now that Beth knew her personally, she was about as far from a princess as a woman could get. "Yeah, Penelope is awesome. Remember that interview she gave Barbara Walters— where she *didn't* cry? She's tough as nails...even Barbara couldn't break her." They both laughed, and Beth continued. "She's strong, but she's hiding a lot of pain."

"Takes one to know one, doesn't it, honey?"

Beth bit her lip. "Yeah, Mom. It does. Are you guys going to be able to come out and visit anytime soon?" Beth wished all the time that she was able to function more normally, especially when it came to her family. She would've loved to have hopped on a plane to visit her parents or her brother, but instead she had to rely on *them* to take the time off and fit it into their schedules to come see her.

"Unfortunately, your father just started a new project. They wanted him to be the foreman in charge on the site."

Beth knew her dad loved construction. He'd started off as a teenager working for a friend, and had worked his way up to being in charge of a team of men that numbered into the hundreds. She was extremely proud of him. "That's great! I know he's thrilled. And it's okay. I understand. Give him my love."

"You know I will."

"Now, walk me through the fried chicken steps again. I'm determined to win this time."

Beth spent the next thirty minutes talking with her mom and relaxing from her stressful day.

Hours later, she paced her small living room, all

relaxed from her conversation with her mom gone. It was ten o'clock and she was expecting Penelope's brother to knock on her door at any moment. Why in the hell she'd agreed to have him come back and help her clean up, she didn't know.

Well, she did…a moment of weakness.

Penelope was her best friend, her only friend here in San Antonio, and she trusted her without reservation. The only reason she'd been able to have a somewhat normal life was because of Pen. Beth had made it to one group therapy session in person, incorrectly thinking that once she'd arrived, she'd be fine. Epic fail on that. She'd completely flipped out when she was supposed to leave and, at the advice of the psychologist who led the group sessions, Penelope had taken hold of her hand until she'd felt stronger.

After hearing that Penelope was nervous to head to her car in the dark alone, Beth felt better about her panic attack. It probably wasn't very charitable of her, but it made her feel not quite so alone in her moments of freak-out. If someone as strong as Penelope had phobias, then maybe Beth wasn't as much of an oddity as she felt.

Pen had been the one to suggest that she attend the therapy sessions remotely, and after only a few months, Beth was feeling better. She still couldn't venture out of her apartment by herself without breaking down, but she could make it through a trip to the store as long as Penelope was with her.

Maybe her trust in Cade—she couldn't see herself

ever calling him Sledge; the name was ridiculous—was just because he was related to Penelope. Maybe it was because he was the best-looking man she'd seen in a long time. He had brown hair much like hers, which fell a bit long over his brow, and light gray eyes. When she'd seen him earlier he'd had a five o'clock shadow, which looked good on him. He was taller than she was, and built. She'd always been attracted to muscular men, and Cade certainly fit that bill.

Maybe it was because he was the first man she'd been attracted to since...it happened. Hell, maybe it was the uniform. Whatever it was, allowing him to come over and help her clean up her kitchen seemed like the right decision earlier today, but now Beth was second-guessing herself.

Penelope was bound to tell her brother about her, what had happened, and that was beyond embarrassing. After learning about her background, Cade would probably show up out of pity rather than anything else. And there was nothing she liked less than people pitying her.

The knock on the door startled Beth to the point she could feel her heartrate speed up and start to get out of control. She took a deep, fortifying breath and forced herself to walk to the door and peer out the small security hole.

She saw Cade standing at her doorstep, smiling. As she watched, he held up two large bottles of what looked like cleaning fluid. Beth took another deep, calming breath and unlocked the two deadbolts, the chain, the lock on the knob itself, and opened the door. Luckily the battering ram had mostly just popped the main lock and hadn't destroyed the door itself.

"Hey."

"Hey back."

"Come in." Beth stood back from the door to give Cade room to enter. He strode into her little apartment as if it was the hundredth time he'd been there instead of only the second. She shut the door behind him and made sure to re-latch the locks before turning to him. Cade had stopped about four feet from her and was seemingly waiting for her to give him a signal as to where he should go or what he should do. She appreciated the courtesy. Her apartment was her sanctuary, and it would've made her feel uncomfortable if he'd just walked in and made himself at home.

It wasn't the most expensive apartment complex in San Antonio, but it wasn't a shithole either. It was three stories high; Beth lived on the first floor, and her neighbors, for the most part, kept to themselves. There was an older single man who lived on her floor who she sometimes saw when she was going shopping with Pen, but otherwise she didn't really get a glimpse of many of the people who lived around and above her.

"I've found some old towels we can use. I also already vacuumed up as much of the powder as I could," Beth told Cade in what she hoped was a normal-sounding voice.

"Sounds good. Let's go see the damage. I don't think

it should take long, as the fire wasn't that large and we got it under control quickly."

Beth led the way to the kitchen and winced anew at the mess. Most of the powder was gone, but the smell of chemicals remained and it was obvious every surface needed to be scrubbed.

"Do you have a bucket or container we can use? I need to dilute this degreasing cleanser."

Beth nodded and reached under the sink for the bucket she used when she mopped. She wasn't the cleanest housekeeper around, but many times when she couldn't sleep, she'd end up cleaning instead.

She watched as Cade poured some of the degreasing liquid into the bucket and then ran some tap water in to dilute it. His biceps bulged as he hefted the now-heavy container to the counter. Beth handed him a cloth and they got to work wiping down the surfaces covered in chemicals and the stovetop. The plates and bowls went into the dishwasher and the pan that had started the fiery mess in the first place ended up in the trash. They didn't speak while they cleaned, but it wasn't an uneasy silence.

After they'd degreased the kitchen, Cade emptied the bucket and started over with some of the liquid from the other bottle he'd brought, again diluting it with water. They spent the next forty minutes or so sanitizing the room with the new mixture.

Beth found working with Cade was relaxing and easy. He didn't talk much, but she didn't feel awkward either. It was as if they'd worked side by side their entire adult lives and not just for the last hour and a half.

Finally, Cade arched his back and groaned. "I think we've got it all. To be on the safe side, I wouldn't put food on any of these surfaces for a while. Not until you've cleaned them a few times."

"Sounds like the smart thing to do. I appreciate you helping me out."

"You're welcome. I'm sorry it happened in the first place. You were lucky. You have to be really careful when you're cooking with oil. I've been to way too many fires that started in the kitchen where people lost everything."

"Yeah, I talked to my mom today and she walked me through her recipe again. I'm sure I'll be better at it next time. I was kinda surprised at how quickly it flared up, that's for sure."

"For an oil fire, never throw water on it—put a lid on the pan and take it off the heat if you can. Do you have a fire extinguisher?"

"No."

"I'll make sure you get one. It's important."

"I understand that *now*. If I had one, I could've saved you guys a trip. But I can order one online. It's not a big deal."

"No way, I'll get you a top-of-the-line one. Even if you have an extinguisher, don't ever be afraid to call nine-one-one. It's always better to be safe than sorry."

"Yeah." Beth looked down at her watch. It was eleven-thirty. "It's getting late. I'm sure you're tired."

Cade shrugged.

Beth didn't know what that meant. He wasn't tired? He wanted to stay? Why would he want to stay…with her? It wasn't as if this was a date or anything, and besides, she'd flat-out told him about her phobia. Why was he still there?

Suddenly she got it. "Pen told you what happened to me, didn't she? You don't have to feel sorry for me. I'm fine."

Cade leaned against her counter and crossed his arms over his chest. His stance should've made her nervous, but the only thing it did was make her stomach do flip-flops. He wasn't wearing a uniform, only a simple navy-blue T-shirt and a pair of jeans, but the way his muscles flexed made her womanly bits— which she'd thought were long dead and buried—stand up and take notice.

"She told me some, but that's not why I'm here." His voice was even and modulated and he didn't look irritated or otherwise put out by her question. "Usually when I'm interested in a woman, I try to find out as much as possible about her. My sister knows you, I love and trust her, so therefore she was the perfect person to ask."

"What'd she say? That I'm fragile? Did she tell you that she has to hold my hand like I'm a three-year-old for me to be able to step foot outside this damn apartment? Did she tell you what I look like when I have a panic attack?"

Beth didn't notice Cade moving until he was right

in front of her. She gasped as he brushed her hair behind her and then put his hands on her shoulders and leaned close.

"No. She told me how fucking proud she is of you. She told me that you were one of the strongest women she knew." His words lost some of their bite as he continued. "She told me how your bravery inspired her to continue to fight her own demons."

Beth looked up at Cade in shock. "She said that?"

Cade nodded. "She didn't use the words, but I know my sister. Trust me when I tell you that she would never speak badly of you. And please let this sink in. You might think you're using her to help you get stuff done outside this apartment, but believe me, she's using you just as much. Helping you makes *her* feel useful...important. The two of you might have had different experiences while you were held against your will, but ultimately I'm guessing you find trusting people just as tough as she does. And the fact that you allow her to help you is huge for her. Understand?"

Cade's words made Beth's heart swell in her chest, but she still pushed. "I wasn't kidding when I said I couldn't go outside by myself."

"I know."

"So why are you still here?"

Cade straightened but didn't move away from her. "Because I want to be. Because I saw something I liked this afternoon, and when I want something, I go after it."

"You just met me. You don't know anything about me."

"And that's why I'm here. I want to *get* to know you."

"Does Pen know her brother is mentally unbalanced?"

Cade dropped his hands, threw his head back and laughed. When he had himself under control, he boldly reached out and grabbed Beth's hand. "Yeah, I think she has an idea. She's known me a very long time."

Beth didn't have a comeback for that as she was being towed into her living room behind Cade.

Ever since she'd realized that holding Penelope's hand and feeling skin-on-skin contact could keep her demons at bay, and make her feel not so alone when she was outside, holding hands had a whole new meaning to her. She was alarmed to realize that the feeling she had with Penelope was magnified tenfold with Cade. His hand was calloused and way bigger than her own. His palm engulfed hers, his heat seeped into her pores, and Beth swore she could feel her blood pressure lower as a result.

Cade sat on the couch and pulled her down next to him. Once they were sitting, he let go of her hand and leaned back, relaxing into her cushions as if he did it every day. "Now...tell me about you. If my sister is comparing you to Penelope Garcia, her very favorite character on television nowadays, you must be good."

Feeling off-kilter, but safe, Beth leaned back and smiled. "She's exaggerating, but I love her for it. I'm sure you're wondering how I can afford this place, or to eat, if I can't go outside by myself. I work from here. I'm not exactly looking for killers like Garcia does on *Criminal Minds*. During the day I work for a website in customer service, answering questions that come in on the chat server."

"And at night?"

"You're a firefighter, yeah?"

"Uh, yeah. You saw me today, right? All dressed up in my costume?"

Beth barked out a laugh. "Sorry, that came out wrong. I didn't mean to insult you."

"You didn't insult me, sugar, just surprised me."

"I just meant, you're not also a cop or anything?"

A look of seriousness flitted over Cade's face. "No, but I have to say, I have friends in law enforcement... and I'm really *really* hoping you're not about to tell me you stay up late breaking the law online."

"No," Beth immediately returned. Then clarified, "Not exactly."

"Then what—exactly?"

Beth looked down at her hands. She picked at a thread on the hem of her T-shirt. "Your sister was right, I'm good at computers. Once upon a time I was working on my computer science degree and I just knew I was going to get a job at Apple or IBM or something, and I'd invent something super cool and everyone would download my app and I'd get rich. But then...you know...and I couldn't go back to school, and I had to get away from California and all the pitying looks I got. When the panic attacks got so bad I couldn't go to work, I started playing around on the Internet. I got good at computer code. Really good. It was fun, something I could do to keep myself busy late at night when I couldn't sleep. I know I could probably still invent apps...but that somehow lost its appeal."

"Okay, that all sounds good so far," Cade prompted.

"Have you heard of the Dark Web?"

"No."

"Well, it's the Internet, but...hidden. There are things called overlay networks, which use regular Internet access, but require specific configurations or authorizations to access. The Dark Web is actually a part of the Deep Web, which is basically a part of the Internet that isn't indexed by search engines. It's—"

"You sure sound like Garcia, and I think I only understand every other word you just said. Break it down for me. Is it legal?"

Beth bit her lip. "Well, some of it is...yeah."

"Hmmmmm."

Reading the disapproval in Cade's tone, Beth hurried on. "I don't do anything against the law. Well, nothing that will hurt anyone else. There's a lot of porn and black market stuff that goes on there, but I don't worry too much about that...unless I run across really sick shit, then I do what I can to get those sickos shut down. But what I really like to do is either find holes in people's firewalls or see if I can track down those weird scammers that send emails to people asking for money, or telling them that they won the lottery in Africa, and alter their code so if anyone is naïve enough to reply, the bad guys never get the response."

Beth risked looking up at Cade. She had no idea what he was thinking; he was staring at her with no expression on his face. She shrugged and tried to downplay it. "It's really not a big deal. I just do it for fun."

"How'd you learn what to do?"

"Learn how to access the Dark Web or find the scammers?"

"Both."

Beth shrugged. "Trial and error mostly. And lots of research." She jumped when Cade reached for her hand and took it in his own again. He brought it up to his lips and kissed her knuckle.

"I have no idea what to say. You're amazing."

Beth immediately shook her head in denial. "No, I'm not."

"You are. Not only did you survive what happened to you, you've taught yourself something that ninety-nine-point-nine percent of people have no idea even exists. I can't say I'm happy about most of it, since it sounds like it could be dangerous if someone ever found out it was you turning them in, but I'm in awe of your intelligence."

Beth blushed and looked away. "So you aren't going to cuff me and turn me in to your buddies?"

"Naw, you're too pretty to go to jail. But I did notice you ignored my comment on the dangerous aspect of what you do."

"It's really not dangerous. I'm just playing around."

"You can deny it, but it doesn't change the facts, Beth. And I know you think you're damaged, but you're not. You might be bruised a bit, but I admire that you're fighting with everything you've got. I'd love to stand by you while you take on that fight."

"Uh…"

"And another thing," Cade went on. "I've got some people I want to introduce you to. No, don't shake your head. I'm not talking tomorrow, or even the next day. I'll take this as slow as you want to go."

Beth could only stare at Cade in bewilderment. Take what slow? What was he talking about?

"But as I said, I have friends in law enforcement and I know they'd kill to have the skills you can do. I know you're not Penelope Garcia and this isn't *Criminal Minds*, but I'm sure the San Antonio Police Department or the Sheriff's Department would love to have someone like you on their side. Hell, even my friend Cruz, who works for the FBI, would move heaven and earth to work with you. And I'll tell you something else…"

He paused as though waiting for her to acknowledge him, so Beth raised her eyebrows as if to ask, "What?"

"Apple and IBM would be lucky to have you working for them. If you can really find holes in firewalls? Any company would be knocking down your door to employ you."

"Actually, there are some people I know from the

web who have been after me to work with them, but I've always stayed away from anything like that since I don't really know who they are and whether they're working for the good guys or the bad ones. It's impossible to tell without meeting them in person."

"Smart. But seriously, if you want to give it a trial run, just let me know and I'll hook you up. I can't promise you a job, but I *can* get you an introduction to the right people. The rest will be up to you to wow them with your knowledge."

"Cade, it's not—"

"It is."

"You don't even know what I was going to say," Beth protested.

"You were going to say that it's not that big of a deal."

Beth blushed. That was exactly what she was going to say. She stayed quiet.

Cade chuckled and squeezed her hand and his voice dropped to a whisper. "Don't let your demons take control, Beth. I'm not saying it's easy, I think you know that, but you are way too amazing of a person to stay locked up in this apartment working for some customer service department."

Beth bit her lip hard in order to keep the tears at bay. "You don't really even know me, but thanks just the same," she whispered back. "Why are you being so nice to me? I mean, don't get me wrong, I'm thankful you helped me tonight and all, but I don't know you. This isn't the typical reaction people have when they meet me. Most of the time they back away slowly, hoping what I have isn't contagious."

"It's the least I can do for someone who has helped my sister as much as you have—"

"Yeah, that makes sense. If it's for your sister."

"You didn't let me finish."

"Oh, sorry." Beth waved her hand in the air between them. "Go ahead."

"I like you, Beth. Sometimes when you meet someone, you just know they're a good person and you want to get to know them better. I felt that with you earlier today. You knowing Penelope was just a bonus. If you've won her over, I know you're someone I want to get to know."

"What if I don't want to get to know *you*? You're being awfully presumptuous here."

"I am." It wasn't a question.

"That's all you're gonna say?"

"Uh-huh."

"Hmmmm. Okay, well. If you must know, now I'm curious about you. I mean, all those stories Pen told me about her older brother going through his GI Joe phase make much more sense now."

Cade grinned. "Hey, GI Joe was the shit."

Beth laughed and told him, "Yeah, okay, you've got me there."

"Okay, now that we've got that straightened out...I really ought to get going. I'm sure you have hackers to find or something and I need to get some sleep before my shift tomorrow. But I promise, next time we'll talk about me, yeah?" Cade told her with a smile.

Beth realized with a start that she didn't know anything more about the man sitting next to her, holding her hand so gently, than she had when she'd let him in earlier that night. All she knew was that he was a firefighter and he was Pen's brother. "I'm sorry, I'm horrible. Isn't one person talking all about themselves what makes people sneak out of restaurants in the middle of a meal?" She didn't go so far as to call what they were doing a date, but she guessed she kinda implied it.

Cade laughed. "I find you much more fascinating than me. But it's only fair for you to know my deep dark secrets. Can I call you?"

Beth shrugged. "It'd be easier if you messaged or emailed me. I'm always online. Besides, I don't have a cell phone. I don't really have a need for one since I don't leave here much. The old-fashioned, plug-it-into-the-wall phone works for me."

"Right." Cade grinned huge at her. "I should've guessed. Give me your email, and I'll find you on Facebook."

"I'm under Elizabeth Parkins. There are about a million of us though, so it might be easier for me to look *you* up."

"I think there are around two million Cade Turners on there. Not sure it'll be any easier for you to find me."

Beth grinned. "Turners maybe. *Cade* Turners?

Doubt it. But honestly, if I can find a hole in a firewall, I can find you on Facebook."

Cade smiled back. "Right. Forgot for a second I was talking to Garcia's twin," he teased, then stood up and, because he hadn't let go of her hand, pulled Beth up with him. They walked to her front door and he watched as she unlocked her locks with one hand.

When she'd gotten all the locks undone, she looked up at Cade. He leaned down, gave her a quick kiss on the cheek and pulled back. His thumb caressed the back of her hand before he let go. "I'll be in touch, Beth. Sleep well."

She never slept well, but she didn't say anything other than, "You too."

He leaned over and picked up the two bottles of cleanser he'd brought and disappeared down the hallway. Beth felt her heart rate increase at the sight of the long hall and quickly shut herself back into her apartment and locked herself in. Feeling safer, she wandered back to the couch and plopped down. She sat right where Cade had been and felt the warmth from his body seep into her skin.

It had been a long, weird day...but interesting. And Beth hadn't had an interesting day in a long time.

And to think it'd all started because of a fire. That had to mean something, but she was too keyed up at the moment to think of what it was.

CHAPTER 3

"STAY THERE, I'LL COME AROUND," Penelope said in a soothing voice a week later.

Beth gave a short nod and took a deep breath. She counted from one to ten in her head and tried to stay relaxed...which was hopeless. She'd thought that going outside would get easier, but it seemed that as the days went by, it actually got harder and harder.

Intellectually, she knew it was highly unlikely that someone was going to jump out of a van or car and grab her as Ben Hurst had, but she just couldn't shake the fear. Who would've thought it could happen to her the first time? It was a fluke...but if it was a fluke once, it could be a fluke twice.

Her door opened and Beth visibly jumped and lurched to the side.

"Easy, Beth. It's me."

Shit. "Sorry, Pen. I know it's you."

"It's fine. Give me your hand."

One thing she liked about Penelope was that she didn't let Beth's weird quirks get to her. She pretended not to see the stares from people who probably assumed because they were holding hands they must be lesbians rather than just good friends. Penelope didn't care if Beth flinched at loud noises or if, like now, because of her fears, Beth completely forgot that ten seconds earlier Penelope said she'd be around to get her from the passenger side of the car.

Beth held out her hand and sighed in relief as Penelope's warm hand closed around hers. The panic didn't disappear, but the feel of another person's palm against hers went a long way toward reassuring her that she couldn't be snatched away easily or without someone else knowing about it.

And that was the crux of the matter. She'd been taken from that Walmart parking lot and no one had known. The only reason someone knew she was missing as soon as they did was because that Navy SEAL team had already been looking for Summer, the woman who'd first been taken by Hurst. Since Beth lived on her own back in California, her parents wouldn't have noticed she was missing for several days, and because her brother lived up in Pennsylvania, he wouldn't have known either. Beth shuddered to think of what Hurst would've been able to do to her if she and Summer hadn't been found.

Penelope's chatter broke through Beth's internal musings as they headed toward the grocery store.

"I swear to God the guys are driving me crazy.

Crash even waited for me after we'd arrived at a medical the other night because he didn't want me to have to walk in by myself in the dark. They're hovering and it's completely unnecessary. I feel like I did right after I'd graduated from the academy and the team didn't completely trust me."

"They're worried about you."

"I know, but it's still annoying."

"How's Moose?" Beth wasn't the most man-savvy person in the world, but even she could tell Pen had a thing for her fellow firefighter.

Penelope shrugged. "Fine."

"Fine, huh?" Beth smiled. Penelope usually had no problem bitching about her friends when they were irritating, but all Beth could get out of her about the tall, extremely good-looking man was "fine."

"Yeah. Why?"

"No reason."

"You're in an awfully good mood today," Penelope observed as they entered the large grocery store.

"Not really. I can't wait to get this over with, but talking about *you* seems to make my anxiety go away."

"Figures," Penelope griped good-naturedly.

Deciding she'd better drop the subject before Penelope switched the attention from Moose to her brother, and asked how she was getting along with Cade, Beth simply smiled at her friend.

The fact was that Beth had communicated with Cade several times since she'd seen him last week. She'd found him easily on Facebook and he'd immediately accepted her friend request. She would've thought it strange that he was as active on Facebook as he was, but his social media habits were good for her, as it allowed them to chat all the time.

He never posted information that was personal, but he shared hilarious videos and some funny memes and firefighter cartoons, with his favorite being by some guy named Paul Combs.

The first night, they'd sent instant messages back and forth for two hours before Beth reluctantly let him go. He'd stayed true to his word and answered all of her questions about him. Beth learned he'd graduated from Texas A&M and had trained extensively at their world-renowned Emergency Operations Training Center. He'd explained that they had several acres set up to train personnel on anything from HazMat emergencies to train derailments, on top of the required annual firefighter training. It all sounded fascinating, especially because it was a world so far removed from what Beth was used to.

The second time he'd caught her online was when she was in the middle of breaking through Exxon's extensive firewall. She'd just wanted to see if she could do it—and she had, but in the back of her mind, she'd known that her actions would set off some pretty intense anti-hacking attacks. She'd had her hands full trying to make sure she got out with her identity and hands clean.

Cade hadn't liked it, but Beth had promised she wasn't doing anything with the data. He'd lectured that what she was doing could land her in jail, and that if she wanted to work on her hacking skills there were safer—and legal—ways to do it. He'd once again told her that he was going to introduce her to his officer friends...but only if she quit hacking into some of the biggest corporations in the world. She could hear in his tone that even though he was teasing her, he was still serious, telling her he didn't exactly relish the idea of visiting her in prison.

Thinking about Cade was enough to distract her from the fact that she was not in her safe apartment, but rather standing in the entrance to the grocery store. Penelope had to say her name twice to get her attention. They each grabbed a basket, as it was impossible to push a cart with one hand, and headed toward the produce section. Beth had no issue getting dried goods delivered to her apartment via the Internet, but fresh fruit, vegetables and meat were another story.

She was more thankful to Penelope than she could ever say; if it wasn't for her, Beth didn't think she'd ever leave her apartment. Beth had asked once what she could do to pay her back and Penelope had gotten pissed, saying they were friends and friends didn't pay each other for doing favors.

Feeling as though she'd needed to do *something*, Beth had used her computer skills to deflect news reporters and other annoying, obnoxious people who constantly bombarded Penelope for interviews and exclusive statements about her time spent as a captive of the infamous terrorist group ISIS. Pen had no idea, but it was worth it to Beth when Penelope had confessed one day that she didn't know why the press had backed off, but she was relieved, and felt like she could finally start to get her life back.

Beth had hacked into Penelope's email and Facebook accounts and answered, blocked, and generally kept the trolls away from her. She let the big networks through—Pen could decide on her own if she wanted to give exclusive interviews to Barbara Walters or Ellen, and she *had* talked to both—but no way was she letting TMZ or Fox News get their claws into one of the best people Beth had ever known.

If a reporter got too aggressive, it was all too easy to unleash a virus on the person's computer, which would make them forget about Penelope for a while. It was illegal, and she knew Cade wouldn't approve, but so far it'd worked, and Penelope was none the wiser. It wasn't much, but it was the only thing Beth could think to do to thank her for all she'd done. Since Pen wouldn't take money, and only occasionally allowed her to thank her, having her back electronically, even if she didn't know it, was what Beth did.

They were headed toward the meat section when Penelope announced, "Oh look, it's Cade."

Beth turned her head and, sure enough, Penelope's brother was headed toward them with a smile on his face. He looked just as handsome as he had the last time she'd seen him. Today he was wearing another pair of jeans, but he had on a polo shirt and Beth could see a light dusting of dark hair on his chest. He looked good. Really good.

"Hey, Squirt...Beth."

"Hi."

Beth mumbled something under her breath, suddenly embarrassed for some reason to be seen out in public with Penelope as she was. She felt under-dressed in her own pair of jeans and oversized T-shirt. She hadn't put any makeup on and had merely pulled her long hair back into a messy bun at the nape of her neck. Not to mention, it was one thing for Cade to *know about* how she needed to hold Pen's hand, but it was another for him to see it up close and personal. She wanted so badly to drop Pen's hand and stand in front of this capable man on her own, but instead she gripped her friend harder.

Just as Cade opened his mouth to say something else, Penelope's cell phone rang. She leaned over, placed the basket of produce on the ground and reached into her back pocket for her phone. Beth listened to her side of the conversation, realizing pretty quickly that this trip was going to be cut short.

"Hello? Hey, what's up? Yeah. Um-hum. Well, I'm kinda busy at the moment. I know. All right, hang on."

Penelope held the phone against her chest to muffle her conversation to the person on the other end of the line. She looked at Beth.

"It's my friend, Hayden. I told her to call the next time she was going to the range. It's not a big deal, but I really wanted her to help me group my shots closer together. Would you mind?"

"Of course not. I can get the rest of what I need later," Beth said immediately. She never wanted to be a burden on Penelope. If she wanted to go and do something else, Beth would never hold her back. Pen had told her a bit about Hayden and she seemed like the kind of person Beth would love to get to know. She was a kick-butt cop in the sheriff's department and sounded hilarious.

"Actually, I thought maybe Cade could help you finish up," Penelope replied in an even tone.

Beth froze where she stood and her eyes swung to Cade's. She couldn't. Pen knew her. She'd seen her mid-panic attack and knew to never leave her alone. Cade didn't know the rules. He didn't know—

"Great idea. I'm happy to," Cade said.

Beth swallowed hard. She wasn't sure about this. At all.

"Look at me, Beth," Penelope demanded. When Beth brought her eyes to her friend's, she continued, "Relax. I wouldn't volunteer my brother if I didn't think he'd take good care of you. He's not going to leave you alone. He's not going to freak out if you have an attack. Okay? You know him. I know you've been talking to him online. It's fine. *You'll* be fine."

"But he doesn't know the rules." Beth's voice trembled and she could feel herself getting worked up.

"Give me your hand," Cade requested in a semistern voice.

As if knowing Beth was incapable of moving, Penelope reached out and transferred Beth's hand from hers to Cade's.

Beth swallowed hard as she felt his ginormous hand engulf hers. She knew it was just a hand, exactly the same as Pen's, but somehow not. Even though she was only a few inches shorter than Cade, standing next to him with her hand in his...she felt protected. Tiny. *Safe.*

If she could've, Beth probably would've torn her hand away from his and hurried out of the store to try to preserve some of her dignity...but she couldn't. And if she was honest with herself, she didn't want to. Cade knew how she was. He might not have seen her in a full-blown panic attack, but he knew enough about her to know it was a possibility. They'd talked about some of what she went through in one of their online conversations.

"What are the rules, Pen?" Cade asked his sister.

As if Beth wasn't standing there, Penelope answered calmly, "Don't let go of her hand. Not to pay. Not to answer your phone, not to reach for something on the shelf. Don't let anyone get too close. Make sure not to—"

"I think he's got it," Beth interrupted, embarrassed beyond belief. She was sure her face was a fiery red.

Beth felt Cade's finger under her chin as he forced her head up to look at him. "I'll take good care of you. Promise."

"I'm not five," Beth grumbled, feeling like the most pathetic person on the planet.

"Believe me, this hasn't escaped my notice," Cade returned in a strange tone.

Penelope put the phone back up to her ear. "Hayden? I'm back. Yeah, I'll meet you at the range in say, thirty minutes? Great. I appreciate you calling. See you soon." She clicked off the phone and hugged her friend awkwardly, as Beth was still holding her basket of food and now Cade's hand.

"Call me when you get home, all right?"

"I will. Thanks for coming with me today."

"*Anytime*, Beth. Seriously."

Beth watched as Penelope strode confidently up the aisle and lost sight of her as she turned left at the end to head for the entrance.

"So...this is awkward. I'm not sure what you expected when you came to the store today, but I bet babysitting your sister's friend wasn't it."

"Don't do that, Beth. Don't belittle how far you've come. You're here and trying to get better. I think you're amazing. And not only was my day made by seeing you, I have an excuse to spend more time with you. Now, what else do you need?"

Beth was glad Cade's tone was no-nonsense and he wasn't going to say anything that would make her want to either hit him or throw up. She decided to ignore his comment about his day being made. He had to have been just being nice. "Ground beef, chicken, some stuff for sandwiches, cream cheese, ice cream, and yogurt."

Cade bent down and picked up the basket his sister had left. "Lead on, my beautiful computer genius."

Beth blushed, but headed toward the meat section of the store without a word. As she finished up her shopping, she couldn't help but compare Cade to his sister. As far as being an interesting shopping companion, they were evenly matched. He had no problem comparing prices of the store-brand versus the name-brand food and discussing the merits of each. He had opinions on which cut of steak was the best, and he even encouraged her to try ground buffalo instead of ground beef.

But when it came to feeling safe, Cade had his sister beat hands down. Beth couldn't say exactly what it was that made her feel that way. Maybe it was how he kept himself between her and the other shoppers. Maybe it was how he intertwined their fingers and squeezed her hand every now and then when he approved of something she'd said. Maybe it was simply the fact that he was a man. Beth hated to be sexist—she'd heard stories about Penelope carrying someone even taller and heavier than Cade out of a fire—but deep in her heart, she knew people would think twice about messing with her when Cade was by her side.

Before she knew it, they were in the parking lot headed for his truck and Beth realized she hadn't even fearfully looked around before stepping foot outside the store. She was with Cade. He wouldn't let anyone snatch her away. It was a heady feeling.

They stopped on the driver's side of a large black Ford F-350. Cade clicked the locks and opened the door, putting her bags on the floor of the backseat then gesturing to her. "Ladies first."

Beth looked up in confusion. "I'm not driving."

"I know." Cade smiled at her as if she'd said the funniest thing he'd ever heard. "But you can crawl over to the passenger side from here since I've got bench seats."

Beth couldn't think of anything to say before he went on.

"That's the rule right? I can't let go, so I'm not. Go on, scoot up and crawl over. I'll be right beside you."

"I'll be fine for the ten seconds it'll take you to walk around the truck. That's what Pen always does." Beth didn't know why she was protesting, except the knot in her stomach was back at his thoughtfulness. The goosebumps springing up on her arms were new though.

"Beth, I got this. Scoot. In."

Okay then. She awkwardly climbed up with Cade's help and moved out of the way of the steering wheel. He hopped up behind her and settled in. When Beth tried to continue moving into the passenger side of the seat, a tug on her hand stopped her.

"Sit there in the middle. There's a seat belt. It'll be more comfortable and you won't have to lean over to keep hold of me."

Beth did as he asked, liking the feel of his thigh against hers, as inappropriate as it was for their second semi-date, if one could call this warped outing a date. Cade reached for the ignition and started the truck as if he did it with his left hand all the time. He expertly backed out of the parking space and headed for the exit. Beth wasn't sure what to say, so she kept quiet and let Cade concentrate on driving.

Keeping her eyes on their clasped hands, which were resting on her leg, Beth realized that she wasn't freaking out. Being inside vehicles sometimes bothered her, but not today. She inhaled deeply, and caught Cade's masculine scent. It wasn't cologne, there was no way he'd wear it, but it must be his soap or shaving cream or something. Whatever it was smelled really good on him.

"You didn't buy anything," Beth blurted out suddenly, thinking about it for the first time. "You had to have been there because you needed food, right?"

"Yup, but I can go back later and get what I need," Cade told her easily, not sounding put out in the least.

"I'm sorry you got stuck with me. You should've said something."

"I didn't get *stuck* with you. I was gonna call you today and see if you wanted to hang out anyway. This just saved me the call."

Beth felt a genuine smile creep across her lips. "What if I'd said I didn't want to hang out?"

Without missing a beat, Cade retorted, "Then it's a good thing I ran into you, isn't it? You couldn't turn me down."

"Blackmail, huh?" It didn't even feel weird to be making fun of herself in this small way. It felt...normal.

Even though she was anything but. Cade had a way of making her phobia seem almost ordinary.

"Hey, anything to get to spend time with a pretty lady."

"As if you couldn't get inside any woman's pants with simply a smile," Beth teased. Expecting a witty comeback, she was surprised when he sounded peeved.

"Just because women have fantasies about doing a fireman doesn't mean I take them up on it. I've never, not once, been as attracted to a woman I'd met while on the job as I am to you."

"I'm sorry. That came out wrong. I merely meant that you...that I was...shit. I just have no idea why you seem to want to hang out with *me*. I'm completely fucked up. I can't go farther than the darn sliding glass door which leads out to the patio in my apartment without freaking and most of the time even *that's* too much. I can't go shopping for food without having to hold someone's hand like a little kid, and I have no idea why being around you makes me feel safer than I've ever felt in my life."

The cab of the truck was silent for a few beats, long enough for Beth to realize what she'd blurted out.

"Jesus, I'm sorry, I—"

"You aren't fucked up. I'd say you're dealing with what happened to you quite well, all things considered. Everyone needs help now and then. And I'm more aroused holding your hand and walking by your side than I've been while completely naked with other women. That you feel safe with me is just icing on the cake."

Cade's words were accompanied by a swipe of his thumb over the back of her hand. Even though his eyes were on the road, Beth could tell that she had almost all of his attention. She opened her mouth to say…something…she wasn't sure what, when he swore.

"Fuck."

It was obvious the word wasn't directed at her. His entire body tensed and his face lost its relaxed look and she could tell he was grinding his teeth together.

Beth looked out the windshield for the first time. They were on the Interstate headed back to her place and up in the distance ahead of them, Beth saw smoke rising from under the hood of a minivan on the side of the road.

CHAPTER 4

"BETH, I have to stop. I have an extinguisher in the back."

Cade's voice was anguished, and though she knew what it would do to her, Beth immediately told him, "Do it."

Even as Cade slowed the truck and began to pull off the road behind the minivan, he tried to reassure her. "I'll be quick. Stay here, lock the doors behind me. I'll do what I can until the fire department shows up. You'll be safe. I'm going to keep an eye on you the whole time." He put the truck in park with his left hand, then reached for her face. He palmed the side of her head and forced her to look at him. "I'll be right here. Okay?"

It wasn't okay, Beth knew what was going to happen as soon as he let go of her, but she'd seen the woman at the side of the car frantically trying to undo a child's car seat through the open back door. Other vehicles were slowing down to watch as they passed, but no one else had stopped. This was what Cade did. He was a hero and the young mother certainly needed one at the moment.

"I'll be fine. Go help her."

The worried look in Cade's eyes made her sit up straighter and try to put more force behind her words. "Go, Cade."

He leaned down and kissed her forehead, hesitating for just a moment before relaxing his hand and letting go of her. Cade opened his door, hopped out, reached in the backseat for the fire extinguisher, clicked the locks on the truck, then slammed the door.

Beth could feel her heartrate increase and her breaths start coming faster, but she kept her eyes on Cade. He ran up to the woman and said something to her. She stepped back from the van as Cade leaned in. Several seconds later, he reappeared holding a toddler in his arms. He handed the child to the mother and reached back into the vehicle. There were now flames shooting up from under the hood.

Beth's gaze went from Cade to the fire. She could see it from over the top of the van, the higher vantage point of the truck helping to give her a good view. Black smoke rolled up with the flames, mesmerizing her.

It was several moments before Beth realized that while she'd been watching the fire, she hadn't thought about anything else. Not about being by herself in the truck, not about being outside, not about someone coming by and kidnapping her. The flames had distracted her. It was fascinating, watching how they seemed to consume everything in their path.

She dropped back into herself with a jolt when she saw the chemicals from the fire extinguisher in Cade's hand pour onto the flames. She switched her attention to the woman. She was now standing back from her fully engulfed van with one child in her arms and another standing next to her, holding on to her leg with both hands. All three were staring wide-eyed at Cade and the fire.

Beth looked past the woman to the row of trees beyond the highway. Didn't the woman realize someone could come out from behind the thick foliage and snatch her or her children? The person could have them far away from the scene before anyone realized they were gone. No one was taking any notice of her or her kids, the fire commanding everyone's attention.

Beth's breaths started coming in short pants without her noticing. She should do *something*. But if she went out there, she'd be grabbed too. She could only watch and hope that the kidnapper lost his nerve.

She heard sirens, but instead of feeling relieved, all she could think about was how the arrival of the firetruck only meant more attention away from the woman. It was the perfect setup for the kidnapper. He could snatch all three of them without any trouble whatsoever. They'd be vulnerable to whatever he wanted to do to them.

Beth didn't feel the sweat begin to ooze out of her

pores or her entire body shaking as if she was standing in the middle of a raging blizzard wearing only shorts and a T-shirt. She didn't realize she was hyperventilating or that her heart was beating as fast as if she'd just run an eight-minute mile. The dizziness from lack of oxygen made her begin to sway in her seat.

Suddenly the woman standing off by herself in the field was *her*. It was as if she was having an out-of-body experience—watching from above as she was about to be kidnapped by Ben Hurst.

He'd take her, knock her out, and she'd wake up tied to the floor of his crappy little cabin in the woods again. He'd inhale his cigarette and laugh when she flinched as he brought it closer to her body. His maniacal laughter ran through her agitated mind as if he was truly standing in front of her.

The door of the truck wrenched open and Beth screamed and scrabbled to the other side of the seat, frantically reaching for the handle. She had to get away! Hurst was going to get her again. He was going to cut off her clothes and—

Cade called himself every name he could think of as he reached for Beth. She was not only having a full-blown panic attack, but a flashback as well, if her reaction to him was anything to go by.

He kept his voice calm and soft, thankful he'd only unlocked the driver's door and not all of the locks on the truck. It'd be a completely different situation if he'd had to chase her down.

"It's me, Cade. You're okay, Beth. Come on, open

your eyes and see *me*. I know I took too long, I am so damn sorry, but I'm here now. Give me your hand. Let me prove it. I'm here, sweetheart. You can do it. Come back to me, Beth. That's it."

It took several minutes. Minutes that ate at Cade as if he was the one torturing Beth.

"C-Cade?"

"Yeah, sweetheart. It's me. I'm here." He reached out and grabbed her hand, surprised at the strength of her grip as she held on to him as if she was hanging off an eighty-foot cliff. "I've got you, slow your breaths down. Close your eyes and concentrate on breathing. We'll do it together. Breathe in slowly...hold it... good...now let it out. Again. In slowly, hold it, then let it out. You can do this. You're not alone, you're safe. I've got you."

Cade continued to croon to her. Walking her through slowing her breathing down. He had a paper bag in his first-aid kit in the back of his truck that usually helped when patients were hyperventilating, but there was no way he was going to let go of Beth long enough to get it.

When he'd seen the minivan on the side of the road, Cade knew he was going to have to break his promise to both his sister and Beth to not let go of her hand. He wouldn't put her in danger by having her get out of the truck with him, and besides, there was no way he could operate the fire extinguisher with only one hand. But he *knew* what it was going to do to Beth.

She did too, and that killed him most of all. She'd

urged him to do what needed to be done, knowing she'd suffer as a result.

But what she didn't realize was that her selfless actions also secured her place in his life. Any woman who would freely let him walk away from her and do his job, knowing it meant she'd suffer, was worth fighting for. Between Beth's bouts of insecurity and self-incrimination, Cade saw her strong-as-steel core. She fought for every inch she gained in her life, even when she slipped back three.

"Is she okay, Sledge?" The male voice came from behind him, and Cade recognized his friend and partner, Moose.

Cade looked up and saw Engine 44 from Station 7 blocking the lane closest to the now smoldering van. Squirrel and Chief were manning the hose and pouring gallons of water on the van's engine.

"She'll be fine. Thanks, Moose."

"Let us know if you need anything."

"I will." Cade didn't watch his friend move away, but sensed when he was gone.

"I'm s-sorry."

Seeing Beth was finally breathing a bit more normally, Cade pulled her into his embrace, not caring if it was too soon or not. She needed to be held as much as he needed to hold her. She'd scared the shit out of him—hell, he was still worried about her. "Don't be sorry. Tell me what happened. Talk me through it."

Beth nuzzled into his embrace, holding tightly to his hand, which was now between them, tucked against their chests, and her other hand snaked around his side, clutching against his T-shirt. "I can't."

"You can. It's like a nightmare…if you talk about it, it loses some of its hold on you." Cade had no idea if that was true or not, but it sounded good at the moment.

"Is the woman okay?"

"Yes."

"No one came out of the trees behind her to get her?"

"No, sweetie. She's now sitting in the ambulance with her kids and the medics are checking her out. She's fine. They all got out in time. My friends have put out the fire. Everyone's safe." He paused a moment. "Is that what you thought? That someone was going to get her?"

Beth nodded and Cade's heart almost burst with sympathy for her.

"No one was paying attention to her. They were w-watching the fire."

Beth's teeth were clattering together and she was shaking in his arms. Cade had seen panic attacks before, but mostly from a distance. He'd never been intimately involved with someone who had them. It was a completely different experience and it was frustrating as hell because there was absolutely nothing he could do except try to help her get through it.

Cade reached over to the backseat, wanting to smile at how Beth continued to cling to him like a baby monkey holding on to its mother, and grabbed an extra bunker jacket. He spread it over Beth's back and held it there with his free hand.

"She's safe, Beth. No one came out of the trees to get either her or the kids." He hesitated, then made his decision. "Is that what happened to you? No one was paying attention and you were grabbed?"

She nodded infinitesimally in his embrace. "No one would've known I was gone except the other woman's boyfriend was looking for *her*."

Lord, she was breaking his heart. "You don't have to worry about that ever again, sweetie. I'll know if you disappear. I'll know, and I'll come looking for you."

His words opened the floodgates and Beth sobbed in his arms.

Neither said anything more. Cade sat with her in his arms as the firefighters made sure the fire under the hood of the minivan was out and, with a wave from Moose, headed back to the station. They sat on the side of the road long enough that Cade watched as the tow truck came and hauled the blackened shell of the van away. He continued to hold Beth as traffic slowly but surely started flowing past them again. It didn't matter. He'd sit there as long as it took for Beth to feel better. Stronger.

He figured she was asleep, and was startled when she finally pulled back and looked around.

"How long have we been sitting here?"

Cade shrugged.

Beth looked confused. "How long would you have sat here waiting for me to get my shit together?"

"As long as you needed."

Cade could see the insecurity in Beth's expression. He put his hand on the side of her face again. "I'm sorry."

"You have nothing to be sorry about," she insisted immediately.

"I do. I knew this would happen when I stopped. But I did it anyway."

"Me too, but I wouldn't have let you go by."

"I know that too." Deciding a change in subject was necessary, Cade said in a relatively normal tone, "Now that the excitement is over, let's get you home. We'll see if we can salvage anything from our trip. I'll replace anything that doesn't make it."

"I should say it's okay to go back to the store now… but I can't. I want to go home."

"Then home is where you'll go. Can you sit up and get your seat belt back on?"

Cade helped Beth sit all the way up, making sure to never let go of her hand, and helped her buckle into the middle of the bench seat again. He eased out into traffic and headed for her apartment.

It'd been a long day, but Cade hoped Beth would let him stay with her for a bit when they got to her apartment. It had been traumatic for her, but it'd been very eye-opening for Cade as well. Yes, she'd had a monster panic attack, but it wasn't nearly as embarrassing as she probably thought it was. Demons were tricky things. They could lay dormant for hours, days, years, but they'd always pick the most inopportune time to raise their ugly heads. There was nothing Cade wanted more than to see Beth relax back into the witty woman he'd begun to get to know.

She didn't realize it, but he was in this for the long haul. He wanted to get to know her better, and not to "heal" her, but because he'd never been as attracted to anyone as much as he was to her. There was just something about her that made him want to protect her from the world one second, then throw her down on the nearest flat surface and ravage her the next.

CHAPTER 5

BETH BREATHED a sigh of relief as she locked the door behind her. Lord, she hadn't felt this wrung out in weeks. She hated feeling helpless. She especially *hated* that Hurst, even though dead, still had the ability to freak her out.

She relaxed her hand, expecting Cade to drop hers, but was surprised when he held on and tugged her toward the kitchen.

"Come on, let's get these things put away."

Beth followed behind him and after he finally dropped her hand, they worked together emptying the bags. The only thing Cade thought should be chucked was the chicken. Everything else seemed to be okay.

Once everything was put away, Cade grabbed her hand again, pulled her behind him to the couch and sat. Beth looked at him curiously. He actually looked more relieved than she was to be back inside her apartment.

"You gonna be all right?" she asked him in a serious voice.

He smiled at her. "Yeah. You?"

"I'm good, now that I'm safe at home, snug as a bug in a rug."

Cade grinned hugely at her. He let go of her hand and Beth couldn't stop the pang of regret that moved through her. It lasted only a nanosecond as he took her head in both of his hands and leaned in. She felt the puffs of air from his mouth as he spoke.

"I want to kiss you, Elizabeth Parkins."

"You do?"

"Yeah."

"Why?"

"Why?" Cade asked in confusion, but he didn't pull away from her.

"Yeah, why? I just had a major freak-out. I'm still all sweaty, and I'm sure you have somewhere you need to be."

"You are sweaty, but so am I...and I'm not afraid of a little sweat. Just wait until you see me after I get back from a call. A fire especially. Our turnout gear might look sexy, but it's hot as fuck. I'm usually drenched by the time I get back to the station. And trust me, you do not want to smell the bunker room; it's downright rancid sometimes. And to answer your question, I've got nowhere I need to be until tomorrow when my shift starts at ten."

"And the freak-out?"

Cade sighed and pulled back a fraction so she was

looking into his eyes. "You freaked out, but even knowing it was likely, you didn't stop me from doing what I needed to do."

"No one else was around to do it."

"I get that, but you should know, if you'd told me you couldn't handle it and asked me not to leave you...I wouldn't have."

"Cade!" Beth exclaimed in shock.

He shrugged. "It's true. You don't realize this yet, but all you have to do is crook that little finger of yours and I'll come running."

"I wouldn't do that to you. That woman needed you more than me. I knew in my heart of hearts that I was safe in your truck. Even if my brain sometimes forgets and zones out on me, I know you and Pen wouldn't let anyone get me."

"Damn straight."

"I still don't like that you had to see me like that. I want you to see me as any other woman."

"Too bad. I don't see you as any other woman."

Beth's gaze dropped from his and she tried to pull away. He wouldn't let her and tightened his hold.

"You could never be any other woman, Beth. You've taught yourself something that people typically take years of schooling to understand. You've helped Penelope deal with what happened to her and I know she's doing as well as she is in part because of you. And now that I think about it, you're probably doing stuff behind the scenes that neither of us know about when it comes to her, aren't you?"

Beth didn't respond, but she could feel the heat bloom in her cheeks.

"Yup, I knew it. I don't want to know what it is, but thank you. She's settled down a bit now that she doesn't constantly have to fight off the tabloids and crazy stalker people who only want to get a glimpse of the Army Princess."

"Stupid-ass nickname."

"Agreed. As I was saying, yeah, you freaked out. But you reached down inside and pulled yourself up by your bootstraps. I liked that. If you haven't noticed, I like *you*, Beth. Now can I kiss you? Please?"

"I don't know much about you."

Cade sighed in mock-exasperation. "If I tell you more about me, will you let me kiss you then?"

"Maybe." Beth smiled to take the sting out of her words. Oh, she wanted this man's kiss, but he was fun to tease, and she really did want to get to know him better. Locking lips with a man she'd so recently met, even if he was the brother of one of her closest friends, wasn't something she felt comfortable with. Talking to him over the Internet was different from hearing about his life from his own two lips.

"I'm assuming you're not working today?" Cade asked, letting go and leaning back into the corner of the couch.

"No, I have the day off," Beth told him, and settled herself into the other corner, curling her legs up underneath her. She was still a little shaky from everything that had happened, but surprisingly she was feeling pretty good, all things considered.

"So, what do you want to know?"

"Everything," Beth replied immediately.

"I think that'll take too long," Cade laughed. "Let's see if I can't condense it a bit. You know Penelope is my sister, she's two years younger than me and we've always been close."

"No sibling rivalry?"

"Not really. She tagged along behind me, and because she wasn't a pain, it was cool. She was a huge tomboy and could actually outplay a lot of my friends growing up. We were both sad when I went off to high school and she was still in middle school."

"That's unusual. My brother is three years older than me, and while we're close now, he didn't want anything to do with me when we were in school," Beth observed.

"I know. I'm not sure why, but we pushed each other to do better," Cade told her, relaxing against the cushions, seemingly not embarrassed at all about his close relationship with his sister. "When I joined the track team, Penelope worked extra hard to make the varsity squad right along with me when she was a freshman. Instead of feeling like she was stifling me, I felt like she had my back, and I certainly had hers."

"I sense a story there."

"Observant little thing, aren't you?"

"I'm not little," Beth protested.

"No, you're not. You're perfect." Not giving her a

chance to disagree, Cade continued, "There was this chick I was hot for my senior year. All she had to do was smile at me and I would've done anything she asked. She didn't really notice me until I became state champion at the end of my junior year. Come that August, she was all over me, and I was thrilled. I knew I was gonna get—excuse my language here—some hot pussy, and couldn't wait to get in there."

Beth laughed, as Cade had meant her to. Watching her relax even more made him feel like he could scale mountains. If he could make Beth forget what had happened, even for a couple of minutes, it seemed like a huge hurdle he'd climbed.

"Well, Penelope heard this chick and her buddies gossiping in the locker room one day. Apparently, they had some sort of sick bet going about who could get pregnant first. They'd decided that they wanted babies, and getting child support from the unlucky daddies was an added bonus. They had no desire to get married, but getting all the cute baby shit from family and friends and being able to tote their adorable babies around to get attention sounded like the perfect life plan to them."

Beth made a gagging noise in the back of her throat. "Seriously? I mean, I know I'm younger than you and all, but really? Most girls I knew in high school were doing everything they could to *keep* from getting knocked up. That sounds completely far-fetched."

"I agree. I didn't believe it either. Who would? It was one of the worst fights me and Penelope ever had.

She told me what she'd overheard and I didn't want to listen to her. I was too caught up in trying to get some."

"Darn teenage hormones."

"Exactly."

"So, what happened? I'm assuming there's not a teenage Cade running around in the world?"

"Hell no. I stopped to really think about it for a second. Penelope wasn't the sort to lie to me. I continued to flirt with this chick, but eventually the fact that I wasn't coming to heel soon enough for her made her look elsewhere. She wanted to win the bet and be the first to get pregnant, and since I was dragging my feet, she moved on to easier prey. The quarterback ended up being the lucky father. I heard she had the baby the summer after we graduated."

"Pen obviously forgave you."

"She made me work for it, but yeah. She still holds it over my head. I love her though. It almost killed me when she disappeared." Cade knew he was treading on shaky ground, he didn't want what he was going to say to bring up her own kidnapping, but wanted to make sure Beth understood his next point. "I saw news reports about some missing soldiers before the Army contacted us to let us know Penelope was one of them. They must've had some sort of advance warning what ISIS was going to do, because the very next day the first video was broadcast of her reading that damn manifesto."

"What about your parents?"

"What about them?"

"I don't remember seeing or hearing much from them while she was gone."

Cade sighed. "Don't get me wrong, I love my parents, but they're more the type to sit at home and wring their hands in consternation. They did everything I asked them to do, but they aren't the take-charge types."

"And you are."

"I am," Cade agreed.

Beth's eyes were wide in her face, but she didn't comment further.

He continued, "I would move heaven and earth to protect my sister. I emailed and called anyone and everyone in the media and government I could find contact information for, I plastered social media with her plight. She wasn't some pretty woman on TV to me. She was my *sister*. My flesh and blood. My parents did what they could, but I wouldn't stop until the President himself did something to try to get her back."

"And you did it. They went in to get her."

"They did. It wasn't easy. I spent a lot of sleepless nights wondering where she was and what she was going through, but honestly, I was lucky."

"Lucky?"

"Yeah. There are so many people out there who never know what happened to their loved one. Kids disappear. Teenagers run away and are never heard from again. Adults disappear off the face of the Earth and are never found. Bones might be discovered, but never identified. I'm lucky. I got Penelope back."

"But she's not the same." Beth's words were whispered now.

"No, she's not. But you know what? I don't give a shit. She's still my sister and I love her as much today as I ever have. Everything in this life changes us. Every experience we have, has the ability to fundamentally alter our path in life. It's how you deal with those changes that's important."

"What if you can't deal?"

"I sure as hell hope you aren't talking about yourself, sweetheart. Because from where I'm sitting, you're dealing exceptionally well."

"I'm not."

"You *are*. Shit, Beth. You're working full time. You taught yourself some seriously tough computer code. You don't sit in here wallowing in self-pity or huddled into a ball. Yeah, you have a hard time going outside, but you don't hide from it. You grab hold of my sister, and now me, and do it with your teeth clenched. That takes guts. Guts a lot of people don't have. You have no idea how strong you are. Don't overlook how far you've come."

Ignoring his words about her, Beth commented, "Pen's lucky to have you."

"I'm the one lucky to have *her*," Cade countered. "Seriously, she's worked her butt off. She followed me into the fire service, then wanted to make more of a difference in the world, so she joined the Army Reserves. She loved it, but in the last few years, it was getting old being sent overseas. She was already planning on leaving, but the whole ISIS thing solidified it for her."

"I can imagine. You never wanted to do anything else?"

"No. I love what I do. No two days on the job are the same. We might have a grass fire, automobile accident and a heart attack on the same day. The next day we might have to help deliver a baby. I love helping people. It's what I do."

"It's dangerous," Beth observed.

Cade shrugged. "Not really. I mean, yeah, there are times when a building is on fire and there's a missing person we have to go in and rescue. But for the most part it's more about the human side of things. Holding someone's hand as they're lying on the ground bleeding. Comforting a husband as his wife is having a seizure. I just like feeling what I do helps others in some small way." Realizing his words might be making Beth feel bad, he quickly tried to lighten up the conversation. "So…what's your favorite color?"

"What?"

"Your favorite color? We've talked a lot about heavy shit…how about if we get to the nitty-gritty. I don't think I can date someone who favors the color black over everything else."

"I didn't realize we were dating," Beth said a bit snarkily.

"Oh, we're dating, sweetheart. You don't think I get to the dugout with just any girl, do you?"

"Get to the dugout? What are you talking about?"

Cade chuckled. "Holding hands...the dugout. I tried to kiss you tonight, but you weren't having it. So we aren't at first base yet...we're just in the dugout."

Beth rolled her eyes at Cade. He was hysterical, but she didn't think egging him on was in her best interest. She steered the conversation back to her favorite color. "I'm tempted to say black just to throw you off, but I'd be lying. Blue. You?"

"Blue. And I'm not just saying that to suck up to you. Food?"

"Pasta. Preferably ramen noodles. I love those things."

"The cheap ones in the rectangle package? You know they're bad for you, right?"

"Don't care. Being cheap is just an added bonus."

"Hummm, okay, pasta. I can live with that. I like a good steak."

"Medium rare?"

Cade smiled, loving their banter. "Is there any other way to cook it?"

"Nope. Okay, let's see...music?"

"Country."

"Ugh, I knew there had to be something about you I didn't like," Beth told him, keeping a straight face.

"Oh come on. I'd get kicked out of the state if I didn't like country." Cade gave her a pouty look.

Beth laughed. "Oh good Lord, don't give me that face. That was the most pathetic thing I've ever seen. I'll let you listen to country, but if you ever start listening to rap, I'll have to break up with you."

"See? Even you admit we're dating. You can't break up with me if we aren't dating in the first place."

Beth rolled her eyes at him again. "And if 'Call Me Maybe' comes on, it's imperative that it gets turned up as loud as it can go so I can lip-sync to it."

"Have you seen that video—"

"The one of the soldiers in Iraq imitating the cheerleaders who lip-synched it?"

"Yup."

"Oh my God, yes. It's one of my favorites. I have it bookmarked. Sometimes I slip it into code for assholes so it pops up when they least expect it on their computers."

Cade laughed until his sides hurt. "You don't!"

"I do. It's either that or the song from *Frozen*." She put a hand on her heart and dramatically threw her head back, singing, "Let it goooooooooooo."

They giggled together, imagining the look on someone's face as the song popped up on their computer in the middle of a porn video or something else, utterly unexpected.

"You crack me up, Beth."

She smiled over at the man sitting on her couch. It was hard to believe she just met him a week ago. She'd heard Penelope talking about her brother in the past, but never expected to have this...connection with him, or any man. It was as if she'd known him for years rather than only days.

"You want to stay for dinner?" The words popped out before Beth could call them back.

"Yes." Cade's answer was immediate and heartfelt.

"I figure it's the least I can do after today."

"No. Today has nothing to do with it. You don't owe me anything. Ask me to stay because you want to get to know me better. Ask me to stay because you *want* me to, not because you think you should. Ask me to stay because you want to get a good-night kiss at the end of our date, not out of any obligation you think you have to me or my sister."

Beth bit her lip, but powered through her shyness. "Will you stay for dinner, Cade? I'd like to get to know you better."

"I'd love to. Thank you for asking."

CHAPTER 6

BETH CLACKED AWAY on her keyboard, occasionally looking over at Cade, who was fast asleep on the couch next to her. They'd had a wonderful dinner. She'd made a bachelor casserole: pasta, cream of mushroom soup, ground buffalo, sour cream, and cheese. It was easy and relatively fast. And he'd been right; the buffalo tasted just like beef, but was healthier.

They'd talked more about their likes and dislikes, and Beth couldn't remember laughing more since she'd left California. After a while, Cade had asked if she'd show him some of what it was she did on the web.

So she'd pulled out her laptop and proceeded to give him an introduction to the Dark Web, trying to explain a bit about how the good guys worked, and what made a bad guy a bad guy. To simplify things, she used the analogy of black-hat versus white-hat-wearing cowboys in old TV shows and movies. They both might be outlaws, but the white hat guys were actually trying to do good. Cade admitted that most of it went over his head, but he'd enjoyed watching her fingers fly over the keyboard as she worked the code scrolling down the screen.

Eventually he'd asked if she minded if he read while she worked. At the shake of her head, he'd pulled out his cell and opened up his reading app. He'd fallen asleep thirty minutes ago, his phone almost falling on his face as he drifted off.

Sitting next to each other, doing their own thing but enjoying spending time together, was new to Beth. She'd never had a boyfriend in high school or college who'd enjoyed hanging out and doing nothing with her. Hell, she'd never had a boyfriend content to lounge next to her and *read* while she worked. It was crazy, but the kind of crazy Beth could get used to.

Cade had his head resting on the back of her couch and his shoeless feet stretched out in front of him. His jeans pulled taut against his legs and crotch, allowing Beth to see the outline of his equipment with no problem. He was a big man, but for once in her life that didn't scare her. Oh, the act of actually having sex with him made her have second thoughts, but his size didn't.

Being six feet tall meant he was taller than her and could help protect her against someone who might want to hurt her, and Beth couldn't help but admit that was a big part of the draw. She wasn't so shallow before being kidnapped, but she figured that was now a part of her psyche and she wouldn't feel bad about it.

Cade's arms were muscular; they'd have to be in

order to haul around the fire hoses he'd talked about earlier. He'd explained some of the physical things they'd had to do to pass the fitness test and what they did in order to stay fit. Being a firefighter wasn't just about breaking down doors and hauling a hose inside a burning building. They had to lift, stretch, climb, and sometimes even run, all while wearing their safety clothes and gear.

Before she'd gotten distracted, Cade had told her about the annual charity stair climb they participated in at the beginning of September each year. To honor the firefighters and police personnel who had perished in the attacks on the World Trade Center in New York City, firefighters around the country climbed a total of one hundred and ten flights of stairs, the exact number of flights in the World Trade Center buildings. They wore all their turnout gear, which weighed at least forty pounds, just as the firefighters on that fateful day had. Beth wanted to support the event, and if she couldn't physically be there, at least she could donate money.

But oh, how she wanted to be able to be there. To stand next to Cade and Penelope and the others who worked at Station 7 would be amazing. She made the decision then and there to make it her goal. She might not ever achieve it, it'd probably be too much for her to be in the middle of a large crowd that would certainly be present at an event like that, but she'd try to work her way up to it.

Being around Cade was already making her want to

do things she never would've considered even a week ago. That had to be a good thing. At least she hoped so.

Turning back to her keyboard, Beth forced herself to concentrate on finding the weakness in the code she was looking at. There were few companies who could make an airtight code, and she'd learned over the last couple of years to keep at it...eventually she'd find a way through. It was a challenge and she always felt proud of herself when she made her way inside.

If she was a bad guy, she could've made off with millions of dollars, and even billions of social security numbers, birthdates, credit card numbers and more, but it was the challenge of getting in that floated her boat. Not stealing. She'd done harmless, albeit still illegal hacks, like upgrading her mom and dad to first class one of the few times they'd flown out to see her, or putting her brother on every bride-to-be mailing list so he'd receive junk mail from bridal companies for the rest of his life when he'd teased her about being a computer geek (which made him totally take it back).

"Gotcha," Beth mumbled under her breath as the entire purchasing history of a large well-known retailer popped up on her screen. It'd only taken her an hour to make her way through the twists and turns in the firewalls to hack into their customer database.

"What'd you get?"

Beth nearly shrieked in surprise as Cade spoke the words in her ear from right next to her.

"Jeez, Cade. You scared the life out of me."

He chuckled, and Beth shivered as his breath washed over her neck.

"Sorry, sweetheart. Who'd you hack now?"

"No one."

"Come on, who?"

"PayPal."

When he didn't say anything, Beth peeked up at him. His mouth was literally hanging open in surprise.

"I didn't *do* anything. I just wanted to see if I could get in."

"Jesus, honey. I know I keep saying this, but seriously, I *have* to introduce you to Dax or Cruz. Your talents are totally wasted in customer service. They'd kill to have you on their payrolls. Now come on, get your cute ass out of their website. It's late. You need to get to sleep."

"I don't sleep much, I told you that."

"Why not?"

Beth shrugged, even though she knew exactly why. "I'll lie down in a couple of hours."

Cade eyed her, but didn't protest or try to convince her to try harder. His next words were much more surprising. "Can I stay?"

"Stay?"

"I know I'm pushing my luck, but I'm beat. My place is across the city and it would take around twenty minutes or so to get there this time of night. I'll be good, I'm perfectly happy staying right here on your couch. I've got to go to work at ten tomorrow…well, today, and I want to replace that chicken we had to throw away before I go in."

"There's no need to go shopping for me. I can get it later. But, yes, you can stay."

"I can go if it makes you uncomfortable."

"It doesn't. As long as you aren't going to pull a Hannibal Lector on me, you're good."

Cade grinned at her serial killer comment, but didn't otherwise say anything about it. "Okay, I'll just stretch out here. I sleep through anything, so don't worry about me."

"I have a guest room."

Cade yawned and settled back on the couch. "This is perfect."

"I'll just move over to the—" She was going to say "chair," when Cade interrupted her.

"Stay. I like you next to me."

She couldn't argue with that logic. "Okay, but the couch pulls out into a recliner on that side. You'd probably be more comfortable that way."

"Oh man, now you've done it." Cade groaned in ecstasy as he found the lever and stretched out until he was almost lying flat. "You'll never get rid of me now. My butt will meld with this cushion and you'll have to get a crane to pull me out."

Beth giggled. "You'll get sick of being here soon enough."

"I wouldn't bet on it, sweetheart."

His words were light, but Beth swallowed hard at

the serious tone of his voice. "Good night, Cade. Thanks for everything today."

"Good night. And you're welcome."

It took a while, but Beth finally pulled her attention away from the gorgeous man sleeping soundly next to her and back to her computer screen. There was one other firewall she wanted to see if she could get around tonight, and she needed to concentrate. She'd heard Cade before when he'd voiced his concerns over her illegal online activities...but the rush she got when she achieved her goal of hacking into a system that was supposed to be hack-proof was hard to give up. It was one of the few things in her life that made her feel proud of herself.

The government frowned when people hacked into their databases—but it was part of the reason she wanted to see if she could do it.

CHAPTER 7

CADE STOOD at Beth's front door and waited for her to look up at him. He honestly hadn't meant to fall asleep, but was thrilled she'd let him stay. He'd woken up around three in the morning and been alone in the living room. He saw Beth's laptop sitting on the table next to her side of the couch and figured she'd finally wandered off to bed.

He didn't like that she didn't sleep well, and as much as he wanted to do something about it, Cade figured it was probably more because her brain wouldn't shut off and she remembered too much of the crap that had happened to her, rather than the fact that she didn't need the sleep.

He was awake when she wandered into the room around seven. She'd made a pot of coffee and he'd left to go pick up some chicken for her. After he'd returned from the store, they'd had a leisurely breakfast together.

It was now time for him to get to work but his heart was beating hard in his chest. He'd been thinking about this moment since last night, and he hoped like hell she was on the same page.

"Thanks for everything. Breakfast, the place to crash, all of it."

"You're welcome."

"Do you think you know enough about me now to let me give you a good-morning-I'll-see-you-later kiss?"

Cade watched her blush, then nod shyly.

Telling himself not to fall on her like a starving, wild mongrel, he took a step toward her, getting up into her personal space. He put one hand on her bicep and the other on her waist, trying not to make her feel trapped. Her hair was down around her shoulders and chest, untamed and messy...and absolutely beautiful.

He leaned in close, as he had the night before, but hesitated, his lips hovering over hers. He wanted to take her. He wanted nothing more than to lean down, capture her lips with his own and take possession of her. She might be sorting through some shit in her head, but she was a good person. Funny, smart, sarcastic, and down-right entertaining. Cade wanted her, but first he was going to start out with a kiss.

He wanted her to want it as much as he did though. He felt like he was pushing Beth, but Cade needed to know she wanted this kiss and wasn't just going along with it because he'd helped her yesterday or because he was Penelope's brother.

Holding his breath, but not losing eye contact, Cade waited a beat. Finally, she moved the inch it took to bring their lips together and he sighed. Every muscle in his body sagged in relief. Thank God.

Without giving her time to give him a small peck and pull away, Cade took what she offered. He fused his lips to hers and licked lightly at the seam. When she gasped, he took advantage and surged inside. She tasted like coffee…and sunshine.

Shit, he was being philosophical, but damn, she was amazing.

It was obvious she wasn't an expert at kissing, but her eagerness and innocence shone through. She turned her head to one side, trying to get closer, and Cade pulled her into him until they were touching from hips to chest, and it still didn't feel close enough. He pulled back momentarily to make sure she was all right, and when she moaned and stood on tiptoes to get closer to him, he took her mouth again.

This time he showed her what to do. His tongue played with hers then retreated, encouraging her to follow him. She did. At the first tentative touch of her tongue against his lips, he groaned deep in his throat. The small sound must've broken her concentration because Beth pulled back, blushing.

Cade put his forehead on hers and closed his eyes, giving her the mental space he knew she needed, but not the physical space. He ran one hand over the side of her head, then curled his hand around her ear, smoothing her hair back at the same time.

"Mmmmm, that was the perfect ending to a wonderful date."

He felt her smile and opened his eyes and pulled back. He wanted to see it for himself. Yup, it was small and tentative, but it was there. "Thank you, sweetheart. That'll keep me going until I can see you again."

Beth pushed a lock of her hair behind her other ear and he could tell it took some effort, but she said, "I'm looking forward to it."

Cade leaned down, brushed a quick kiss over her now swollen lips and stepped back. He wanted more, but he was patient. She needed to know that he wasn't going to rush her into anything she might not be ready for. The last thing he wanted to do was scare her. "I'll message you later. I have three days on and two days off this week, so I won't have a lot of free time to see you, but I'll touch base electronically...all right?"

"Yeah. That sounds good."

"If you need anything, though, let me know and I'll take care of it."

"I'll be fine."

"I know you will. Do me a favor?"

"What's that?"

"Try not to hack into the President's email until I can get you on the FBI's payroll, okay? Courting you while you're in prison would cramp my style."

Beth laughed, as he'd meant her to. "Can't promise, but I'll see what I can do."

"I'd appreciate that. Have a good day, sweetheart. I'll be in touch soon."

"Bye, Cade."

"Bye."

* * *

The next few days went by fairly quickly for Beth. She chatted with both Penelope and Cade when they had some down time at the station, and got back into the swing of dealing with questions from customers for her day job.

She'd even made time to call her brother, David, as well. Living up in Philadelphia, he was in the marketing department for a large accounting firm. He'd always said that it was very interesting to be a creative type of person working with a bunch of mathematicians.

"Hey, Beth, how are you?"

"I'm as good as I can be, I guess."

"I received a subscription to a magazine called *Girls and Corpses* last week...you wouldn't know anything about that, would you?"

"Nope, but you might like to know for your birthday, you may or may not be receiving *Teddy Bear Times* magazine as well."

David laughed. "It's been too long since I've talked to ya, sis. Now...seriously, how are you?"

"I'm better."

"Really?"

"Yeah, really. I've had a few setbacks, but nothing that wasn't expected."

"Oh, Beth."

Ignoring the sorrow in her brother's voice, she continued quickly, "I met a guy."

The silence on the line was almost deafening.

"A guy." David didn't say it as a question, but Beth had no doubt it was.

"Yeah. He's Penelope's brother. Penelope being the firefighter I told you about who's in my therapy group. Her brother's also a firefighter."

"How'd you meet him?"

"Hummm, yeah, well, I was trying to make Mom's fried chicken."

"You didn't."

"I did. I almost burned the place down and the fire department showed up to save my bacon. He was there, then he came back and helped me clean up."

"So you're dating now? Does he know about your agoraphobia?"

Beth sighed in exasperation. "Yeah, I think we're dating. But I'm taking things slowly, so you don't have to get the shotgun out yet."

"You *think* you're dating?"

"Yeah."

"And the other?"

"Yes, I told him about the panic attacks. He's Pen's brother, she told him about what happened to me."

"And you're okay with that?"

"Surprisingly, yes. I'd rather she tell him than have to rehash it all myself. David, I like him."

"I have some time saved up, I want to come and visit."

"I'd love that! As long as you're not planning on scaring Cade away."

"His name's Cade?"

"Yeah. Cade Turner. When are you coming?"

"Not for a while. I'm just letting you know it's on my to-do list."

"How are *you*? Anyone special in your life?"

"There's a new accountant here I have my eye on. He's kinda nerdy and straightlaced but I've glimpsed a wicked sense of humor under his stern countenance."

Beth had never given a crap about her brother's sexual orientation; he was just her older brother. "Well, good luck with that."

"It was good talking to you. Take it slow with this guy, okay, sis? I worry about you. I don't want him taking you somewhere and then not thinking it's a big deal, abandoning you or something."

"He'd never do that. Ever."

"Okay. Call me more often, would ya? I miss you."

"I will. I love you."

"Love you too, Beth. Bye."

"Bye."

Beth had hung up the phone and smiled. She loved David and was thrilled he was at least trying to get into the dating scene. She wanted to see him happy as much as he wanted to see *her* happy and healthy.

* * *

It wasn't until the third night after Cade had slept over, when she was bored with the Dark Web and looking for something to do, that she really thought about the minivan that had been on fire. She hadn't reflected on what had happened because she'd been dealing with the aftereffects of being with Cade, the panic attack...and his kiss.

But now, sitting in her dark apartment, she had an epiphany.

While she'd been sitting in Cade's truck watching the flames shoot up toward the sky, she hadn't been scared until the fire had been snuffed out. Was it a fluke?

It gave her an idea.

Beth put her laptop aside and headed into the kitchen. She rummaged through two drawers before finding what she wanted. She went back into her living room and sat on the edge of her couch, pulling the coffee table closer.

She struck one of the matches. It lit and Beth held it up in front of her as it burned down. Before the flame hit her fingers, she blew it out, watching as the smoke rose lazily in the air.

She dropped the burnt stick to the table and reached for another.

The flame caught with the first strike and Beth felt her eyes go blurry as she watched this one burn. Again, with one gust of air, the flame was extinguished and disappeared with a puff of smoke.

She did it again. And again. Until the entire pack lay in burnt sticks on the table in front of her.

Beth felt her heart beating strongly in her chest. It wasn't pounding, but it was steady. *She* felt steady. The control she had over that flame was heady. She knew it was only a match, but *she* decided when it would burn and when it would die.

There wasn't much else she felt like she had control over in her life.

She wasn't in charge of her body when she had to venture outside her four walls. She'd had no control over Hurst when he'd been hurting her. She even felt out of control, albeit in a good way, when Cade had kissed her.

But this. This was different somehow.

She stood up abruptly and went back to the kitchen. After ten minutes of searching, Beth went back to her couch in defeat. She didn't have any more matches in the house, not even one of those propane lighter clicky things.

Ignoring the blackened stubs of wood scattered around her coffee table, she sat back and powered up her laptop, feeling excited.

She might not have them right now, but she could have as many as she wanted tomorrow. Thank God for overnight shipping.

CHAPTER 8

A WEEK LATER, Beth relaxed on the couch with Penelope and Cade. Cade had called from the firehouse the day before and asked if she might like to hang out and watch a movie with him. She'd told him she would've loved to, but she already had plans with his sister.

He'd told her to hang on and she'd listened as he yelled for his sister across the fire station.

"Yo, sis!"

"What?" Penelope's voice was faint and muffled.

"What time are you heading over to Beth's place tomorrow?"

"Six. Why?"

"Mind if I come too?"

"No."

He'd come back on the line and Beth swore she could hear the smile in his voice. "I'll see you tomorrow?"

Of course she'd agreed. She'd looked forward to

seeing them both again. They made her feel normal, and that in itself was amazing.

It'd been a while since she'd remoted into one of the group therapy sessions she and Pen attended, and Beth knew her friend would be on her case about it tonight. She kept meaning to, but hadn't been able to get up the nerve.

She wanted to talk to someone about her new discovery, but felt weird about Penelope knowing. She *fought* fire, and Beth instinctively knew she wouldn't understand and would try to talk her out of it. But Beth had no idea how something that made her feel so... free...could be bad.

It was fine. She was doing much better. She didn't need the therapy as much anymore anyway.

Beth looked over to the sliding glass door in her living room. It'd been the big white elephant in her life for a while now. The curtains had been kept firmly closed and she'd even put a bookshelf partially in front of it. This morning she'd taken a deep breath and made the first step toward trying to live a more normal life. She'd moved the heavy piece of furniture.

Pen hadn't commented on it when she'd arrived, but Beth could see she wanted to. The room was a bit brighter, even though the curtains were still drawn. Beth knew if she was ever going to be able to attend the Memorial Stair Climb event, or otherwise be able to step foot outside her apartment without holding someone's hand, she had to start somewhere.

In actuality, it freaked her out. Anyone could break

the door, it was only glass. The patio opened up into a large courtyard at the complex. There was a small concrete pad outside each ground-floor apartment, which gave way to a grassy field. Beth frequently heard kids playing, dogs barking, and the occasional group get-together, but in the past she'd merely turned up the television or the music she was listening to and tuned it out.

But sometime over the last week or so, she'd begun to realize how much she was missing out on in her life —and she'd gotten pissed. Damn Ben Hurst for making her this way. It wasn't fair that she was still suffering for something that bastard had done.

"...don't you think?"

Beth had completely missed Penelope's question. "Sorry, what?"

"I said, this movie would've been a lot better with Chris Pratt in it, yeah?"

"Of course. *Every* movie would be better with some Chris in it. Preferably with lots of butt shots."

Penelope giggled at her comment and Cade simply shook his head, obviously used to his sister's quirks.

"So, what have you guys been up to? Anything exciting happen at work?" Beth asked, twisting in her seat to face them. Cade was sitting in what Beth was quickly coming to think of as "his" seat, and Penelope was in the comfortable armchair next to the couch. Beth knew the nature of being a firefighter wasn't all go-go-go. It was a lot of sit-around-and-wait-for-something-to-happen. Pen had told her that some days they could get one call, and others they'd be on the go nonstop for the entire shift.

Cade seemed content to let his sister answer, and didn't interrupt as she talked about their week.

"First off, Taco broke his own record for the number of tacos he could eat in one sitting. I swear to God that man has a parasite or something. He never gains a pound, but he ate fifteen of those things today. Gross. Most normal people would've been puking if they ate that much in one sitting. Other than that, we had three car crashes, one bicycle wreck, and four grass fires. People annoy me. I mean, why would you throw a lit cigarette out the window when things are as dry as they are around here?" Penelope shook her head in disgust, then continued. "Seven false alarms, two reports of smoke that turned out to be nothing, one structure fire, three lift-assists, and thirteen medicals."

"Wow, that seems like a lot for only a couple of days."

"It's actually about average," Penelope told her after taking a sip of water.

"What's a lift-assist?" Beth was fascinated. She and Penelope had hung out before, of course, but they'd rarely talked details about her job. They usually talked about how Pen could help her with an upcoming shopping trip or other innocuous topics.

"It's where someone falls and can't get up by themselves."

"Oh, like older people?" Beth asked.

"Yeah, or those who are overweight."

"Really?"

"Uh-huh. I hate those the most. Not because I blame the person. I mean, if they could lose the weight easily, I'm sure they would. No one wants to weigh five hundred pounds. But let's just say all our working out really helps in those situations."

"I had no idea people called the fire department for help with that sort of thing."

Cade spoke up for the first time. "People call for help in all sorts of situations, Beth. There's no harm in asking for assistance when it's needed."

Beth looked at him, knowing what he wasn't coming right out and saying, but sorta coming right out and saying it anyway. "You know, you're not as subtle as you might think you are."

Cade chuckled. "That did come out as sounding awfully 'preachy' didn't it? I honestly didn't mean it to though. Think about it. If you weighed six hundred pounds and you slipped and fell and couldn't get up on your own...what would you do? You might crawl around on the floor, if you were able to, but if you couldn't pull yourself up, you'd end up dying there. Most of the time their loved ones do try to help them, but without a lot of muscle, it's just not gonna happen."

Cade leaned forward and continued his passionate speech. "I don't care if it's helping someone off the floor who can't do it themselves, or climbing a tree to get a cat down that doesn't really need the help anyway. It could be a kid whose mother is having a seizure, or an elderly woman who's lonely so she calls us for a small cut on her finger just so she has someone to talk to for a couple of minutes. Helping is what I do—I was born to do it. Don't mistake my comments as directed solely at you...although if *you* need help, you sure as hell better call me."

"You mean call nine-one-one."

"No. I mean call *me*."

Beth could only stare at Cade. His words settled in her soul and made her feel almost lightheaded. She knew she could count on Pen to give her a hand when she needed it, but to hear Cade so passionately and earnestly speaking right to her heart, scared her to death.

Deciding it was beyond time to change the subject —when Cade made goosebumps break out all over her arms, it was definitely time—she said, "Pen, you really shouldn't use the same password for all your accounts. I've headed off three hackers in the last week who would've gotten into your PayPal, bank, and electric company accounts."

"What?"

Penelope was obviously confused at the change in subject, but Cade merely relaxed back in his seat and kept his eyes on Beth as she fidgeted uncomfortably.

"Using PenisGod isn't a good username for things like Amazon and eBay. And you really need to delete your craigslist account because calling yourself a penis god is only attracting weirdos. You probably don't even remember you had that old ad up when you were trying to sell your bicycle. Well, it's one of the most clicked-on ads on the site for San Antonio. I'm not exaggerating either. You had four hundred and sixty-nine messages—and I'm not even going to comment on the sixty-nine thing. But three hundred and fourteen of those contained pictures of men's dicks. Fifty-seven contained marriage proposals, most from overseas; twenty-seven were from women who were interested in a threesome with you, fifty-five were spam, people trying to get you to click on links or buy some crap product, and the remaining sixteen emails were religious in nature, telling you to repent for your soul."

"I should probably be pissed you got into my account, but I trust you, so I'm not. But it's not penis god!" Penelope exclaimed huffily. "It's Pen IS God."

Cade burst out laughing. "Seriously, sis? Penis god? Just wait until the guys hear this!"

Penelope was on Cade before he could protect himself. She'd pushed him over and was tickling him mercilessly, threatening bodily harm and other nefarious tricks that she'd use to get back at him if any of the guys at the station found out.

Beth breathed a sigh of relief that the tension in the room had been broken. Cade finally got the upper hand on his sister, being eight inches taller had a great deal to do with it, and they settled back into their seats, still giggling.

"Okay, Miss Smarty Pants...I knew you were good at the whole computer thing, but you're way better than I'd thought, aren't you?" Pen asked, still breathing hard from her tussle with her brother.

"I'm pretty good," Beth said, shrugging and down-playing her abilities.

"She hacked PayPal's firewall the other night," Cade informed his sister smoothly, with a hint of pride in his voice.

"You did not!"

Beth shrugged and nodded. "It wasn't a big deal."

"Not a big deal? Okay, that's it…" Penelope pulled out her phone and began hitting buttons as if she were possessed.

Beth looked at Cade with her eyebrows raised in question.

"Don't look at me, I have no idea what she's up to."

Putting her phone down, Penelope smiled and folded her arms in front of her. "I give it ten minutes."

"You give *what* ten minutes?" Beth asked.

"You'll see."

Beth rolled her eyes. "Always the drama queen."

"She's been that way her entire life, if you didn't already know. You should get used to it," Cade told Beth without malice.

"You really did stop people from getting my info?" Penelope asked, ignoring her brother.

"Yeah. Your passwords should be different, and you should use special characters, upper and lowercase letters, and never use a real word."

"But I'll never remember them if I do that. It's handy because now I can log into all my accounts and never forget which password goes with what."

"It's also handy for any ol' hacker to get into all your

accounts too. Write them down then, but not on your computer. It's way too easy to hack in through a back-door and read anything you've got stored on your hard drive."

"People *do* that?"

"*Yes*, Pen. People do that. How long have we known each other?"

"Um, I knew there were hackers out there, but I didn't know they did that shit."

"They do."

"Have *you* done it?"

"Yes."

"Yes?"

Beth wanted to laugh at the horror in her friend's voice. "Pen. I do it for fun, to see if I can. Others do it to find stuff to blackmail people with or to steal from them."

"Whose computer have you hacked into?"

"I don't think you want to know."

"Mine?"

"No."

"Why not?"

Beth thought about clarifying how hacking into her email server was different from getting into the files on her computer, but decided it was easier to deal with the question at hand.

"Why not? Pen, it's not a challenge. I could probably guess the password to your computer in like three seconds. Besides, you're my friend, I wouldn't do that to you. But…see this little piece of paper over the built-in camera on my laptop?"

Both Cade and Pen nodded after Beth turned her screen to face them. "I meant to ask you about that," Pen told her.

"It's because anyone who hacks into your hard drive can take it over and if you don't have your webcam covered, the hacker can use it to spy on you and record whatever it is you're doing in view of the camera."

"What? *Seriously?*"

"Seriously."

"That's so gross." Penelope visibly shuddered. "I can't believe people would do that. I know, I shouldn't be surprised, but I am anyway."

Beth smiled at her friend's naiveté—then looked down at her computer when the alarm she'd programmed in to let her know when someone was trying to enter it through the backdoor went off. "What the fuck? Oh no you don't, you bastard."

"What?" Cade's tone lost any and all teasing. He looked around as if there was a physical threat in the room.

"Some asshole is trying to access my hard drive. Heh, he's obviously a novice, he should've seen the trap I had set up. What's he doing…oh shit, no way. Okay, it's on, you piece of shit."

Penelope and Cade looked at each other. Cade noticed the smirk on his sister's face and narrowed his eyes, wondering what brought it on. She was up to something, but he had no idea what. At the moment, he was more concerned about Beth.

Her fingers were flying over the keyboard and she was muttering under her breath. He could see lines and lines of code scrolling across her screen. Cade had no idea how she was able to read anything because it was moving so fast, but she obviously could, because she alternated between being happy when she'd done something to keep whomever it was out, and swearing when the other hacker got around the blockades she put in place, as quickly as she put them up.

It was obvious she'd tuned everything out but whatever was going on with her computer. It was cute as hell, but also a bit unnerving that she could forget he and his sister were even there.

Finally she sat back with a disgruntled huff and swore. "Dammit all to hell."

"What?" Penelope asked.

"He got in."

"And? What does that mean?"

"He won."

"Did he get your info? Are you gonna be broke now? Am I gonna have to visit you at the homeless shelter downtown?" Penelope joked.

Beth looked at her friend in disbelief. "You think I keep *anything* sensitive on my computer? No way. As soon as the alarm went off, all my passwords were automatically changed, and they'll continue to update every forty-five seconds until I stop the program."

"How will you know what they are so you can log into your stuff?"

Beth didn't bother to answer, just rolled her eyes.

"Okay, so you've figured that out already. How do you know he won? Was it really a competition?"

"How do I know he won?" Beth turned her screen again so both Pen and Cade could see it. There were electronic fireworks going off on the screen and the words "I WON" were flashing on and off as well.

Cade coughed into his hand, trying not to laugh. It really wasn't funny, if Beth's pissed-off face was anything to go by, but whoever the hacker was had a pretty good sense of humor.

Penelope's phone pinged with a text. She looked down and grinned.

"What's so funny?" Beth asked, obviously still upset.

Penelope turned her phone to Beth and showed her a picture of a computer screen, which looked exactly like Beth's did. The text message under it read, "Tell Elizabeth, I win."

CHAPTER 9

"WHAT THE *HELL*, Pen? You know who did this?" Beth asked in disbelief, looking ready to lurch across the room and strangle her friend.

"Yup."

When Penelope didn't say anything more, Beth put her computer to the side and stalked over to her friend. Before she got to her, Cade grabbed her hand and pulled her down next to him. "Easy, sweetheart. You can't kill my sister in front of me. I'd have to call my friend Dax and I'd be an accessory to murder and do twenty to life. Then you'd be the one visiting *me* in the penitentiary."

Cade felt good when Beth didn't pull away from him, but gripped his hand hard.

"Who is it?" Her question was geared toward Penelope.

"My friend, Tex. He's a computer genius who

helped get the teams in to save me. I've only met him once, but have talked to him many times."

Beth's eyes narrowed. "So why did he hack into my computer?"

"Probably to see if what I told him was true."

"Pen, I love you, but I swear to God if you don't start making sense, I'm gonna email every news agency I can come up with, pretend to be you, and tell them you're dying to finally tell your side of your story."

Cade saw his sister pale, and squeezed Beth's hand in warning. "Beth…"

He saw the remorse on Beth's face as soon as the words left her mouth. "I'm sorry, Pen. You know I wouldn't do that. But shit. Really? Who *is* this guy?"

"Look. All I heard from the men who rescued me is how great this Tex person is. How he can hack into anything, how much he's done for them, and how no one is as good as he is. I just…when you were talking about getting into my computer and keeping those jerks from accessing my info, I wanted to introduce you to Tex. *All* I said was that you were good and maybe you could help him out someday." Penelope fingered the pendant around her throat nervously as she spoke.

"And he hacked into my computer as a result?"

Penelope shrugged. "I guess he wanted to know if I was exaggerating or not."

"So, now that he got through, I guess he knows you were exaggerating."

Beth's computer made a weird dinging noise again,

and Cade let go of her hand as she lurched across the cushions to pick it up. Her fingers darted over the keys again and she said under her breath, "I'll be damned."

"What now?" Penelope asked, leaning forward to try to see her screen.

Beth looked up. "He restored my firewall and repaired the hole he made. Not only that, but, look…" She turned the computer and showed Cade and Penelope the note on the screen.

Tiger was right. You're good. Want a job?

"I don't get it. Who's Tiger?" Beth asked in confusion.

"That would be me. It's what the guys who came in to rescue me called me," Penelope said sheepishly.

"Hmmmm. Wonder what kind of job he's talking about?"

"Uh, one with computers?" Penelope said as if Beth had a couple of screws loose in her head.

"Hey! I haven't had the chance to talk to Daxton or Cruz yet about you working for them," Cade complained. "But now that I think about it, it's probably better if you work for him. You know…with your penchant for illegally hacking into Fortune 500 databases and all."

"She doesn't do it to steal stuff," Penelope huffed, sticking up for her friend.

"Well, I'll think about it and contact him later."

"What? Beth! You should take Tex up on it!" Penelope urged.

"I'm busy. I'm hanging out with you guys. Besides,

my heart hasn't gotten over the shock of someone breaking into my computer yet."

Cade smiled. It was amazing how different Beth was when she was at home in her own space and comfortable. He liked it. He liked *her*.

Penelope hadn't told him much about the men who'd rescued her, and she certainly hadn't mentioned anyone with the unbelievably cliché name of "Tex." He'd have to talk to his sister privately about the man. While he was proud of Beth's computer abilities, what she was doing *was* illegal, and the last thing he wanted was for her to get caught. She had enough on her plate as it was…she didn't need any more hassle.

Wanting to get Beth's thoughts off her computer, he asked, "What's with all the candles?" Cade liked it when Beth was relaxed, and now that she knew some random hacker wasn't messing with her data, she'd put the computer aside again and had folded against him. But with his question, he felt her tense up. He hurried to reassure her. "I wasn't making fun. I like them, it's just that I haven't seen them before."

Cade looked around the room and noted just how many there were. There were some tealight candles on the kitchen counter, and a variety of colors and sizes of them in a box on the floor next to the sliding glass doors that led into the courtyard.

"Now that I think about it, you have a ton of them, Beth," Penelope chimed in. She leaned over and picked up one from the coffee table and smelled it. "This one isn't even scented."

"Uh, yeah. I thought they were...but I bought the wrong ones."

"I have a friend who sells the really good kind. I can hook you up if you want?" Pen asked, trying to be helpful.

"It's okay."

"Well, if you want more, just let me know."

"I will."

Cade felt Beth relax against him again as they turned their attention back to the movie, now that the drama of the night was over. Something niggled at the back of his mind, but he pushed it aside, lost in the softness of Beth's body against his.

* * *

Three hours later, well after Penelope had left, Cade stood at Beth's door looking down at her. "I feel like we spend a lot of time standing here."

Beth smiled and wrinkled her nose. "I know, right? It's just a door, but sometimes it feels like I really am in jail."

"You really shouldn't be so hard on yourself."

"I'm trying to get better."

"I know."

Beth looked away, then brought her eyes back up to his. "What if it doesn't ever get easier? I don't want to be like this for the rest of my life."

"All you can do is go one day at a time. Don't borrow trouble, sweetheart."

Beth sighed and slowly leaned into Cade, resting her forehead against his chest. "I want so badly to be like everyone else."

"I like you just the way you are."

Beth felt his words rumble through his wide chest and into her own body. "If I was like everyone else we might have normal dates."

"I don't know. This one was pretty good. We hung out, watched a movie, laughed, and now we're going to kiss each other good-night."

His words brought her head up, and she saw the blinding smile aimed at her. "First, I'm a total computer geek. I love it, but unfortunately it's not exactly the sexiest thing in the world. Second, it might have been a good night here, but I want so badly to be able to hang out with you in public. A restaurant, a bar...your place."

"Done."

"What?"

"We'll start with my place. I'll come and get you and we can hang over there. It's not as cool as your apartment is though. It's a bachelor pad."

"I'd love to see your place," Beth said wistfully. "And meet your friends. You've talked about them so much, I feel like I know them."

Cade laughed. "You can meet them, but I swear if Driftwood or Crash hit on you, I won't be responsible for my actions."

"They're the playboys, right?"

"I guess that's as good a label to give them as any," Cade said easily.

Beth wrinkled her forehead. "Who are the others again?"

"Let's see. Firefighters first. Taco was here at your place when you tried to super-fry your chicken. He wasn't the asshole who tried to force you outside though, just making that clear, that was one of the new guys who, thankfully, I don't work with much. Squirrel is who you might call our resident geek. Tall, skinny, and wears glasses, but he's the best medic we've got. There isn't a medical situation he can't figure out and take control of. If I ever have a heart attack, get my arm cut off, stab myself or get shot, I'd want Squirrel to be at my side."

"He's that good?"

"I once saw him triage and treat eight people at a bus wreck site. We were all there, but it was utter chaos. Every single person he touched that night survived, and every single one sent him a thank you note. And just so you know, this is highly unusual. People are thankful we're there to help them, but only one percent actually follow up to say thank you."

"I've been meaning to get those thank you cards sent," Beth said with a small smile.

"You can thank me with a kiss, sweetheart. I'll pass your thanks on to the rest of the team."

"What about the others?"

"Ah, you're killin' me. Okay, there's Chief and Moose."

"Moose is the one who was at the minivan fire the other night and who Pen likes, right?"

"Yes. But the two of them are so stubborn, I don't know if either of them will ever pull their heads out of their asses long enough to do something about it."

"And these cop friends I keep hearing about?"

"Daxton is a Texas Ranger. He rescued his girlfriend, Mackenzie, from being buried alive. Cruz is with the FBI. He met his girlfriend when he went undercover in a motorcycle club."

"She's a biker?" Beth asked incredulously.

"Good Lord, no. She's the sister of a woman who was in too deep with the club and... Anyway, no. I'm sure you'll hear the story sooner or later from Mickie herself. Then there's Quint, who's with the San Antonio Police Department, and his girlfriend is blind, but she rescued herself when she got into trouble, which is totally awesome. By the time he showed up to save the day, Corrie had already gotten away. Then there's the rest of the crew, who are all still single, and if they flirt with you, I'll have to hurt them. Hayden, the lone female in our close-knit group, you might remember from the grocery store the other day. She's the one Penelope was going shooting with. Then TJ is with the Highway Patrol, Calder is a medical examiner, and Conor, who's a game warden."

"How did you guys get so close? I didn't think firefighters hung out with cops."

"It was inevitable. Our paths cross so much. There aren't a lot of calls we go on that don't have some sort of law enforcement involved. They're all great guys, and now that some have girlfriends, it's even more fun to hang out with them. You'll meet them all eventually. I know you'll like them though."

"I *hope* I'll get to meet them. I want to be able to go to that softball tournament you've told me about so often. It sounds hilarious."

"You will. We'll work our way up to it. Although the game is only funny because the damn cops can't play fair to save their lives. We have to resort to under-handed techniques to keep them from cheating," Cade told her with a smile.

"I'd do anything to be able to be casual about being outside this damn apartment. To be a normal person and able to meet you at the bar and have a drink or two before we headed off for a night at the movies or with your friends."

"Stop. If you were this fictional 'normal' that you keep talking about, we might never have met. You wouldn't have been in that counseling session with Penelope and I wouldn't have offered to help you clean up your place after that fire."

"You wouldn't have?"

"No, contrary to what it seems, I don't go around helping all the people I meet on the job after hours. I fully admit I enjoy being there when folks need help, but it's not something I purposely set out to do when I go home. You knew my sister; that, along with the attraction I had for you, pushed me to want to see you again."

Beth licked her lips and looked up at the amazing man in front of her. He was so much braver than she was. She'd been attracted to him as well. The fact that he was Pen's brother also made her let her guard down around him. She most likely wouldn't have opened up to him otherwise.

"So…you said something about kissing?"

Cade's smile lit up his face. "Yeah, I believe I did. Put your arms around my neck."

Beth stood on her tiptoes so she could clasp her fingers together at his nape.

"Hold on, sweetheart."

Cade lowered his head and did what he'd wanted to do all night. Watching her bite her lip as she cyber-battled with Tex, as she licked her lips after drinking from the water bottle, as she smiled while he and Penelope bantered back and forth, almost pushed him over the edge several times.

Now that Penelope wasn't there to act as a chaperone, Cade took Beth's mouth as if it would be the last time he'd ever touch her. He wasn't gentle and didn't ease into the kiss. He devoured her mouth with all the passion he'd been suppressing all night.

Beth met his tongue with her own, curling around it and sucking. Cade could feel her fingernails digging into the sensitive skin on the back of his neck and he growled in approval. She learned quickly what he liked and what made herself feel good. He slanted his head and took her deeper, tasting and nipping. He probably shouldn't have been surprised at her eagerness, but he was.

The last time he'd stood at her door and kissed her,

he'd gotten the impression she wasn't that experienced, but tonight she seemed much more confident. It was if she was a different person, and the dichotomy entranced him.

Finally, knowing he needed to pull back before he stripped her naked and took her against the infamous door she hated, Cade licked her lip one last time before ending their kiss. They were both breathing hard and he rested his forehead against hers.

"Wow."

He smiled at the breathy word. "Yeah, wow."

Her fingers continued to caress him in what he thought was an unconscious act on her part. He squeezed her waist where his hands had crept during their kiss. They were resting under her shirt on her bare skin and Cade could feel goosebumps rise as he caressed her.

"I feel like I could take on the world when you kiss me."

Cade's fingers involuntarily clenched and he forced himself to relax, not wanting to hurt her. Her words were so sad. Cade couldn't help but feel both elated and so very sorry for her at the same time.

He put one hand under her chin and forced her to look at him. "Then I'll have to make sure I kiss you more often, won't I?"

Beth smiled weakly up at him. "I guess you will."

Cade brushed his lips across hers in a chaste caress. "I'll talk to you soon, okay?"

"Okay. Drive safe."

"Always." Cade pulled away and dealt with the locks on her door, reaching out and squeezing her hand once more, before heading down the hallway toward the exit that led out to the parking lot.

Beth watched from her door until the panic threatened to overtake her. She closed the door, locked it, and immediately went into the kitchen to get 'one of the extra-long matches she'd ordered online.

She lit it and watched as the flame slowly burned down the eight-inch stick until she blew it out right above her fingertips with one hard puff.

Beth put her head on her arms on the counter and breathed out a frustrated sigh. Her lips still tingled from Cade's kisses and she swore she could still feel his fingers on the bare skin of her waist.

Interestingly enough, she was more afraid of stepping foot outside her apartment than she was of getting involved with Cade. Even though Hurst had hurt and tortured her, she wasn't afraid of Cade. Intellectually, she knew that sex with him wouldn't be like what Hurst had done to her. She hadn't been a virgin when she'd been kidnapped and wasn't afraid of the act, per se. Cade was going out of his way to take things slowly with her, and she knew to the marrow of her bones he wouldn't hurt her. He'd be gentle and would make sure she was comfortable and taken care of before he'd even think of getting off himself.

She wanted to be his girlfriend. Wanted to be by his side as he hung out with his buddies from the station. Wanted to be able to drive to his place and be waiting for him when he got off work. Wanted to go to one of the infamous firefighter versus police officer softball games she'd heard so much about.

But until she managed to kick the stupid agoraphobia in its ass, she wasn't going anywhere. She was a prisoner in her own home.

Beth picked up her head and reached for another match. They were the key. They'd be crucial to getting her out of her head and into the real world. If the flame kept her from concentrating on her fear, she'd use it to help her get better.

Despite the small voice deep down that was telling her it wouldn't be that easy, Beth was pleased with her decision.

CHAPTER 10

BETH STOOD STILL on the little patio, her back to the glass door behind her. Her legs were shaking, her breaths coming too fast to be healthy, but she was outside. By herself.

It was two in the morning and Beth stared at the flames licking upward in the small circular grill she'd bought online.

She'd started out lighting a piece of paper over the sink inside her apartment and watching it burn down to ash. Then she'd assembled the grill in her living room, put a short stack of paper in the bottom and watched as that too went up in flames. It was over too quickly and had produced a lot more smoke than she realized it would. Afraid her smoke detector was going to go off and wake the entire apartment complex, and, more horrifically, make Cade and his friends come busting into her apartment and find out her dirty little secret, Beth had carried the grill to the patio door and cracked it open.

It'd taken a week, but after slowly moving the grill farther and farther back onto the concrete pad, she'd been able to stand in the doorway and watch the flames. Now, she was finally all the way outside. She'd done it.

Beth knew she was a long way away from being able to function outside her apartment by herself, but she felt like she'd taken a giant step forward. Dismissing the small voice inside that mocked her by saying watching shit burn was not only *not* forward momentum, but was actually a scary, creepy backward leap, Beth took a deep breath.

Things were going very well in her life recently. She'd gotten ahold of the mysterious Tex and he'd been putting her through some tests to make sure she had what it took to work for him...or for whoever he was grooming her to work for. She still hadn't decided if she *wanted* to work for Tex, she wasn't even sure exactly what it was he did, but the possibility of doing what she loved for a living, rather than customer service, was exciting.

Beth had a blast trying to work through the challenges Tex put forth for her. She passed most of them with flying colors and when he'd typed "good job" one night, Beth had felt like her heart was going to burst with pride. She sensed that he wasn't a man who gave praise easily, so earning those two little words from him had meant a lot.

The thought of being able to quit her customer service job and work full-time with code, trying to prevent cyberattacks, was a dream come true. And while she wasn't there yet, she felt good about where she was headed. Beth had no idea how to thank Penelope for hooking her up with Tex—even if he'd bested her in getting through her safeguards on her personal computer.

Her relationship with Cade was also moving forward in a good direction. He'd come over and taken her shopping again, not once letting go of her hand, and with no crises on the way to or from the store. She'd felt more relaxed the entire time they'd been out and about than she had in the last year.

Even though she didn't see her parents or brother much, she was very close to them. They were frustrated because they didn't know how to help her work past what had happened, but she'd been making an effort to call them more often lately too.

The only thing Beth felt was holding her back from being completely happy was her stupid fear of being outside. She knew it was a million to one shot that anyone would kidnap her again, but it was that *one* that was holding her back. She wanted to be able to confidently walk outside and not constantly have to look around her, but she'd take being able to be outside of her apartment and not turn into a blubbering basket case.

She'd done tons of research online and knew there were various drugs she could take that might be able to help her, but Beth was stubborn. She wanted to be herself again, without having to resort to Xanax or something similar. Her first therapist back in California had prescribed it, and Beth hated how it had made her feel. Granted, it had been useful in enabling her to get to Texas without completely freaking out, but as soon as she was settled, she'd stopped taking it.

Beth supposed her abhorrence for taking the drug was why she latched onto the idea of fire now. It gave her a similar sensation...a feeling of looking at herself from far away. While that flame was flickering and dancing, she didn't feel scared or anxious. Both wins in her book.

The problem was that Beth had no idea how to translate the peace and calm she felt while watching flames crackle and spit as they devoured whatever was burning, into her everyday life. She'd tried closing her eyes and imagining the fire, but it wasn't the same. There was something about the slight burn in her eyes from the smoke and the smell of whatever was smoldering that made her not think about anything else going on around her.

Not to mention, she hadn't told Penelope or Cade about her new therapy, knowing they wouldn't approve and would try to put the kibosh on it. Things with Cade were going well and the last thing she wanted to do was mess it up. It wasn't as if she was a pyromaniac or something. She wasn't setting buildings on fire or anything and she wasn't hurting anyone. But she still knew, *knew*, it would affect her relationship with both Cade and Penelope.

Looking around, and seeing no one in the dark blackness in the middle of the night, Beth took a step toward the grill, then another. She'd had to light it, so it wasn't as if she hadn't been out this far, but this felt different. The flames mesmerized her and made her feel so much more in control. *She* decided when they'd stop. The control was heady.

She poured a bottle of water over the flames and they hissed and spit, but were snuffed out, leaving only a thin trail of smoke behind in their wake. Beth looked up into the sky, filled with hundreds of stars, and took a deep breath. She could do this. She *would* do this. She'd be normal again if it killed her.

* * *

"So...we've watched four movies at your place, gone shopping three times, and talked on the phone over two dozen times. Don't you think it's about time you see where I live?"

Cade's words were lazy, but Beth could hear the underlying tension in them. She'd been putting him off, but he was right. They'd been getting along wonderfully. Each kiss made her fall for him harder. He'd been patient and hadn't rushed her into anything beyond what he'd previously called "the dugout" and first base.

The last time he'd been over, they'd made out like teenagers on her couch and she'd actually fallen asleep before three in the morning, snug and safe in his arms. She'd woken up around four with a crick in her neck from their awkward position on the couch, but hadn't even cared.

She really liked this man and was more than curious about where he lived. He'd claimed it was "only a bachelor pad," but she figured he was probably downplaying it a bit. Pen had told her Cade lived in the Potranco Ranch area, a community on the northwest side of the city with half-acre home sites. He'd bought the house a couple of years ago when it was a buyer's market. Beth was dying to see it.

"I'd love to see your place, Cade," she told him, gripping the phone so hard she was afraid it'd crack under the pressure.

"Great. Tonight?"

Beth could feel the panic building inside at his suggestion. "Tonight's not good. I have to do a thing for Tex and—"

"You can do it at my place. I'll come and get you early, before dinner. We'll stop and get takeout and bring it home."

Beth was silent. She so wanted to come up with a hundred excuses for why tonight wouldn't work, but couldn't.

"Please, Beth. Trust me. I'm gonna be with you the entire time. I know this is hard for you. I *know* it. But I think if you get the first time out of the way, you'll feel so much better."

It was the please that did it. And the fact he was

right. She'd built it up so much in her mind, that it was merely the thought of being in his space and not her own that was making her uneasy. "Okay. But don't blame me if I freak out or if you have to bring me back here or keep hold of me all night."

Beth could just imagine her having to hold Cade's hand even in his house. What a disaster.

"Don't you get it? There's nothing I'd like better than holding on to you all night, sweetheart."

God, he was so wonderful.

"Do you have a preference for dinner? There's a great Thai place on my way home. Or we could do pizza or Chinese. Really anything you're in the mood for, I can arrange."

"Can we stop at Whataburger?"

Cade laughed. "Of course."

"I haven't had one in forever," Beth said wistfully.

"Then one big, juicy Whataburger is what you'll have. I can't wait to see you. I'll be there around five-thirty."

Beth looked at her watch. Two. She had three and a half hours to freak out.

"Great!" she told him in a high voice, trying to act excited.

He obviously saw right through her. His voice was soft and easy, not accusatory or pushy at all. "Beth, if this is too much too fast, just tell me. I'll back off and we'll continue to hang out at your place. It's not a big deal."

Beth took a deep breath. "No, it's okay. I can't

pretend I'm not nervous as all get-out. But you're right, it's time. I need to get out of this apartment, otherwise I'll never leave. Even my counselor said if I didn't push myself I'd get more and more comfortable where I am…and would have a harder time breaking free."

"I worry about you."

"I know. Thank you. But Cade?"

"Yes, hon?"

"If I freak out—"

"If you have an attack I'll be right there. Okay?"

"Okay," Beth whispered. "Thanks."

"Bring your computer with you…you have that thing to do for Tex and it'll make you more comfortable. If nothing else, you can lose yourself in work. I'll see you in a few hours. Try not to stress about this. It'll be fine."

"See you soon."

"Bye."

"Bye."

Beth hung up her phone and took a deep breath. Then another. Then one more. She felt a bit calmer, but reached over and grabbed the disposable lighter sitting on the table. She flicked it on and sighed when the flame burst to life. She held it until her thumb hurt from the pressure it took to hold the fuel lever down.

She was so screwed.

CHAPTER 11

So far, so good.

Cade had showed up exactly at five-thirty, taken hold of her hand and hadn't let go yet. They'd stopped at the burger chain and picked up dinner. Beth couldn't help but be impressed with his neighborhood. The houses weren't mansions, but they weren't shacks either.

Cade's was a two-story with a porch that wrapped around the front and one side. His yard was hurting from the lack of rain, but was nicely manicured and it was massive. There was what looked like a forest behind his house, which turned out to be some sort of nature refuge. He'd explained that he'd purchased two lots, wanting room between him and his nearest neighbor. The neighborhood was still being built and at the moment the lots around his house stood empty, waiting for someone to buy the land and design their dream house. Since no one could build on the land behind the house, because of the nature refuge, it was like living out in the country, but having the convenience of being close to civilization at the same time. Beth loved it on sight.

He didn't let go of her hand even when they were inside, merely towed her into his kitchen. Cade dropped the bag of food on the counter then turned to her. He finally let go of her hand, only to sandwich her head in his hands and lean in.

"You seem to be all right. Yeah?"

"I'm okay, thanks, Cade."

"Good. I have a surprise for you after we eat."

"Uh, I'm not that good with surprises."

"That's because you haven't had enough practice with the good kind."

Beth couldn't remember the last time she'd had a nice surprise. "That's probably true, but I'm reserving the right to get payback if it all goes downhill."

Cade laughed and kissed her lightly on the lips. He leaned down and nuzzled behind her ear. Beth helped by tilting her head to give him better access. The goosebumps that raced down her arms made her shiver. "It's not going to go downhill, but feel free to hold me down and have your wicked way with me if it makes you feel better."

Beth laughed and pushed lightly. "Goof. Come on, I'm starved, and the smell of that burger and fries is making me want to gnaw my arm off."

"Can't have that. Dig in, sweetheart."

Beth forced herself to back away from Cade. He

was way too addicting. She had enough issues in her life and didn't want to add crazy stalker girlfriend to the list.

Dinner went well. Beth couldn't remember the last time she'd enjoyed a fast-food meal so much. It wasn't just the food, but Cade. He was funny and Beth relaxed just being around him.

Cade gave her a tour of his house, and Beth was very impressed. It *did* look like a single guy lived there, but it wasn't over the top, there wasn't one foosball table to be seen. There were three bedrooms, with one set up as a workout room. The guest bathroom was clean and it even looked like there was a full roll of toilet paper on the roll—and the paper was actually hanging over the top instead of under it. He got bonus points for that.

The master bedroom was huge and Beth immediately felt at ease in it. He had a king-size bed, which was mostly made. The comforter was thrown over the sheets, and it looked extremely comfy. There were at least six pillows, and Beth couldn't resist teasing Cade about it.

"Enough pillows there?"

Cade didn't take offense. "Hey, what can I say? I like to cuddle at night, and if a pillow is the only thing available to snuggle up to, it'll have to do...although I prefer a human to curl up with."

Beth blushed. "I walked right into that one didn't I?"

"You did, and I couldn't resist." Cade gave her a one-armed hug. "But seriously, you should know I haven't had a woman at my house in over two years."

Beth looked up at Cade in amazement. "First, why? And second, I'm not sure why you're telling me that."

"Are you kidding? Sometimes I can't tell when you're being sarcastic and when you're serious."

"I'm being completely serious."

Cade turned to her, his face not showing any of the easy-going Cade she'd gotten to know over the last few weeks. "Beth. I'm telling you this because it's true. Because I like you...a lot. Because we're dating. Although if you have to ask why I'm trying in my ass-backward way to let you know I'm not a manwhore, I'm not sure we're on the same page."

Beth swallowed hard. If he could be honest with her, the least she could do was give it back to him. "I... it's been a really long time for me...since my freshman year in college. I thought he liked me, but he was drunk and didn't even remember me in the morning."

"Dumb college-asshole fuck."

Beth's lips twitched. She couldn't help it. Cade's disgruntled words were kinda funny. "I don't think you're a manwhore."

"Thank you."

"And I like you too. A lot."

"Good."

"But I'm not ready to hop into bed with you."

"I know, but you know what? I'd be disappointed if you were. I like the pace we're going. You're still dealing with a lot of stuff in your life, and I really, *really* don't want to be some sort of rebound guy," Cade told her, sincerity coating his words.

"You're definitely *not* a rebound guy, Cade. In fact, you're more like my start-my-new-life guy."

"I hope that's a more permanent position than rebound guy, because I'll tell you right now, Beth, I plan to be around for a very long time. You don't get to be my age and not hang on with everything you have to a good thing. And, sweetheart, you are *definitely* a good thing."

Beth's breath hitched at his words. God. Her thoughts came out soft and low. "I wouldn't necessarily start carving our names into that huge tree on the side of your house, but I'm thinking that making sure we have the necessary tools just in case wouldn't be amiss or inappropriate at this point."

Cade pulled Beth toward him and wrapped his arms around her. "Good. I'm sure I've got tree-carving tools around here someplace."

Beth snuggled into Cade, buried her nose against his neck and inhaled. He always smelled so good, even when she saw him right after his shift when he stopped by with groceries for her. Feeling her nipples peak at the thought of what he'd smell like all over, and the thought of getting her hands on him, she shifted in his hold.

Cade drew back a fraction of an inch and looked down at her. "I know, standing next to this huge bed makes me want to try it out too, but I promised you a surprise. Come on, sweetheart. I have no doubt we'll eventually make it up here and we'll spend hours getting to know each other, inside and out, and hitting a home run, but right now, I want to show you something."

Beth ran her finger over his collarbone and coyly looked up at him. "You could show me something right here…if you wanted."

Cade barked out a laugh. "Lord, if I thought you were ready, I'd have you naked and under me so fast your head would spin."

"I'm getting there. You know, I once thought what that asshole did to me would make me afraid to get naked with anyone ever again, but I'm finding that prospect not so scary with you. I have a feeling you'd cut off your own arm before you'd do anything that would scare or hurt me."

"Damn straight. And you have no idea how happy I am to hear that. I won't ever hurt you, and I'll do what I can to make sure it's only the two of us in our bed, but tonight we're going to enjoy your surprise, then I'll take you home."

"Can I stay here?"

"What?"

"Not *here*, here. But in your house. I'll stay downstairs because I know you have to work tomorrow, but I can set up my computer at your kitchen table and I'll sleep on the couch. If it's not too much trouble, you can drop me off at my place before you go into work."

"My place *is* your place," Cade told her seriously. "I'd like nothing more than for you to feel as comfortable here as you are in your apartment. I wasn't sure if you were ready for that. I know your place is your safety net. I wouldn't ask you to do anything that would make you uncomfortable."

"I like your house. It feels...safe to me, especially if you're here. I'm not sure why."

"You can stay as long as you want. Tomorrow, if you think you'd be okay, you can hang around here while I go to work."

"Really? You aren't scared I'll go through your things or anything?"

"No. Because I've got nothing to hide. If you want to hack into my computer, go for it."

"I already have."

Cade looked taken-aback for a moment, then recovered. "Right...see? Nothing to hide."

Beth let loose the smile she was holding back. "I was kidding, Cade. I wouldn't hack into your hard drive."

"Brat." The word was said affectionately and Cade followed it up with a long, wet kiss that made Beth's legs weak.

When he finally pulled back, they were both breathing hard. "Come on. We need to get out of my bedroom, and I have that surprise I promised you."

Beth followed Cade down the hall and stairs back into his living room. He sat her on one of the leather couches then went into the kitchen. He popped some popcorn and got them both a beer. It seemed like an odd choice of snack, but Beth didn't say anything. He was obviously on a mission.

After setting the popcorn and beers on the coffee table, he went to the TV and messed with some of the equipment. Finally, he came back over to where she was sitting and settled next to her. He clicked on the television and sat back, pulling her with him.

"A movie is my surprise?"

"Not a movie. Watch."

Beth smiled huge when the video started playing. She looked at Cade incredulously when she realized what she was watching.

He shrugged. "We've talked about it, I figured until you feel strong enough to get to one yourself, this would do."

Beth threw herself into Cade's arms, but didn't take her eyes off the screen. He'd put in a recording of what was obviously one of their officers versus firefighters softball games. The video wasn't the best quality, and made her slightly sick to watch with the shaky movement from whoever was filming, but it was the best present anyone had gotten her in a long time. The popcorn and beer made sense now.

They watched the entire game, and Cade gave her a running commentary on what was going on offscreen that she couldn't see. Both teams flagrantly cheated, but it all seemed to be a part of the fun. Beth giggled until tears coursed down her cheeks when Penelope flashed the officers while wearing her sports bra to divert their attention, and Driftwood stole home and scored the winning run for the firefighters.

"It looks like you guys really do get along well."

"We do. There might be a rivalry between us and the cops, but every single one of us knows any of the others would lay down their lives for us if it came to that. We work together. Many times when we show up to accidents or fires, one of them is already on the scene," Cade reminded her, talking about the law enforcement officers.

"And we watch their backs when we can. It's almost crazy how much our paths cross when we're doing our jobs."

"Is what you do that dangerous then?" Beth asked, worried.

"No, sweetheart. We tend to stick to helping others. I won't lie and say it's always one hundred percent safe...dealing with fire is never safe. It's unpredictable and even when you think you've got it under control, it can flare up and bite you in the ass. I've studied it, I know the science behind how it works, but even I'm still taken by surprise every now and then. We only pretend to control it, but in reality, the flames are always in charge."

Beth was surprised by his words. That hadn't been her experience at all. She was easily able to decide when to put her little fires out, but she kept quiet as he went on.

"It's just that when there's a car accident and we get called, usually one of our friends is already there working the scene. If there's a domestic incident, we get called in for medical assistance, but again, our boys in blue are usually already there and they've got it under control. I've even seen them jump in and help with water when we need it at a scene. We're in it together and I wouldn't change what I do for the world."

"You love it."

"I do."

They were silent for a moment as they watched the firefighters celebrating on the screen in front of them. "Do you think your friends would come over here one night...you know, if you had a cookout or something... so I could meet them?" Beth thought she was probably overstepping, but she wanted to meet his friends so badly. They looked fun. She didn't have enough fun in her life. Once upon a time, back before everything that had happened, she'd loved to hang out. She used to be the life of the party. Watching the tape and seeing everyone joking around and having fun, she realized she missed it.

"Yes. I want to show you off."

"That's not quite what I meant." Beth chuckled nervously. "I just thought that—"

"It's fine. I'll see if we can set it up this coming weekend. All right?"

"Yeah. But can I ask a favor?"

"Anything."

"If I start to lose it, will you take me into your bedroom or something? I don't want them seeing me that way. I mean, they probably all know about me already..." Her voice trailed off as if asking for confirmation. When Cade nodded, she continued, "But as you know, it's one thing to know about my agoraphobia and it's another for them to see it in person, especially the first time I meet them. Sometimes I get nervous around a lot of people, and even though I won't be outside, every now and then I still panic."

"Beth, they're all medics. And the cops may not have seen a panic attack, but they've seen much worse in their line of work. It's not going to faze them."

"But they haven't seen *me* have one."

"Okay, I promise to take you into another room if it happens. But I think you're going to be fine. Within ten minutes of them being here, you're going to think you've known them forever."

"I hope so."

"I know so. But just remember, you're my girl—and I'll tell you right now, if any of those yahoos even *thinks* about stealing you away, they'll have me to deal with."

Beth giggled and rolled her eyes at Cade. It sounded as though he was completely serious, but she thought she was pretty safe from his friends hitting on her.

Cade hugged her again and leaned in so his lips were at her ear. "In case I forget to tell you later, I like having you in my space, sweetheart. I like everything about you. Knowing you want to meet my friends and get to know them? Icing on the cake."

Beth shivered as his breath caused goosebumps to rise on her arms. Darn it, she always reacted to him that way. It was amazing and somewhat embarrassing at the same time. "If they're your friends, I know I'll like them."

"As long as you like me better, I'm good with that."

Cade kissed her again, this one inching up to and past second base before he pulled back, taking a deep breath. Beth could feel how much he liked kissing her because his erection was pressing against her stomach.

"God, you make me lose my head. Come on, let's get you settled. Pull out your laptop and I'll put in a movie."

Beth smiled and did as he suggested, reaching for her bag from where she was sitting on the couch, while Cade fiddled with the TV to put in a DVD. She was still smiling thirty minutes later when she looked over and saw him fast asleep next to her. He'd put his hand on her leg as he'd settled in beside her, and it was still there, limp and heavy against her. Her smile grew bigger as she turned her attention back to her laptop and the firewall she was trying to break.

CHAPTER 12

THE FOLLOWING WEEKEND, Cade welcomed all of his friends from Station 7, as well as some of the law enforcement officers he'd told Beth about. Dax and Mack had been able to come, along with Hayden and Conor. After a few minutes of introductions as each arrived, his friends fell into their usual routines, teasing and joking around. It wasn't long before Cade saw the stress lines smooth off Beth's face and she began to relax enough to tease them back.

"I am not a circus freak to be brought out to perform tricks for your amusement," Beth said with a completely straight face.

Driftwood looked shocked for a second, but when Beth couldn't hold back the grin that had been threatening to appear, he sighed in relief. "Shit, woman, I thought you were serious!"

Hayden and the rest of the group howled with laughter.

Penelope smirked at Driftwood, but didn't say a word.

Beth felt sorry for Cade's friend now. "I could totally hack into your online dating site and get the personal email addresses of all the women you've flagged...but then you'd find out that half of them are at least ten years older or younger than their profiles said, a fourth are actually men, and the other fourth are already married. I don't understand why you're even using an online site. You're hot. Are you really telling me that you can't find a date?"

"He can find a date; it's just that he's a one-night kinda guy, and he's already tapped most of the women he knows. So to avoid having them get the wrong idea and think he'd actually date them for more than one night, he's trying to find a new pool of women," Taco helpfully explained.

Driftwood did actually look a bit guilty, but he didn't deny his friend's justification of his need for an online dating service. "I'm not the only one who has a profile, just so you know. What's the saying, 'those that live in glass houses shouldn't throw stones'?"

Crash piped up, defending himself. "I only went on that one time because we were bored on that shift. I didn't actually answer any of the messages I got. I like to check out my dates in person before I decide to spend the evening with them."

"Dating? Is that what you're calling what you do now?" Chief asked, smirking, looking relaxed with a beer in his hand, his hip leaning against the wall.

Squirrel cleared his throat, and Beth smiled at him. He didn't look like any of the other guys on the squad. His tall, skinny frame and glasses made him seem as if he should be working alongside her on the computer rather than running into burning buildings. "Technically it *is* a date. He meets them at a bar, pays for their drinks, and food if they want it, then they go to her place, have intercourse, and the night ends."

Beth suppressed a giggle at the word "intercourse." Squirrel totally should be buried in a company working on a computer somewhere.

Moose choked back a laugh and slapped Squirrel on the back. "You're so right, my man. That's a date in my book."

Cade decided to cut in. Now seemed like a good time to change the subject before his squad got into a deeper discussion about what constituted an official date. "Just because my girlfriend's a computer genius doesn't mean you now all have a get-out-of-jail-free card. Behave yourselves."

Everyone laughed and went back to their individual conversations. Beth leaned into Cade and whispered, "I'm having a good time."

Cade would've laughed, but he knew how hard this afternoon had been for her. He'd picked her up the day before and brought her to his house. They'd spent yesterday afternoon getting ready for the barbeque. Cade had run out to the store to get last-minute supplies and when he'd gotten home, Beth had finished cleaning the kitchen.

He could tell she was keyed up because she'd had a hard time sitting still. She'd finally settled down with her computer after her new friend Tex gave her some "homework." As much as he'd wanted to take her up to his bed and spend the night making love to her, it still hadn't felt like the right time, and she'd admitted she wasn't ready. So Cade had gone to bed by himself, leaving Beth muttering to herself as she tapped away on her laptop.

It was the oddest relationship Cade had ever been in, but it seemed right to take it slow with Beth. She was very important to him and the last thing he wanted was to rush her into something she wasn't ready for.

Although their make-out sessions were getting more and more...involved, for lack of a better word, he still held back from taking her all the way. They'd rounded second base and were well on their way to third before Cade had pulled back.

But he knew in his gut their time was coming. She'd whispered in his ear just that morning that she thought she was ready for him. But he didn't want her to *think* she was ready, he wanted her to *know* she was—and to desire him with a passion that couldn't be denied.

She hadn't panicked even once since his friends had come over. She'd greeted them as if she'd known them her entire life. No one commented on the tight hold she had on his hand and they hadn't teased him at all for being connected at the hip to his new girlfriend.

He picked up her hand to kiss her fingers—and then froze, gripping her fingers tight so she couldn't pull away from him. "What happened?" he asked in concern, frowning down at the obvious burn marks on her fingers.

"Oh, it's not a big deal."

"It's a big deal to me if you're hurt," Cade retorted, then repeated, "What happened?"

Beth glanced around and bit her lip before reluctantly answering him. "I was cooking the other day and grabbed the pan, forgetting it'd be hot."

Cade didn't say anything for a beat, sensing that she was lying to him. "Do they hurt?" he finally asked.

She shook her head. "Not so much anymore. They blistered about a day after it happened, but they're obviously gone now."

Bringing her hand up to his mouth, he gently kissed each finger. They were red and if they'd blistered, they'd most likely been second degree burns. It had to have hurt like a bitch. Cade hated, absolutely *hated*, that she'd been hurt and he hadn't been there to care for her.

"I take it you're not Betty Crocker," Moose drawled sarcastically.

It was enough to break the tension in the room.

"Uh, no." Beth looked up at Cade.

Realizing by the furrow in her brow that she was embarrassed to talk about the burns, Cade let it drop. He smiled at her, remembering the fried chicken she'd been trying to make the day they'd met.

As if she could read his mind, Mackenzie asked, "How did you guys meet?"

The guys were mostly watching the football game, and it gave the four women, Beth, Penelope, Hayden and Mackenzie, a chance to girl-talk for a bit.

"I almost set my kitchen on fire and he showed up to put it out."

"Seriously? Wow, that's amazing," Mackenzie gushed. "That's so much cooler than how I met Daxton! I literally ran into him at a charity event I was hosting, then I got pulled over by TJ—have you met TJ yet?"

"Nope."

"Oh, well, he's hot too, but I got pulled over by TJ, and Daxton was in the car with him. He didn't realize it was me until I'd already gotten my warning and left. He illegally got my phone number from TJ and called me. It's a good thing, because I totally never would've had the nerve to call him if I knew he was there and I probably would've died of embarrassment at the same time. Seriously, it's cliché, but it's all good because I love him a whole lot and he saved my life."

Beth just stared at the other woman. She was shorter and curvier than her five-eight, but she had the confidence of someone at least six feet tall. She liked her immediately. Penelope had warned her beforehand that Mackenzie had a tendency to ramble, and she certainly hadn't lied.

"Cade said something about that. Saved your life?"

"Uh-huh." Mackenzie nodded. "Do you remember Jordan Charles Staal?" At Beth's blank look, Mackenzie waved her hand dismissively. "It doesn't matter. Anyway, this guy was pissed at the Rangers and stole me from work. Daxton and the rest of the guys found me before he could do any lasting harm."

"Yeah, it wasn't quite as easy as that," Hayden said, exasperated. "But that's the gist of it."

"But you're all right now?" Beth asked, concerned.

"Oh yeah. It sucked, but whatever. He's dead, I'm not, and I get to have Daxton in my bed every night. What's better than that?"

"Oh good Lord, please don't talk about Dax and bed in front of me," Hayden complained. "I have to see him on an almost daily basis."

"You just need your own man," Penelope told her friend. "It'll be different then."

"I'm not sure that's in the cards," the deputy said completely seriously.

"Uh, what?" Beth broke in, feeling comfortable with the group. "You've got beautiful red hair, you're stacked and built...what are you talking about?"

"I'm one of the guys," Hayden returned immediately. "And I wouldn't want to date any of my fellow LEOs anyway. Too weird to see him at work and then go home to him as well. Besides, men in general don't see me as female. I wear my uniform for most of my waking hours. I'm too busy to date. What else...?"

"Hey, you never know," Mackenzie broke in. "One day you'll be going about your business then BAM, there will be a guy who falls hard and fast. You'll be in a relationship before you know it."

Hayden rolled her eyes and took a small sip of the

beer she'd been nursing. "Being around you is exhausting sometimes, Mack."

Mackenzie beamed as if Hayden had just complimented her. "Thanks!"

They all laughed. Mackenzie was like Teflon—words just bounced right off of her and didn't seem to faze her at all.

"Anyone want something else to drink?" Beth asked, standing up.

"I'm good."

"No, thanks."

"Nope."

Beth smiled at the women and headed into the kitchen, grinning all the way. She couldn't believe she'd been nervous about meeting Cade's friends. So far they were great and hadn't made her feel awkward at all. Besides some basic questions about what she did for a living and commiserating about her agoraphobia in passing, they hadn't seemed to care she wasn't like most people.

"You okay?"

Beth turned and grinned at Cade. "I'm great. Thank you for tonight. I love your friends."

"I knew you would."

Cade held his arms out and Beth snuggled into him. "This is the first time since I moved to San Antonio that I feel like I really made the right decision. I've missed having friends." She looked up at Cade and repeated, "Thank you."

"You don't have to thank me, sweetheart. It's my pleasure. And I have ulterior motives."

Beth arched her eyebrows at him. "Ulterior motives?"

"Yup. I figure if you like my friends, you'll be more likely to keep me around."

She rolled her eyes then, and put her head back against him. "Whatever. And for the record, I'm keeping you."

"Good."

They stood in each other's arms for a while, enjoying the moment. Finally, when Dax called out, "Where's my beer, Cade?" they broke apart reluctantly.

Cade kissed Beth quickly, but with feeling. "Come on, we can't keep the vultures waiting, they'll be circling for blood if I don't get back out there."

Beth didn't think she'd smiled so much in years. The rest of the night was just as easy and fun. Each of the women told her they couldn't wait to hang out some more, and the men had been equally as enthusiastic when they'd left.

All in all, it was a great start to her new life. Beth didn't know what she had to thank for it, but she would hold on to it for as long as she could.

* * *

A week after his friends and coworkers had visited and they'd stuffed their faces with as much barbeque as they could stand, Beth and Cade were getting ready to head out. Cade had a three-day shift coming up where he only got eight hours off before he had to work again. Usually when this round of shifts came, Beth went back to her apartment, since all Cade did when he got home was sleep until he had to get to the station again.

"You can stay here, I don't mind."

"I appreciate it, Cade, but I'd feel more comfortable at my place this time."

"Okay, but I hope you know the day is coming when I'll want you here all the time."

Beth looked at Cade in shock. "It's only been like two months since we met."

"And?"

"And don't you think it's too early?"

"No." When Beth just continued to stare at him, Cade went on. "Beth, where do you think this thing between us is going? Do you think I'm just stringing you along until we make love, then I'm going to dump you?"

She shook her head, biting her bottom lip nervously.

"Right. I'm not proposing, sweetheart. But I like waking up to you in my home. I like working alongside you in the kitchen. I like cuddling with you and I certainly like the way you feel in my arms."

"We haven't had sex yet."

"I'm well aware of that. And we will. Soon. But I don't feel the way I do about you because of sex. It's because of *you*."

"I...I feel the same way. But I'm still having a hard time believing it."

Cade smiled and kissed Beth's forehead. "I'll still be here when you *do* believe it, sweetheart. Let's get you home so I can get to work on time. The guys'll give me shit if I'm late."

Cade loved the blush that bloomed over her cheeks. He could guess what she was thinking; that they'd think he was late because they'd been having sex.

He reached for Beth's shoulder bag that held her laptop and cursed when the strap broke and it tumbled to the floor, spilling the contents everywhere.

"Shit! I'm sorry. Is your computer going to be okay?" Cade asked fretfully as he crouched down to help her pick up her things. Amongst the pens and the sticky pads she was forever scribbling on, there were three packs of matches and two disposable lighters. He held one up and teased, "You take up smoking and not tell me?"

He frowned when Beth didn't answer him, but instead snatched the lighter out of his hand and stuffed it back into her bag. She stood up, holding her case in front of her defensively. "No."

She didn't elaborate and Cade hurried to soothe her, not wanting to piss her off. "Okay, no big deal. You ready to go? You have your overnight bag?"

Beth nodded and gestured to her small gym bag sitting at the base of the stairs. He really wanted her to unpack her things and leave some of her stuff here so she didn't have to continue to carry it all back and forth, but that would come in time, too.

Figuring she wasn't used to others being nosy and questioning her about her things, he merely grabbed her overnight bag and came back to her. Taking a gentle hold of her elbow, he steered her out of his house. As soon as his door was locked, he shifted so he could hold her hand, walked toward his truck, helped her into it, and headed for her place.

They arrived without incident and as soon as they entered her apartment, she went to the patio door and pulled back the curtain. She'd told him that she was working on trying to make sure she didn't live in a dungeon. Cade saw her take a deep breath, as if fortifying herself against the view outside the sliding glass door, but she stuck it out and left the curtain open as she stood there.

He walked over to her and hugged her from behind, resting his chin on her shoulder. He didn't know what she was looking at, but he knew her perception of the view was very different from his. He saw a big grassy field with people relaxing and playing catch with a football; she most likely saw danger lurking from behind every tree and bush.

About to pull away and let her know he really did have to get to work, Cade took a second look at the area around her patio. There was a grill sitting at the edge of the concrete that he hadn't noticed before...

But the thing that concerned him was that the grass

around it was scorched black, as if there'd recently been an out-of-control fire.

"What's that?" Cade asked her sharply.

"What's what?" Beth asked, looking up at him from within the circle of his arms.

"Did you have a fire?"

"What?" Beth's tone was a bit less relaxed, and he felt her stiffen in his arms.

"The scorch marks around your patio. Did the neighbors use your grill and the barbeque got out of control?"

Beth shrugged. "I guess so."

"Idiots. They could've burned down the entire complex. You'd think they'd be a bit more careful with it, being as dry as it has been. You have that extinguisher I brought you still, right?"

Beth nodded, but didn't say anything.

"Good. I'd recommend bringing that grill inside so they can't use it without your permission, or getting rid of it altogether."

"I will."

Cade went on, "If you need help, just let me know. You've been getting better at not panicking when you step outside, but I don't want you to overdo it. Now, I really do have to get going, sweetheart. I'll call you tonight if I can."

Beth turned in his arms. "But you have the overnight shift."

"Yeah, and it gets boring when we don't get any calls. I'd rather talk to you than sit around and listen to

Driftwood or Crash blabbering about their online dating profiles."

She smiled at the exasperation in his voice. "Then I'd love that. If you get the chance, that is. No big deal otherwise."

"I'll talk to you later. I can guarantee at some point over the next three days it'll be slow enough for me to get in my Beth time."

She grinned at that. They spent their normal amount of time standing at her front door making out before Cade reluctantly pulled his lips away from hers. One of his hands was resting on her ass under her pants, and the other was holding one of her breasts while his thumb caressed her hard nipple. Both of her hands were under his shirt, clutching at his lower back, her nails gently scraping the tender skin there as she pulled him into her so they could both feel how aroused he was by their kisses.

Cade groaned and reluctantly moved his hands to rest at her waist, much safer territory, as he caressed her warm skin. "I hope once we make love, our ritual at this door never changes. I swear I just *see* your door now and I get hard."

Beth giggled and took an unenthusiastic step backward, breaking their hold on each other. "I know. I'm looking forward to you having those two days off after your shift this week."

Cade smiled. "I'm all yours, sweetheart."

"Good. I'm ready."

He ran a finger down her cheek lovingly and stated,

"On that note, I'm out of here. I'll call you." Cade stepped toward her, kissed her hard, and then stood back before she could get her hands on him again. Knowing if she touched him, he'd end up doing something drastic, like taking her where she stood, Cade opened her front door and said, "Be safe. I'll talk to you later."

"You too. Thanks for bringing me home."

"Anytime. Bye."

"Bye."

Beth watched until she couldn't see Cade anymore, congratulating herself for being able to stand at her entryway by herself for as long as she did and not freaking out.

She shut the door, immediately went to her purse and grabbed one of the lighters. She sat back on her couch and flicked it on, taking a deep breath as she stared at the flickering flame.

Beth hated lying to Cade, but she didn't think he'd understand anything about how the fire by her patio had started.

She'd been happy with how she'd been able to go farther and farther out on her patio. She'd started out with very small fires in the grill set right by the door, where she could watch them burn from inside her apartment. Gradually she'd worked herself up to bigger and bigger fires. It was getting a little easier to be able to stand outside—*outside*— by herself, not touching the sliding glass doors. Every time it happened, she was amazed that she was actually doing it.

Concentrating solely on the flames and not on who or what was around her, Beth felt almost normal for the first time in a long time. The wind on her face felt good and she couldn't remember the last time she'd stood outside and felt so free.

Of course, the wind on her face should've been a warning, but it wasn't until the entire grill was blown over by a gust of wind and the fire went tumbling out and onto the dry grass that Beth had come back into herself with a jolt. The flames licked at the grass and quickly began to consume everything in their path.

Luckily, Beth had reacted quickly, spinning and heading back inside to grab the fire extinguisher Cade had given her. She'd pulled the pin and sprayed the chemicals on the fire, just as he'd shown her. The fire went out in seconds, but the damage had been done.

The black grass remained as a reminder that she wasn't normal. That Beth had to resort to being a pyromaniac in order to cope with her life.

She certainly didn't like it. She didn't like the implications of how addicted to fire she was becoming, and she knew down to the marrow of her bones that if she ever wanted something with Cade to work, she had to give it up...but it wasn't as easy as that. He would be appalled at what she'd resorted to in order to deal with her anxiety.

It was like quitting smoking or drinking; some people could stop cold turkey, but the majority of people came back to it time and time again. Fires weren't a drug, but they felt like it all the same.

The flame from the lighter flickered and, as her thumb tired and lost the pressure on the fuel lever, went out. Beth threw the lighter on the coffee table, went into the kitchen and opened the cabinet where she'd been hiding all of the candles she'd bought. She'd gone a bit crazy online the other night and had bought them in bulk. There were tall ones, short and fat ones, tealights, birthday candles...all unscented and all waiting to be lit.

Beth grabbed a handful and brought them back to the table. She carefully set them up in a line and flicked on the lighter again. She lit them one by one, smiling as the wicks caught fire and burned. She'd just let these burn down, then she'd stop.

CHAPTER 13

"I'll see you in a bit, sweetheart."

"Don't you need to go home and get some rest?" Beth asked, knowing Cade probably hadn't had a lot of quality sleep. He'd completed his third day of the long shifts and he'd told her how they'd had one call after another the night before.

"I'd rather see you than sleep."

Beth smiled and swallowed hard before answering. "Okay. It's hard to argue with that since I feel the same. Drive safe and I'll see you soon then."

"I will. I've missed you."

"Me too."

"Bye."

"Bye."

Beth hung up and hugged herself. They'd spent the last three nights talking over the phone. Cade had called as he said he would, and last night they'd even managed to sort of have phone sex. It wasn't *exactly* phone sex, as neither of them got off, but they'd shared some sexual fantasies, and when Beth had heard Cade grunting a bit, she'd asked if he was touching himself.

She probably should've been more weirded out than she was, but with the amount of porn she spent time looking at online—and trying to screw up the links to so the sicker stuff, like sex with kids, couldn't be viewed anymore—knowing Cade was thinking about her and touching himself didn't even register on her weirdo-meter.

Her question had led to him asking if she'd ever had phone sex before, and when she'd answered negatively, they'd spent some more time talking about what turned them on. Just when Beth told Cade she'd undone her pants and was touching herself, the tones for a call rang through the station.

They'd both groaned unhappily and Cade had said quickly before hanging up to head out, "It's just as well, I think *I* want to be the one to make you go off our first time together."

Now he was on his way over to her apartment. Beth looked around and noticed for the first time in three days that her place was a mess. There were burnt matches all over her coffee table, not to mention the burned-to-the-stub candles that were strewn across her apartment.

Looking at the mess, and feeling ashamed, made her really think about what she was doing for the first time.

Making a split-second decision that she knew she

should've made long before now, she groaned under her breath and went into the kitchen to grab a trash bag. Knowing deep within her heart if she was embarrassed to let Cade or Pen or any of the others see how low she'd sunk to try to deal with her agoraphobia, it wasn't healthy.

She stuffed the candles and the matches into the trash bag. In a fit of panic, she flung open the lower cabinet where she kept more candles and swept those into the trash too. The drawer above was thrown open, and the brand-new ten-pack of lighters was tossed in as well.

Breathing as if she'd run a five-mile race, Beth frantically looked around, trying to make sure she'd removed all evidence of her temporary insanity.

She closed the bag and set it in the corner of her kitchen. She'd have Pen take it to the trash bin later.

Leaning over the kitchen counter, Beth rested her head on her hands and tried to control her breathing. It was ridiculous how sad she felt at the loss of the paraphernalia. For the first time in a long time, she felt normal—at least when she was controlling the fires. It was as if the candles and matches mocked her from inside the trash bag. She swore she could almost hear them calling her name, urging her to release them and put them back in their cabinet home.

Ignoring the siren call of the bag in the corner, Beth stood up straight and stalked into her bedroom. Cade was going to take her back to his house, she wanted to be packed and ready to go when he arrived. She needed a break from the demons in her apartment, and if she wasn't mistaken, she and Cade would most likely be sleeping in the same bed for the next two nights.

She was finally ready. More than ready. She *wanted* Cade to make love to her more than she wanted or needed the sweet seduction of the flames.

She was a bit nervous about her scars from her time with Hurst, but she and Cade had talked about it one night, and he'd even shown her some of his scars from various fires and accidents he'd had. He knew just what to do and say to make her feel better, especially when he'd told her, "As much as I want to see your body, it's *you* who I connect with."

She just knew that while in Cade's arms, thoughts of the scary outdoors, what had happened to her, and the stress over knowing that lighting fires wasn't the answer she was looking for, would all disappear. She couldn't wait.

When the knock came at her door fifteen minutes later, Beth was ready. After verifying it really was Cade, she quickly opened the door and threw herself into his arms. He smelled like he'd recently taken a shower... fresh and clean. Cade walked them inside her apartment and shut the door with his foot. Without letting her go, and keeping her feet off the ground, he pulled back and looked her in the eyes.

"Hi, sweetheart."

"Hi."

"You seem happy to see me. You okay?"

Beth nodded. "I'm very happy to see you. And not

because anything is wrong. I'm just glad you're here. I missed you."

Cade groaned and leaned down to her. Beth met him halfway and the sparks that seemed to fly in the air as their lips met crackled around them. Pulling his lips away from hers after a moment, Cade commented wryly, "This damn door will be the death of me."

Beth smiled and licked her lips seductively. She never thought she'd want to do anything seductive again, but being around Cade made her suddenly remember all the ways she used to tease men before she'd been kidnapped.

"You ready to go?"

"Definitely. My bag is right here."

Cade looked down at the duffle bag she packed, then back up at her. "I'm torn."

"Torn?"

"Yeah. To get to my place, I have to put you down and pick up that bag. That means I won't feel you next to me the whole time I'm driving. And in case you hadn't noticed, I like you against me."

"Is that what that is? I thought you had one of your firefighting tools down your pants or something."

"Oh, it's a tool all right…"

Beth giggled at his retort. "Well then, how about you put me down, let's get to your place, and you can put that *tool* in its proper place."

Cade shook his head in amusement and reluctantly loosened his grip so she slid along his body until her feet were on the ground. "I've missed you too, sweetheart. And before we go anywhere or say anything else, please know that as much as I want to have you in my bed, we'll go at your pace. I won't do anything to put you back in that bad place."

Beth put her palm on his cheek. "I know. I'm ready, Cade. You've been patient and slow with me. You haven't once made fun of me or been impatient when I've had an attack. I trust you…more than anyone I've trusted since I was kidnapped. I can't promise not to have any flashbacks, but I feel stronger in your arms than I have in a very, very long time. I want you. I want to feel you inside me. I want to orgasm with someone other than myself. I want to be intimate with you, in every way."

"Good Lord, sweetheart. Are you trying to kill me?"

"No. The last thing I want is you to be incapacitated before we get to the good stuff and round home base. Hanging out at third base has gotten old. I'm ready to hit a home run."

Cade laughed and leaned over to grab her bag. "Go get your laptop and let's get out of here. I'm feeling kinda tired after all…I need to get home to my bed."

Beth smiled all the way from her front door to Cade's house, for the first time in a long time thinking more about what was about to happen than what might be lurking outside hunting her down.

CHAPTER 14

BETH STOOD next to Cade's bed and shifted nervously. She wasn't scared of him or of what they were about to do, it'd just been a long time since she'd been naked in front of anyone and a long time since she'd had sex, so it was all just a bit overwhelming.

Sensing her unease, Cade gestured to the bed behind her. "Lay down, sweetheart, relax."

She went to take off her shirt and Cade caught her hand in his. "Don't worry about that, just lay back."

Feeling cowardly, but relieved at the respite, Beth scooted back onto his mattress and waited for him to make the first move. She watched as Cade stripped his T-shirt over his head and she gasped at her first look at him.

Cade had a light dusting of dark hair on his chest, but it did nothing to distract from his body at all. Beth had had her hands on his sides, back, and even his belly, but seeing it all unfettered for the first time made her catch her breath.

He wasn't perfect, that was the first thing she noticed, but that actually made this easier, because she was far from perfect as well. He wasn't in his twenties anymore, and along with that came a little extra weight on his sides. He didn't have eighteen-pack abs either, but he was in no way overweight. The scars he'd told her about were obvious as well, but again, they didn't take away any of her appreciation of his physique.

His upper body was sculpted and almost perfect though. The lifting of equipment, and apparently people, went a long way toward keeping him in shape. The muscles in his arms bulged as he moved to get into bed next to her. His pectoral muscles rippled as he shifted over her as well. Somehow, even though he didn't look like a bodybuilder, he oozed testosterone and masculinity all the same.

Cade had left his jeans on, and they sat low on his hips, as if waiting to be unzipped and tugged off. Beth swallowed hard and looked up at him, wondering how this was all going to go. She might not have had sex in a while, but even she knew that they'd both need to remove some more clothes if it was going to work.

"Relax, sweetheart," Cade told her in a calming tone as he eased himself down next to her.

"I can't."

He chuckled and rested one hand lightly on her belly as the other propped up his head. "What's making you nervous?"

163

"Uh…everything?"

"Specifically. We'll work through them one at a time."

"I know I probably sounded…experienced back at my apartment, but I've only done this twice—and you know about one of those times."

"And you might not believe me, but I've done this a lot less times than you're probably thinking." At her look of disbelief, he continued, "And guys are easy. You touch us, rub against us, and we're good to go. It's women who are scary. You have special places that need to be touched and caressed. We could do it too hard, or too soft, and it won't work. It's harder to tell when you're aroused enough so that we won't hurt you when we get inside. It takes a lot to hurt me, but women aren't built the same way. I could easily cause you pain, and that's the last thing I want to happen. So we'll learn together what works best for us…okay?" Not waiting for her to answer, he went on. "What else?"

The thought that Cade might not be as self-assured as he looked went a long way toward relaxing Beth— that, and his warm hand caressing her belly as they talked. "I don't work out. I sit around a lot and work on my computer."

"And?"

"I don't look like you. I have a pooch, and then there are my scars."

Cade took one of Beth's hands in his and brought it to his side. He held it to him and squeezed the flesh there. "Feel that?" At her nod, he commented with absolutely no self-loathing, "It's extra skin. Flab. Love handles. My muffin top."

Beth giggled. "You don't have a muffin top! Jeez!"

"I do. You can't imagine the number of side sit-ups I've done to try to get rid of it, and it just won't go." He brought her hand up to his chest and pressed her fingers to the small scars there. "And I've got my own scars, sweetheart. I know we've talked about it, but we'll discuss it again, as much as you need to make you believe me when I say that the scars on your body will make absolutely no difference in how I feel about you. You don't feel less about me because of mine, do you?"

"Of course not. But Cade, yours are from your job, from doing something good for others."

Cade didn't lose eye contact with Beth as he tried to articulate what he was feeling. "The point is that neither of us is perfect. But I can tell you, I've never been as attracted to anyone as I am to you. *You*, Beth. Yes, I want to see every inch of your body, but it's what's inside you that I love, not the package it comes in."

Beth stared at Cade wide-eyed as he continued. She had no idea if he knew what he'd just admitted or not, but he didn't give her a chance to ask.

"You have scars from what someone else did to you, but I don't see them as scars, more like life medals. Life throws a lot at us. The more scars a person has just means they've survived more of what life threw at them. It means that they're stronger than the average person. Mine are piddly compared to yours. You are the most amazing, strong, pigheaded, controlled, smart, *stubborn* woman I've ever met. And I mean all of that in the best way possible. If you weren't all of those things, you wouldn't have made it through what you have. You've spit in the face of death and come out the other side. I will love your scars because they made you who you are today."

"Cade…"

"Let me see you?"

Beth could only nod. She didn't see herself that way —obviously—but it was breathtaking that Cade did. She suddenly wished with all her heart that she *was* that woman. She *wanted* to be that woman for Cade. She didn't want to ever do anything to make him think otherwise.

Suddenly grateful she'd packed up all her fire paraphernalia—she never wanted him to know how weak she'd been—she made a promise to herself to try to be the woman Cade saw.

She held her breath as Cade slowly pushed her shirt up and over her head. Raising her arms to make it easier for him to get it off, Beth let her breath out in a whoosh as his warm palm spanned her lower belly. She looked down at it, loving the sight of his tanned skin on her pale body. When he didn't move, she brought her eyes up to his.

He was looking at her face, instead of her body. When he caught her eyes, he murmured, "Okay so far?"

Beth nodded, and, taking the initiative, arched her

back and reached under herself to undo the snap of her bra. It was now or never, and baring herself all at once would be easier than doing it by increments. Like pulling off a Band-Aid...she wanted to get it done. She unclasped the two hooks, drew the cups down her arms, and threw the material on the floor.

Cade's eyes finally moved downward, and she heard him inhale as she exposed herself to him.

His hand finally moved, inching higher and higher, finally covering her naked breast with his palm.

"Perfection," he breathed as he stroked and caressed her. As though he knew right where Hurst had hurt her, his fingers moved to each scar and lightly traced them. They'd faded over time because of the creams she'd used, but they still seemed to stand out to Beth.

Cade leaned into her and began to kiss each and every mark. It wasn't sexual, so much as reverent. The cigarette burns on her breasts got the same treatment as the fading slice on her side from the killer's knife. It was as if his touch could erase what had happened to her. And in some ways, it did just that.

Eventually his caresses changed from tender and healing to erotic and arousing. When he drew one of her nipples into his mouth and sucked gently, Beth swore she felt it down to her toes. She could feel herself getting wet and she shifted under him. His large hand held her breast to his mouth as he feasted on her. Not able to stand it any longer, Beth complained, "Cade...I want to touch you too."

Cade immediately turned over on his back,

bringing her with him. Beth found herself half on top of him, and she propped herself up on her elbows, careful not to dig them into his chest.

"I'm all yours, sweetheart."

Beth didn't hesitate, too aroused to worry about what she might look like as she dove toward his nipples. If she liked the feel of his mouth on her, he'd probably like it just as much. She nibbled and bit at his nipple as her hand roamed his body. When her hand wandered too close to his hard length, he turned them until she was under him once again.

"I want you." His words were blunt and guttural, as if her ministrations had pushed him to the edge.

"Yes."

Cade kneeled up on the mattress and unsnapped the button on his jeans and lowered the zipper, never losing eye contact with her. He shoved his pants and boxers down together, falling to one hip to remove them, before getting back up on his knees next to her.

Beth's eyes widened as she visually caressed him. His dick was hard and it bobbed up and down with his movements as if it was waving hello. She reached out a hand and ran a fingertip over the mushroom head, watching in fascination as it jerked at her touch and a bead of pre-come materialized at the tip.

"As I told you earlier, sweetheart, guys are easy. You can tell when we're aroused, it's kinda hard to hide. And we're fairly easy to please. Soft touches, hard ones…we like it all. Does this scare you?" Cade asked, vaguely gesturing to his naked body hovering near hers. He was amazingly nonchalant, considering he was completely bare before her and obviously aroused. His lack of outward urgency went a long way toward reassuring her he wasn't about to lose it and pounce on her.

She shook her head. "No, I'm not scared of you, Cade."

"Good. I want to see the rest of you."

And just like that, Beth wanted the same thing. She wanted to be naked with Cade. Wanted him to see all of her. It'd been so long since she'd made this kind of connection with another human, and suddenly she wanted to be skin-to-skin.

Her hands moved to her waistband and she shoved her sweats down her legs and kicked them off. She wasn't as talented as he was though, and had to take the time to push her plain pink cotton panties off after the sweats. Finally, she lay back naked as the day she was born.

Cade didn't make her wait to let her know what he thought.

"Absolutely fucking amazing." His words were reverent and oozed sincerity.

Beth was ridiculously relieved he still seemed to be as aroused as he was before they'd shed their clothes. He was right in that he couldn't hide his reaction to her. Beth wrapped one hand around his thigh and with the other she gripped his erection. His breath came in short pants as he leaned over her and nuzzled her belly button.

Without words, they learned each other's bodies. He stayed kneeling next to her hip as he caressed her upper thighs and legs while she did the same to him. He leaned over, spreading his legs to give her hand room to move on his shaft, and licked her belly, blowing on her wet folds. Beth's hand rubbed his pre-come over the head of his shaft as she caressed him. He finally moved until he was lying between her legs.

Beth looked down at the amazing man about to learn her body up close and personal. He spread her folds apart gently with his thumbs as he leaned in and licked her.

At her jolt when his tongue touched her, Cade looked up and reassured her. "Ummmmm, I swear to God I've never wanted to do this as badly as I want to do it to you. Has anyone eaten you out before, sweetheart?"

Beth shook her head, not able to squeeze words out of her constricted throat.

"Good." Cade's voice was possessive and hard. "I get to be first. I love that. Hold on. I might not be an expert, but I think I can make you feel good."

As Cade got to work, Beth thought she was going to die. Her toes curled and her knees came up as he licked and sucked and...*worshiped* between her legs. It all felt good, but when he shifted upward and started licking her clit, Beth could only groan in ecstasy. She liked his mouth on her, but this was something different.

When his mouth eased away, her hips pressed up, trying to follow him. She needed more, more pressure, more attention on her clit. She knew if he paid just a little more attention to it, she'd be there. She'd had orgasms before, at her own hand, but having Cade be the one to throw her over the edge was almost scary. He had complete control over her pleasure, and she wanted him to be the one to make her explode.

"Harder, Cade. Right on my clit. Please, I'm almost..." Her breath hitched as Cade did just as she begged. He concentrated on the small bundle of nerves, using his thumb to pull the hood out of the way so he had unfettered access to the sensitive bud underneath. He licked her hard and fast, over and over. Her hips bucked up against him, but he didn't lose her. His hands held her still as he closed his lips over her and sucked at the same time as he lashed at her with his tongue.

Beth balanced on the precipice of a monster orgasm, needing just a bit more to throw her over the edge. When he eased one finger inside her tight sheath and pumped in and out of her as he sucked, that was all it took.

She shuddered in Cade's grasp as he continued to lick at her. Just when she thought it was over, he flicked her clit once more and she trembled with another mini-orgasm. Finally, after she was weak with pleasure, he lifted his head and she watched as he put the finger that had been inside her into his mouth and licked it clean.

"Delicious."

"Oh my God. You didn't just do that."

Cade scooted up until he was hovering over her sated body, supporting himself on his elbows. Beth could feel his erection, hard and wet against her inner thigh. He was smiling, a broad grin that she'd pay to see on his face all the time. "I did do it. You *are* delicious."

Beth wrinkled her nose at him and he chuckled. "It must be a guy thing."

"Must be," she agreed.

He got serious. "You okay? No bad memories?"

"No!" Beth told him immediately and with heat. "Nothing you did came close to anything that happened that night."

"Good. And I feel I must warn you, I liked that…a lot."

"Yeah?"

"Yeah. Eating you out, you telling me exactly how you like it and what you needed to get off, you orgasming in my mouth. All of it. I have a feeling I'll be doing it a lot."

"I want you."

"Tonight was about you, sweetheart."

"And it was awesome. Stupendous. Wonderful. But I still want you."

"I don't want to rush you."

Beth started to get pissed. "Look. I get that you don't want me to have a panic attack, but I'm so far from that, it's not even funny. And while I know you just gave me the best orgasm I've ever had, now I want to have one with *you* inside me. I've heard it's really awesome to orgasm while being filled with a hard cock. I don't have that firsthand knowledge, mind you, but I have to admit that the second you put your finger inside me, I wanted it to be your dick."

"Jesus Christ, Beth," Cade said, lurching toward the small table next to his bed. "I swear to God you're going to kill me. I was all prepared to be noble and finger you to another orgasm, but you had to go and open your mouth."

He ripped open the condom packet as he mumbled to himself. Beth wasn't sure he even knew what he was saying, or that he was talking out loud. She lay patiently, waiting for him to come back to her.

"You had to go and tell me you've never gotten off while being fucked. First, I was the only man to tongue that delicious pussy of yours, and now this. Shit, I can't wait to feel your hot muscles squeeze my dick, you have no idea how amazing it was to feel you tighten around my finger."

Cade got on his knees and pushed her legs open, Beth complied and assisted him by bending her knees to give him more room to work. She smiled as he continued his mini-rant under his breath.

"You are so beautiful and responsive. I can't believe anyone would ever hurt you." His eyes roamed her body, one hand caressing her chest as he spoke. Grabbing hold of himself with his free hand, Cade touched the tip of his now-covered cock to her folds and inhaled as he slipped the head inside her. It seemed to bring him back to his senses, as his eyes snapped up to hers.

"Beth, I—"

"Yes, Cade. Fuck me. I want you, and I'm more than ready for you." She lifted her hips a fraction, showing him with her actions as well as her words that she was really okay.

Without another word, Cade eased more of himself inside her, stopping every couple of millimeters, letting her acclimate to his size. When he was fully seated inside, he took a deep breath and leaned down to kiss her long and slow. In seemingly no hurry, he took his time, devouring her mouth without moving a muscle. It wasn't until Beth tore her mouth away and dug her nails into his sides and said, "Cade...please," that he spoke again.

"What do you need?"

"You."

"You have me."

"Move. Fuck me."

"There's no fucking here, sweetheart," Cade told her, sitting up and gliding in and out of her as he spoke. "I said it earlier, and I'll say it again in case you didn't catch it. I love you."

Beth's breath hitched as she looked up at the man who had changed her life.

"I'm in awe of you, and I don't know if I can ever live up to the amazing woman you are. But I'll spend every moment of my life loving, protecting, and standing by your side."

Beth whimpered as his speed picked up and he

thrust in and out of her, as if wanting to make his point.

"I don't care if I have to dig a hole in the side of a mountain for us to live in, or if you can never set foot outside our home without my hand holding yours. I'll gladly do it for the rest of my life. Holding your hand is no hardship." He groaned then as Beth threw herself upward and wrapped herself around him.

Thrown off balance, Cade fell backward, holding Beth against him as he ended up under her on the large mattress. Their heads were now at the bottom of the bed, but he didn't care.

"You love me?"

"Yes." His answer was immediate and confident.

"I love you too."

At her words, his eyes closed for a moment as if in relief, then opened again. "Fuck *me*, Beth. Take me how you need it."

"But I've already gotten off."

"I told you earlier, men can orgasm much easier than women can. Take me the way you need to, I'll come, sweetheart, pretty much no matter what you do. I can guarantee you that."

Beth smiled, feeling powerful as she looked down at the man she loved and who loved her back. She swiveled her hips, loving the groan that came out of his mouth at her actions. "Tell me what to do. I've never done it this way."

"Jesus. Another first for me. I'm a lucky bastard. Ride me, Beth. Up and down. Hard and fast." Cade's words were guttural and desperate. He might claim that he'd be able to orgasm no matter what, but it was obvious some actions were better than others.

Beth raised herself almost all the way off, then powered down on him, taking him to the hilt.

"Fuck yeah. Again."

She did it again, liking that he was giving her some direction. Beth found that the harder she took him, the better it felt for her too. She threw herself enthusiastically into the new experience, bouncing up and down on Cade's cock as if she were riding a mechanical bull at top speed.

"Lean back," Cade ordered, seemingly out of the blue.

Startled, Beth did as he asked, bracing herself on his thighs behind her. She didn't understand why he wanted her in this position, as she couldn't move as easily, until his thumb landed on her clit and began to rub against her hard. She no longer had the right angle to ride him, but she could grind herself against him as her hips shifted under his ministrations.

"Cade!"

"That's it, rub against me. Uh...yeah...fuck. I can feel you squeezing me. You're close...do it...come for me, sweetheart, while I fill you with my cock."

His dirty words and thumb were all it took for her to come for the third time that night. She vaguely felt Cade's hands grip her hips and hold her to him tightly as she writhed and jerked in the midst of her orgasm. Finally, feeling boneless, she sat up and Cade pulled her toward him so she lay motionless on his chest. She straightened out her legs, groaning at the relief in her knees as she moved to a more comfortable position.

The words came unbidden to her lips. "They were right; it does feel so much better with a hard dick inside me."

Cade barked out a laugh and squeezed her affectionately. "I'm not sure who 'they' are, but I think that's why dildos and vibrators were invented, sweetheart."

"Hummm." Beth felt positively lethargic. "I can't imagine a plastic toy would feel better than a flesh and blood man."

"As long as it's *my* flesh and blood that's inside you, I can't argue with that logic."

Beth picked up her head. "It was good for you too, wasn't it?"

"Lord, sweetheart. If it was any better, I'd have passed out."

"So you came?"

"Yeah. I came. The second I felt you quivering and shaking around me, I couldn't hold back anymore. I blew harder than I have since I was sixteen years old."

"I love you."

Cade sighed with contentment. "I love you too. Come on, we're all turned around. Let me get up and take care of this condom and I'll come back and we can nap for a while. Sound good?"

"Um hum."

"You're already half asleep, aren't you?"

"Um hum."

Cade smiled at the woman in his arms. He'd never been happier. Beth might not seem like the ideal girlfriend to some, but to him, she was perfect.

He hadn't lied earlier when he said he'd be happy with her no matter if she overcame her phobias or not. He remembered thinking so long ago that he didn't think it would work out between them because he didn't want to give up his outdoor activities. But now? He didn't give a rat's ass about camping or otherwise being outside. He was completely honest when he'd told her he'd live in a cave with her. He loved her just the way she was.

He couldn't imagine her doing anything that would change his mind.

CHAPTER 15

THE LAST TWO weeks had been idyllic for Beth. There were times she had to pinch herself to make sure it was all real. She spent Cade's time off with him and sometimes the guys at the station. She and Cade spent every night they could together, making love in as many ways as possible. It was as if once they'd made it to home base, they wanted to get there every night.

Beth had even shown Cade a video she'd found one night while trying to shut down a porn site that featured child porn, as well as the regular variety of videos. The clip that caught her attention was of a woman giving herself orgasm after orgasm. She and Cade had discussed at length, amazingly without embarrassment, whether or not it was real, and finally, in order to prove to her that women could orgasm nonstop, Cade had bought a Hitachi Magic Wand and demonstrated the power of the vibrator. He'd kept the thing on her clit until she'd had at least half a dozen orgasms and had begged him to stop.

He'd thrown it to the side without bothering to turn it off and had fucked her brains out, managing to wring one last orgasm from her as he took her from behind. Lying limp and exhausted in his arms, she'd had to admit that the video was probably authentic.

The bag of candles, matches, and lighters still sat in her kitchen, mocking her. Every time she stayed at her place, Beth had to force herself to stay away from the bag. Even though things were going well between her and Cade, she still fought the urge to go out and get her grill and light up another fire. Every day she promised herself she'd get Penelope to take the bag to the dumpster for her, but so far she hadn't been able to. It was a crutch...one Beth was ashamed of, but couldn't seem to shake.

Tonight Cade was working part of a shift for Taco, so he wouldn't be leaving the station until midnight. Since Beth had been neglecting her late-night hacker sleuthing recently, they'd decided to meet up in the morning. That way Cade could get some sleep and they'd have the entire day together. Many times when they stayed the night with each other, they were up way too late making love and ended up sleeping half the day away.

That night, Beth woke with a jerk. She glanced at her clock, saw it was three-thirty in the morning. She'd only been asleep for about forty minutes and wondered what had disturbed her.

A scream broke through the silence of the night and Beth let out a small shriek of her own. It had sounded close, too close.

She bolted out of bed and into her small living room. She whipped back the curtains, for once with no thought to her own phobias, and saw an eerie orange glow. She knew immediately what it was; she'd seen and studied it enough recently.

Fire. And it was big, much bigger than the small fires she'd dabbled in. And close.

While she wanted to find out where it was coming from, at the moment all she was concerned about was the person behind the scream. Were they in trouble? Hurting? Being taken against their will?

Long ago Beth had sworn to herself that she'd never sit around and do nothing if she had the ability to prevent what occurred to her from happening to someone else, agoraphobia be damned.

She cautiously opened the sliding glass door and peered out. She saw a group of people standing in the courtyard pointing up at one of the apartments over her head. She glanced up.

One of the balconies on the third floor was completely engulfed in flames.

For a beat, Beth stared. There was so much more fire than she'd ever had the guts to build...although she'd been working her way up to bigger and bigger flames before she'd quit. She could see embers lazily floating off in the breeze while the wood that made up the balcony glowed bright orange.

The gathering of people was getting larger and Beth could see several on their cell phones, hopefully calling for assistance and not filming the damn thing for their social media profiles.

Beth struggled with her psyche. On one hand, she should get outside, join the others in the relative safety of the courtyard, but the thought made her shake. On the other hand, she knew if she concentrated on the fire, she'd be able to do it—but what happened when it was extinguished? She'd be trapped out in the open with nothing to distract her.

She was getting better. Cade and Penelope had worked long and hard, giving her the courage to take risks. But the longer she stood in her doorway, the more and more people gathered.

Beth whirled around and raced back into her bedroom, throwing on a pair of jeans, socks, tennis shoes, and a long-sleeve T-shirt. She stuffed one of the knives she'd bought online into her back pocket, just in case, and grabbed one of the two fire extinguishers Cade had given her "for emergencies."

Not knowing what she was going to do with it, Beth went back to her patio and stepped outside. With her gaze fixed upward, she stood at the very end of the concrete pad. It was a compromise of sorts; she was outside, so she wouldn't get trapped in her apartment, but she could dash back inside at a moment's notice if needed.

Beth bit her cheek and concentrated on the flames hissing above her head. She could see them licking the eaves of the roof when she first heard the sirens. She wondered if Station 7 was responding, and who was on duty. Cade should be off, but maybe Pen or one of the other guys she'd been getting to know was working.

Beth purposely kept her breaths long, focusing on breathing in and out rather than on the people all around her. Hugging the extinguisher to her chest, she counted to eighty-seven in her head before she heard the first firefighter.

"Everyone back up! You need to get farther away from the building."

One of the firefighters was shouting at the residents gathered in the courtyard. It was only a matter of time before someone noticed her. Beth's breathing quickened in panic. They'd make her move, she had no doubt.

"You're Beth, right? Come on, let's get away from here."

The voice was low and calm. She turned to see one of her neighbors. She had no idea what his name was, only that she'd seen him before. He was older than her by around twenty or so years. His hair was receding and graying, and currently tousled from sleep. His voice was melodic and soothing. Most importantly, he was holding his hand out to her.

Beth's mind reeled. It could be a trick. Ben Hurst hadn't been young...he was older, and when she thought about it, kinda looked like her neighbor. The man standing so patiently with his hand outstretched for her could snatch her away...except she'd seen him.

She knew him. He lived there with her. Well, at least on the same floor as her. They'd made eye contact and exchanged greetings as she came and went with Cade over the last couple of months.

Damned if she did and damned if she didn't.

She reached out her hand, hoping like hell he was one of the good guys. If not, she knew she'd never recover from being kidnapped a second time.

* * *

Cade's tires squealed as he hit the brakes and pulled haphazardly into the first available parking spot. He was still two blocks away from Beth's apartment complex, but with the number of emergency vehicles, he knew he wouldn't be able to get any closer.

He'd been off-shift when the fire had been reported. He was dead to the world sleeping when Penelope had called him, frantic. She'd been up and had heard the call on the scanner. Cade had barely taken the time to pull on a pair of sneakers and a T-shirt and rushed out of his house. The fifteen minutes it took him to get to Beth's place—thank God for light traffic in the middle of the night—were the longest of his life.

Just last night, he and Penelope and the rest of the guys had talked through his suspicions about Beth.

He couldn't ignore the signals anymore. She was doing better with her agoraphobia, but he realized with the kind of insight he'd spent his adult life cultivating with his job, it was most likely because she was purposely setting fires.

Cade hadn't made much of it when it'd happened, but he remembered once early in their relationship he'd woken up in the middle of the night and wandered into the living room to check on her—and found her sitting on the couch watching a dozen candles flickering in front of her. She'd lit them all and was leaning forward on the couch, fixated on the flickering flames. He'd called her name three times before she'd realized he was standing there.

She'd quickly blown out the candles and had stammered some excuse, but he'd begun to put two and two together.

He'd had his suspicions, but hadn't wanted to accuse her of something that might not be true. When he'd finally put all of the incidents and clues together, he finally realized with a sinking feeling in his belly that all the coincidences with her and fire weren't actually coincidences at all. It was suddenly as clear as if she'd flat-out told him.

And how he wished she *had*.

It was apparent that Beth had merely swapped one demon for another. He wouldn't go so far as to call her a pyromaniac...but she was definitely heading toward something that would be tough to come back from, tougher than her fear of being outside around people.

From the candles, buying a grill when she was terrified to step foot outside her apartment, the lighters in her purse, the burn marks around her patio, her burnt fingers—which couldn't have come from grabbing a hot pan; her palm would've been burnt, not her fingers —the signs were all there, and it was heart wrenching.

He was a firefighter...he *fought* fires for a living. He had no idea how he could trust Beth if she continued down the path she was on. Just last week he'd been on the cusp of asking her to move in with him, but if he had to worry about coming home to nothing but ashes, or her scorched body, or if she'd move on to burning buildings, it could never work between them...and that broke his heart.

Cade saw the smoke lazily rising into the sky as he ran; it was lit up by the spotlights from all the emergency vehicles as they concentrated their beams on the apartment. It looked like the fire itself was out, but it'd been a good-sized one, from what he could tell. He entered the large courtyard and looked toward Beth's building. It looked like the bulk of the damage was on the upper floor, but there were scorch marks all the way down the outside of the building, including around her apartment. Cade didn't want to believe it, but he had a gut feeling that Beth had been involved. She was known to stay up until very early in the morning and she was obviously fixated with fire.

The firefighters were concentrating on her building, using the ladder truck to pour water on the roof and the external walls.

Tearing his eyes away from the scorch marks on the building, Cade frantically looked around for Beth. Even with the doubts coursing through his brain, he needed to make sure she was all right. He hadn't decided what he was going to do. He'd only just realized the extent of her problem.

There were groups of people standing everywhere, and Cade didn't immediately see Beth. For the first time he got an inkling of what she might feel when she had her panic attacks. He could feel his heart rate increase, and the adrenaline coursing through his veins made his hands shake.

Just as he was sure she was huddled inside her apartment, afraid to step foot outside, even if her apartment was burning down around her, Cade saw two people standing a bit off to the side of the mass of spectators.

He immediately made his way toward them, recognizing Beth's body language even as he stalked over to the couple. She was standing about a foot and a half away from the older man, but her arm was outstretched, holding his hand. Cade recognized him as one of her neighbors; he'd nodded at him when he'd been visiting Beth in the past.

Her face was pale and she was staring wide-eyed up at the roof of her building as if she couldn't tear her gaze away. Cade ran his eyes over her as he approached, trying to see if she was injured in any way. She was wearing a pair of jeans with one of his long-sleeve Station 7 T-shirts, which swam on her smaller frame. One hand was gripping her neighbor's for all she was worth, and the other arm held one of the fire extinguishers he'd bought for her. Beth was standing stiffly and while she looked extremely uncomfortable, Cade could see she wasn't freaking out...yet.

"Beth? Are you all right?"

Beth's eyes immediately shifted to him, and Cade sighed in relief at the look of recognition in her eyes. He held out his hand and she immediately leaned over to put the extinguisher on the ground, and then reached out to grab it. Cade noticed that she didn't let go of her neighbor until he had her hand firmly in his.

Cade felt her sigh as she melted into his embrace, burrowing her face into his chest. She shook as she nuzzled into him, holding on for dear life.

"Shhhh, I've got you. You're okay." Cade turned to her neighbor. "Thanks."

"You're welcome. I've noticed she's a little gun-shy when it comes to being around people and that she doesn't go outside much. I figured I might serve as a stand-in until you got here."

Not surprised the man had noticed—after all, he'd been at Beth's apartment a lot over the last couple of months—Cade gave him a chin lift in thanks.

Now that he knew Beth was safe in his arms, Cade recalled all the other things he'd thought about in the last couple of days. He had a million questions, but now wasn't the time.

They stood in the courtyard watching as the firefighters finished hosing down the building and did their walk-through, looking for hotspots. They finally came out and made an announcement that while the damage looked localized, the people who lived in that building wouldn't be able to go back to their apartments until at least the next day. The fire marshal and building inspectors would be checking over the structure in the coming days to make sure it was safe. Red Cross shelters were being set up for the displaced residents.

Beth hadn't moved at the announcement, except perhaps to burrow farther into his arms. Not releasing her hand, Cade hugged her closer to his chest. He wouldn't abandon her, but he had no idea how he was going to manage having her in his house and space without making love to her.

He'd made the decision that night after the discussion with the others at the firehouse that he needed to back off from their relationship until she could get her firebug tendencies under control. He wasn't giving her up for good, but she had to want to get better, to want to stop the fire thing before he could go any deeper into their relationship.

Cade wanted to snort at himself. He wasn't sure how much deeper he could go. He loved her. And knowing she'd turned to fire to help control her fears killed him. Having her in his home was not going to help with his decision to back away from their intense relationship for a while.

"Come on, sweetheart, let's get going. It's late, you have to be exhausted."

She looked up at him. "I don't have any of my stuff."

"We'll get anything you need later. I'll take care of you, Beth."

"I know you will. I'm trying to take this all in stride…but I'm having a hard time. If I can't go back, I just…"

"It's going to be fine. You'll get through this. You've been doing a lot better. Hang in there."

Beth looked up at Cade with questions in her eyes. Cade knew she was probably expecting more out of him. Hell, a week ago he wouldn't have hesitated to tell her to make his home *her* home; he'd been about to do that very thing earlier this week. But he had too many questions now. He steeled himself against the lost look in her eyes.

It was for her own good. She needed more help than he could give her.

"Come on. I had to park a bit away from here because of the traffic. Things will look better in the morning."

Beth nodded and they set off for his truck. Cade had no idea what the next day would bring—hopefully answers to some of his questions. For better or worse, they had to talk about her issues, and where the two of them were going from here.

CHAPTER 16

"Why don't you go ahead and go in and get comfortable. I'll be in after a while."

Beth paused on the stairs leading upstairs. She'd been pleased with how she'd been handling everything. She'd trusted her neighbor, he hadn't kidnapped her, she'd stood outside with him for who knew how long before Cade showed up, without majorly freaking out. She had no idea if she'd be able to get back to her apartment, her safe place, the next day or not, and she'd done it all without using the lighter she'd taken to carrying around again.

The damn bag in the kitchen held all of her fire tools, except for one lighter. Finding that every once in a while she could use it to calm herself, she couldn't bring herself to throw it away yet. It wasn't as if she was actually setting fires with it...but the flame relaxed her enough so she could push the panic attacks away.

But this—she wasn't sure she could handle Cade

pulling away from her on top of everything else. He was her rock, even if he didn't realize just how much she relied on him. She wanted to be whole for him.

Beth felt her heart kick into gear and her breathing increase. She curled her hands into fists and tried not to panic. "You're not coming?"

"I'll be up later."

"Cade? Are you all right?"

"We'll talk later."

Shit shit shit. "We have something to talk about?"

"Yeah, but it's fine, Beth. Just get some sleep. It's been a hectic night and I know you're probably on the verge of collapsing. I'm just keyed up right now."

Beth took a deep breath. There was no way she was sleeping at this point. "I think we should talk now. If you've got something to say, then you should get it off your chest."

"Not now."

Beth studied Cade. He was a long way from the easy-going man she'd gotten to know over the last few months. They'd disagreed in the past, but not like this. Dread worked its way up her spine and made her mouth dry. "I think now is the perfect time. Do you not want me here? Is that it?"

Cade clenched his teeth and Beth saw the muscle in his jaw tighten.

"That's it, isn't it? You should've said something when we were still at my place, Cade."

"It's complicated."

"Complicated." Beth laughed bitterly. "Is that code

for 'it's not working out'? No wait, let me guess. It's not me, it's you, right?"

Cade leaned against the kitchen counter with his arms crossed. "No, it just means it's complicated."

"You don't have to babysit me. I thought we were past this."

"I thought so too."

Now Beth was getting pissed. He was talking in riddles and Beth knew she was missing something big, but had no idea what. "Spit it out, Cade. If you're sick of having to hold my hand, literally, all the time, just say so. I'm a big girl. I might be afraid of a lot of shit, but I'll never stay with someone who resents me."

"How did the fire start tonight, Beth?"

"What?" Beth was confused at the seemingly abrupt change of topic. "I have no idea. I was in bed when I heard shouts and the fire alarm went off."

The look on Cade's face didn't change. "What about the fire on your patio a few weeks ago. How'd that start? And the burns on your fingers? I know that didn't happen from you grabbing a pan. Did you hold a match too long? Get too close to one of your fires? What about all the candles you suddenly had around your place?"

Beth swallowed. Hard. She'd thought she'd been discreet. Obviously having a firefighter for a boyfriend meant he noticed those things. "What about them?"

"Are you seriously going to stand there and tell me they have nothing to do with tonight?"

"They don't."

Now Cade looked defeated. "Go to bed, Beth."

"Cade. That fire tonight had nothing to do with me," Beth said firmly, hoping against hope he'd hear the sincerity in her voice.

He didn't say anything, but continued to stare at her, his gaze piercing as if he could see right to the heart of her.

Her voice dropped to a whisper. "I admit I'm... going through a-a phase where I find watching flames...soothing. But I *didn't* start this fire."

"Soothing. Are you listening to yourself?" Cade pushed off the counter and paced. "Beth, you can't see what's right in front of your face. I admit I was slow picking it up myself, but normal people don't light matches until they burn down to their fingers and scorch them. Normal people don't find fire comforting. *Normal* people don't light trash on fire on their grill just to watch it burn."

Beth had no idea if Cade purposely chose his words or not, but it was a moot point. They'd struck her with the force of a ten-ton truck. He continued on as if he hadn't just ripped her heart out, trampled it, then tried to hand it back as if nothing was wrong.

"And that lighter you carry around? I suppose that's just in case someone needs to light their cigarette?" Cade's voice gentled as if he finally understood that what he was saying could be hurtful. "You can't trade one crutch for another, sweetheart."

"Is that what you think *you* are? A crutch?"

"Yeah. And Penelope. And your neighbor tonight.

We're all your crutches. And that's okay; I have no problem with it. But I *do* have an issue with you using *fire* as a crutch. I've spent my entire life understanding and fighting fire. Faulty oil heaters, Christmas tree lights that overheat, cooking accidents from oil getting too hot." He smiled sadly at the last example before continuing, "I have no problem being the hero and rushing in to save the day. But the deliberate setting of fires is something I can't wrap my mind around."

"I had nothing to do with the fire tonight," Beth repeated for what felt like the hundredth time.

"Maybe. Maybe not. But the bottom line is that someday you *might* have something to do with a fire I get called to if you continue down this path. What if the next one kills someone? Will that be worth the high you get from it?"

Beth knew she should be freaking out. Should be panicking, but she was too busy trying to keep her heart from breaking open and bleeding all over Cade's floor to worry about a pesky thing like breathing. Cade didn't understand that she wasn't getting a "high" from the flames; quite the contrary. They soothed something inside her, made it so that she felt she had some control in her life. Made it so she could function. She wanted to explain it. Tell him what the fires did for her, but she was scared. She didn't want to lose him, but she couldn't think straight. It seemed Cade had made up his mind, and he actually thought she had started the fire at her apartment complex tonight, no matter that she'd told him differently.

"So, this is it?" Her voice was flat and toneless.

"No. Hell no! That's not what I'm saying. I don't *want* this to be it. Beth, I love you. I love you so much this is hurting me more than it is you." Cade ran his hand over his hair, obviously frustrated.

Beth doubted that, but he kept going.

"But I can't leave you in my home wondering if today's the day I'm going to get called back here to find the house ablaze. To find your dead body in a back room because you panicked at the thought of going outside. To find third-degree burns all over your body because one of the fires you started to 'deal' with things in your life got out of control. I love you too much for that."

Beth bit her lip and didn't speak. It was obvious Cade thought he had her all figured out.

"You need help, sweetheart. More than I can give you. I thought I was helping being there for you, letting you lean on me. But I see now that ultimately I wasn't. You need professional help. Probably more than just your therapy group."

"I'll be out of your hair tomorrow," Beth said, without losing eye contact with Cade. He stepped toward her, reaching out to put his hand on her shoulders, but Beth backed away before he could touch her. "You have no clue, Cade Turner. None. I wish you could walk just one day in my shoes. Just one. I didn't start the fire tonight. Yes, I've been struggling with this new obsession with fire, but that fire on my patio a few weeks ago scared the shit out of me and I've been managing it since then. I'd planned on talking with Penelope about it...then you. But you jumped to conclusions, and the main thing I got from everything you just said is that you don't trust me."

"It's not about trust," Cade implored. "It's because I love you so much and want—"

Beth waved his words away. "I remember the first time you took hold of my hand in the grocery store. I was with Penelope and she wanted to go do something with Hayden. I was nervous as heck but didn't want to hold Pen back. You smiled at me and took my hand and I swear to God I felt my worries drain out of my body and onto the floor. I even looked back to see if I'd left a puddle behind us as we walked away. Not once have I ever thought I was a burden to you...until just now.

"The last thing I ever wanted to be was a liability. Why do you think I left California? My parents had no idea how to help me and I could see it was tearing them up inside. My brother wanted to move back home to help 'take care of' me. I don't want to be taken care of, Cade. All I've ever wanted was to be loved for who I am."

"Beth—"

She spoke over him, knowing if she didn't get it out now, she might never be able to. He wanted to talk? Fine. She was talking. "I get why you'd think I started that fire tonight. I do. And I don't blame you for it. But all I've wanted since Hurst raped me, since he stuck a knife in my side, since he put out burning cigarettes on my body...was to be *normal*. I thought I was making pretty good progress toward that until about three minutes ago, when you told me otherwise. I might never be able to stroll casually through the aisles of Walmart without a care in the world, but that doesn't mean I don't deserve to have someone by my side supporting me while I make the attempt.

"I love you, Cade. I might be younger, but right now I feel as if I've got years on you. You have no idea—" Her voice cracked, but Beth powered through it. "You have no idea what you've done. I'm sorry I didn't tell you about the matches. And the candles and the lighters. I'm sorry I was trying to do everything possible to be the kind of woman you needed. The kind who could sit in the stands during a softball game and cheer you on. The kind of woman you'd be proud to hold her hand and walk next to, not because she needed the contact to keep from freaking out, but because you couldn't bear to be next to her and *not* be touching her. All my fire stuff is in a trash bag in my apartment. I did it two weeks ago. I've been working my way up to having Pen throw it out for me. I had an appointment set up next week to talk to my counselor about it all. I should've talked to you. I know that. But I didn't want to disappoint you. Big fail on my part."

Beth shrugged and stopped talking. She didn't have anything else in her at the moment. She'd said what she needed to say.

"Get some sleep, Beth. We'll talk in the morning. We'll work this out. I don't want to lose you. All I ever wanted was for you to be confident in yourself. To see yourself as the amazing person I see. And who Penelope, and Tex, and all my friends see."

Knowing she'd never sleep, Beth nodded anyway and headed up the stairs. She slowly walked to the bedroom, hoping against hope that Cade would bound up the stairs apologizing. She entered the room which held so many wonderful memories of the two of them and shut the door. The latch of the knob sounded loud in the quiet room. Final.

As much as she was hurting, Beth knew Cade hadn't meant to upset her. He was frustrated and worried about her. She couldn't blame him. If she'd thought he might burn her place down, she'd have second thoughts too. But it didn't change anything.

He'd been right about one thing. She *had* been using Cade and Penelope as crutches. It was as clear as ever to her now. If she was going to get better, she had to help herself. She couldn't rely on anyone else to make her better. It was up to her.

CHAPTER 17

CADE TOSSED and turned on the couch for the rest of the night...well, morning. He replayed his conversation with Beth over and over, and mentally kicked himself each time. He'd said things all wrong. He didn't mean to imply she was abnormal, or that she was using Penelope and him. He'd only been worried about her, and about how she was coping.

A part of him worried about his own reputation as a firefighter, but now that he really thought about it, he knew his friends wouldn't treat him any differently if they knew Beth was a firebug. They'd probably rally around him even more and do everything in their power to help both him and his girlfriend. Besides, he was more equipped than most people to handle her addiction. And he knew the others would do whatever they could to help, not ridicule either him or her.

She'd been through hell and back and he'd just thrown it in her face. Cade felt like shit and he couldn't wait to make things right between then. He missed her, and she was right upstairs. Cade didn't like the feeling. Not at all.

As soon as Beth got up, he'd make sure she understood where he was coming from, that he loved her and wanted her to get better. They'd get her help together. He'd take her to her appointment next week with her counselor and do whatever it took to get them back on track.

He wanted Beth in his life, however he could have her. He couldn't stand to lose her now, not after everything they'd been through. He loved her and it would devastate him if he'd said something that made her backslide in her recovery.

Needing to see her, and make things right between them, Cade finally went upstairs and knocked lightly on his bedroom door. Looking at his watch and seeing it was nine o'clock, even with their very late night, he figured Beth would've been awake by now. He knocked again.

When he got no answer, he opened the door a crack and looked in.

Alarmed, he opened the door all the way and scanned the room. His bed was made and there was no sign of Beth. The bathroom door was ajar and it was obvious she wasn't simply taking a shower.

Cade's head spun as he stood there for a moment trying to process what he was seeing. Where was she? It wasn't as if she could leave on her own...could she? How in the hell did she get by him?

Jesus, he was an idiot.

He stalked back downstairs and into his kitchen and picked up his cell, calling Penelope. Without giving her time to chat, he asked as soon as she answered, "Where's Beth?"

"Good morning to you too, Cade. What do you mean, where's Beth? She went home with you."

"She's not here. Did you pick her up?"

Penelope sounded a bit less nonchalant now. "No. What happened?"

Cade sighed and ran his hand through his hair. "We talked last night about her fire thing."

"I take it that didn't go well."

"It didn't go well."

"She didn't call me, Cade. Who else would she call?"

"Your counselor? Her parents? Brother? I don't know, sis."

"Okay, we'll divide and conquer. I'll call. You see if you can get ahold of her parents."

"I don't know their number."

"Shit. I don't either. Okay, she had to have gotten ahold of someone, right? It's not like she could've walked back into town."

"She probably used the phone in my room. I've got a landline in there but I never use it, so I forgot about it. I'll see if Cruz can help me."

"That's not exactly legal. Why don't you swing by her place and see if she's there before you bring in the FBI? She's probably there licking her wounds. I'll call her doc and meet you there. Okay?"

"Right. See you soon."

"I'll call if I hear anything."

"Thanks, Penelope."

"We'll find her, Cade. Try not to worry."

"Bye."

"Bye."

Cade clicked off his phone, rushed into his bedroom, and threw on a pair of jeans and a clean T-shirt. He quickly got into his truck and headed for Beth's apartment. He hadn't scoffed at his sister's words, but he wanted to. Not worry? Not possible.

The no-trespassing signs hung by the fire department the night before were still up at Beth's apartment complex, but Cade ignored them, waving to the fire marshal. Luckily the man recognized him and didn't seem to mind him being there.

Cade knocked on Beth's door, but didn't get an answer. He pulled out the extra key she'd given him and entered.

He knew immediately she wasn't home; there was a silence that only came with emptiness. Cade looked around, trying to decide if she'd been there since the fire last night. He walked into the kitchen and saw a garbage bag sitting on the floor next to the tall trash can.

Cade peeled back the plastic and looked inside.

There were dozens of candles and what had to have been a carton of kitchen matches, still inside their jackets. There were also at least two propane sticks that he could see, amongst the other paraphernalia. Cade swallowed the bile that rose in his throat.

Beth hadn't lied to him; she really was trying to give it up.

She'd done this sometime before the fire last night. It was obvious from the water damage in her kitchen, from the water thrown on the flames last night. He looked up. The ceiling still had some water dripping in places—including on the bag that held all of Beth's demons.

He dropped the plastic bag as if it'd physically burned his hand and stalked into the living room. There was water damage in there as well, but not as much as in the kitchen. Seeing nothing out of place, Cade pushed open her bedroom door. The bed covers were thrown back as if she'd just climbed out of it.

As if she'd been woken up in the middle of the night by screams, just as she'd claimed, and had scrambled out of bed.

Not sure what he was really looking for, Cade peered inside her closet, then her bathroom. Again, nothing stuck out as missing.

Realizing with sudden clarity what he *should* be looking for, Cade's eyes swept the room. Not finding what he was seeking, he hurried back into the living room, knowing with a glance she'd been here and was now gone.

Cade settled onto the soggy couch, ignoring the dampness of the cushions, and put his head in his hands.

Penelope and Moose found him that way ten minutes later. The counselor wasn't with them, but it didn't matter now anyway.

"Cade?" Penelope asked with concern.

"She's gone," Cade said without lifting his head. "I fucked up and she's gone."

"How could she be gone?" Penelope asked in confusion. "She hasn't gone anywhere without one of us with her for the last couple of months. I talked to the doctor who leads our group and she hasn't heard from her, but that doesn't mean Beth *won't* contact her."

"I guess humiliation and hurt are powerful motivators."

"Sledge, man, come on. I'm sure it wasn't that bad," Moose said, putting his hand on Cade's shoulder in support.

Cade looked up at his friend. "I told her she wasn't normal. I said she was using me and Penelope as a crutch."

"I'm sure you were trying to make her see that she needed more help than we could provide." Penelope tried to ease her brother's obvious pain.

"I was, but it came out all wrong. I love her, Squirt. What if she's having an attack right now? What if she's out there, hyperventilating and scared someone is going to snatch her off the street? What if she turns back to fire because of what I said?"

"Do you have any idea where she might have gone?" Moose asked, trying to get Cade's mind away from the pit he was spiraling toward.

"No. All I know is that she's gone. She took her computer. She wouldn't go anywhere without it."

"That's it! Cade, you're a genius," Penelope exclaimed, pulling out her phone.

Cade could only stare at his sister in confusion. He'd known the second he'd seen Beth's laptop bag was missing that she'd fled. She wouldn't go anywhere without her precious computer. It was her lifeline.

Penelope held up a hand, preventing Cade from asking the questions she knew he was dying to ask as she waited for someone on the other end of the line to answer.

"Hey, it's Penelope. I need a favor. Please call as soon as you can."

"Who was that?" Cade asked after she hung up.

"Tex. If he could find me in the middle of a Turkish hell, he can find Beth."

"I don't know; she's pretty good with that electronic shit, I'm sure she can hide from him."

"No way. From everything I've heard, Tex is the best. And Beth might be good, but Tex is better. He has to be."

Cade felt hope for the first time that morning. Beth had made it back to her apartment, so she had to be okay. Where she was now, he had no idea, but he'd find her and make her listen to him. He loved her. He did remember telling her that last night, but he'd prefaced it with so much shit, it was no wonder she didn't believe it.

He trusted his sister and this Tex person, but it

wouldn't hurt to call Cruz, Daxton, and Quint as well. They'd certainly be willing to help look for her if needed. They'd only met Beth once, but knowing how Cade felt about her, they'd definitely do what they could to track her down.

Having Mackenzie, Mickie, and Corrie around would help Penelope as well. She acted tough, but not knowing where Beth was would wear on her. The women could band together and help give Penelope comfort.

The guys at the station would help, of course. They'd blanket the city and find her. If she was holed up at a hotel somewhere, they'd all take turns calling places to see if she'd checked in. He and Penelope both had some awesome friends—but all Cade wanted was to see for himself that Beth was all right.

He'd driven her away with his words, and now he needed to right that wrong.

Four days later, Cade paced the length of his living room. He'd spoken with Cruz, Quint, and Daxton, and they'd assured him they'd do what they could to find Beth for him. It was driving him crazy that he had no idea where she was. He wasn't sleeping and he'd taken a week off work. There was no way he could concentrate enough to make sure he wasn't a danger to himself, his friends, or any patients they might have to deal with.

Cade knew Beth had to be nearby. She'd been getting better at being outside, but he didn't think she'd be able to get on a plane or bus yet...not with her panic attacks. She *had* to have another person here in San Antonio who she felt she could turn to in order to help her. She hadn't talked about any other friends in the area, but that didn't mean she didn't have them.

Cade started to panic, thinking about different scenarios. Maybe she'd gotten close to one of her hacker friends and had gone to him or her...and if that person turned out to be a psycho, he might never see or hear from her again. The thought made his stomach turn.

His phone rang and Cade quickly swiped the screen and brought it up to his ear. Expecting it to be his sister, he asked without saying hello, "Did you find her?"

"Beth is fine, she just needs some time."

"Who is this?" Cade asked in confusion, not recognizing the deep voice on the other end of the line.

"Her brother, David."

"Have you spoken with her? Can I come see her? I need to see her!"

"Yes, of course I've talked with her, and as I said, she's fine. She doesn't want to see anyone right now. Some guy named Tex got in touch with me and said you were worried about her, and that I should contact you."

Cade eased himself onto the couch. He had a million questions, but didn't think the irritated man on the other end of the line would put up with all of them. "Thank you. But when? When can I come and see her?"

"I don't know. It's up to her. If it was up to *me*, you'd never come anywhere near her ever again," David said in a stern voice. "She didn't tell me everything that happened, but for the last few months she's sounded happier and better than she's been in a long time…ever since that fucking asshole kidnapped her. When she called me the other morning, it was as if she'd reverted to the person she'd become right after her ordeal. She couldn't stop crying and she was barely making sense. Something happened, and if I wasn't more concerned about my sister, I'd fly down there and kick your ass."

"Where is she?" Cade's voice broke as he asked the question that had haunted him for four long days.

"Somewhere safe."

"Please, man, I get that you're pissed. Hell, I don't blame you. I've been kicking my own ass for the last couple of days. I just need to know where she is and that she really is safe."

"Pennsylvania."

"What? How'd she get there?"

"It wasn't easy. She had stuffed herself with so many drugs, I'm not sure she even recognized me when I picked her up at the train station."

"Jesus," Cade breathed. "Anyone could have messed with her while she was like that. Is she with you?"

"No. She checked herself into a hospital up here that specializes in treating agoraphobia. I have no idea how she got in, as they have a waiting list at least six months long, but I've learned over the last few years not to ask when it comes to computers and my sister."

Cade chuckled without much humor. It sounded just like something his Beth would do. Hack into the database and get herself a coveted spot in a treatment center. "You're in Philadelphia, right?"

"Don't even think about coming up here, Cade. I'm only calling because Tex insisted you needed to know. I wouldn't have bothered otherwise."

Realizing how pissed Beth's brother was at him, Cade treaded carefully. "I admit I said some shit I probably should've waited to talk to her about. But she pushed. And again, before you say it, I know that's no excuse on my part. But I was worried about her. I was afraid she was stuck inside her apartment as it burned down around her. I didn't think I'd *get* to see her again. So when she insisted I tell her what was bothering me, I spoke out of stress and my concern for her. I love your sister, David. I've never felt as much fear as I have the last four days, not knowing where she was, if she was all right. I'll keep my distance as long as she needs me to but I'm not giving up on her. She's it for me."

"And if she isn't able to live a normal life again?"

"Then I'll make her normal *my* new normal."

"Just like that?"

"Just like that. I love her. Did you not hear me? I don't care. I'll do whatever it takes."

There was a slight pause before David spoke again in a tone a bit more congenial than he'd used a moment ago. "She's at The Anxiety and Agoraphobia Treatment

Center in Bala Cynwyd, Pennsylvania, outside of Philadelphia."

"Thank you."

"She doesn't want to see you."

"I know. I get that. I'll give her time, but I'm not giving up on her."

Cade heard David sigh. "For what it's worth, she loves you. You hurt her, but even almost comatose from the amount of Xanax she'd taken to get up here, her first concern was for you. She was worried about disappearing on you and how you'd take it. She would've called you right then if she had a phone."

Hearing that made Cade feel a smidgen better. He didn't feel good about any part of this situation, but knowing that Beth was worried about him made him feel as if maybe he still had a chance to right what he'd done wrong. "You'll keep in touch, let me know how she's doing?"

"We'll see."

Cade wasn't happy with his answer, but couldn't blame the man. "Okay. If you see or talk to her...tell her I love her and I'm here waiting for her."

"I have to go," David said abruptly.

"Thanks for calling. Seriously. You have no idea how much it means to me and her other friends down here."

"Bye."

Cade wasn't surprised David had ended the conversation so abruptly. He ran his hand over his face and took a deep breath. He had to call Penelope and the others and let them know Beth was safe. Now it was a waiting game to see what would happen next. He hadn't lied to Beth's brother; he wasn't giving up on her. He'd wait for as long as she needed, but he wasn't going to let her go without a fight.

CHAPTER 18

CADE SAT on the couch at the station staring at the football game on the television, but not seeing it. It'd been two weeks since he'd spoken with Beth's brother, and he hadn't heard anything from either Beth or David since. He'd accepted that the not knowing and waiting would be hard, but he'd had no idea it would be *this* tough.

"Heard anything, Sledge?" Chief asked from next to him.

Cade sighed. "No. Nothing, but I'm assuming she's okay."

"Why?"

"Because for the last week or so I've been signed up for no less than five online dating sites."

"Huh? What's that have to do with anything?" Squirrel asked from a recliner next to the couch.

Cade had admitted to all his buddies what had happened and all the shit things he'd said to Beth that night. They'd sympathized with him and hadn't made him feel worse about it, for which he was thankful.

"Beth gets...bored easily. I can just imagine what it's like being in a hospital filled with others who have misgivings about stepping foot outside."

"How can you be sure it's Beth who signed you up?"

"One profile described me as being an 'overbearing Neanderthal who spoke before thinking.'"

"Ouch," Taco chimed in, trying to hold back his snicker, with little success.

Cade smiled, even though that one had hurt a bit. "I have high hopes she's thawing toward me though, because the last one described me as 'misguided, but with my heart in the right place.'"

"Does it bother you that she can so easily hack into anything electronic you've got? What about your privacy?" Crash asked.

Cade didn't mind the question and didn't hesitate in answering. "Hell no. I've got nothing to hide from her. If she wants to hack my credit card and go on a spending spree, I'm all for it. It took me thinking she was dead to realize that I'd give her anything she wants...even if she doesn't ask and just takes it."

"That's kinda fucked up, man," Squirrel stated with a shudder.

"No, it's not. Because I know her. She's not ever going to steal from me. She's not that kind of person. But I'm an open book to her. If she wants to hack my phone and read my texts? She's welcome to it. She wants to check out my browsing history on my computer? She can knock herself out. I've got nothing to hide. Nothing. I love her. I've missed her more these last two weeks than I can possibly explain."

"Yeah, going without sex for two weeks would kill me, man," Taco teased from across the room.

"It's not the sex," Cade tried to clarify. "Don't get me wrong, I'm not sleeping well without her in my arms, but it's more that I miss being able to talk to her. To discuss work, what she did during the day, seeing her smile. You guys don't get it now, but I swear you will when you find a woman of your own."

The room was silent for a moment. The other guys finally seemed to get that what he had with Beth wasn't a casual relationship. She was it for him.

Before anyone could say anything, Cade's phone buzzed with an incoming text. Looking down, Cade's breath caught.

You hurt me, and I'm still mad...but I can't stop thinking about you.

Cade swore he felt his heart stop beating for a moment. He immediately texted back.

I'm sorry. I love you and think about you every day. I hope you're okay.

He waited but she didn't text back. He sighed, and decided to take her reaching out as a good sign. He wasn't going to push his luck, but now that he had her number—she'd obviously gotten a cell phone sometime in the last two weeks—he wasn't going to let her get away. He cared too much about her to give up now.

The tones rang out in the station and Cade had to

put aside his thoughts of Beth and her text for the moment, but deep down he was formulating his plan to make sure she didn't forget about him while she was gone.

* * *

Beth read the text message that came in and couldn't stop the chuckle that escaped.

You wouldn't happen to know anything about the box of men's thong underwear that just arrived on my doorstep would you?

"Something funny?" Dr. Neal asked from the chair across from her.

Beth nodded. "Cade. He got my latest present."

The doctor smiled at Beth. "I understand that he's down in Texas, but I'm thinking it's time he came up and had some sessions with you. Since you reached out two weeks ago and let him know how you felt, you guys have been talking almost every day, right?"

"Talking via text, yeah. But you know as well as I do that I only contacted him because it was a part of my therapy."

"True, but at no point did I tell you that you had to *keep* talking to him. And he was the one who, once you texted him that first time, kept at it until you responded back."

Beth blushed. Darn it. She hated that her doctor knew everything. Well, okay, she didn't *hate* it, it was just hard to lie to her. "I wasn't sure he would care."

"It seems like he cares quite a bit to me. Beth, I can count on one hand the number of single men who would do what yours has done if he didn't care. The fact that you have not only your family's support, but apparently a man who loves you very much as well? A lot of people don't have that. I'm not saying this to make you feel bad, not at all, but I urge you to really think hard about it."

Beth bit her lip in consternation. "He told me I wasn't normal. That I was using him as a crutch."

"And we've been over this. The truth is that you *aren't* normal and you *were* using him as a crutch. I'm not trying to be harsh, but Beth, you know what happened to you is what caused this. You aren't doing it on purpose and you're here, doing what you can to get better. I'll be honest, I could drug you up to your eyeballs and you'd be able to walk around all on your own…but if you can't feel anything, what's the point of living?" She paused, then brought up an unrelated topic.

"And I haven't talked about it before now, but I have to tell you, I have a sneaking suspicion that you being here wasn't a stroke of luck…am I right? I know how long the waiting list is—and you, my sneaky friend, weren't on that list until a couple of hours before you arrived."

Beth didn't say anything, but the flush moving over her face probably gave her away, and she wouldn't meet Dr. Neal's eyes.

"For such a smart person, you certainly can be clueless at times. Beth, while I don't approve of your actions—taking the spot of someone who has been waiting months wasn't the fairest thing you've done—now that you're here, I'm going to do everything in my power to help you. Beth, you might never be 'cured,' but the tools you've learned here will help you when you go back to Texas."

Ignoring the part about hacking her way into the facility, Beth said in surprise, "Back to Texas?"

"Yes. Back to Cade. He loves you, Beth."

"But my brother is here. He can help me."

"He is, and he's been a wonderful support for you, but you need more. You need someone to always be by your side and to help you when you slip, and to keep you headed in the right direction. I'd really like to meet Cade, Beth. It's time."

Beth's breathing sped up and Dr. Neal was immediately next to her. "No, don't panic, remember your training. Take deep breaths, close your eyes and think about your safe place. That's it…good. You've gotten so much better at controlling your attacks. You're going to get out of here much sooner than almost anyone I've treated. I fully believe it's because of the confidence being with your Cade has given you. Now…are you ready to talk about him visiting?"

Beth opened her eyes to see her doctor kneeling in front of her. "Yes."

"Good. I'll expect to see him at your next session in two days. Make it happen, Beth."

"Yes, ma'am."

* * *

Beth forced herself to stay seated on the balcony of her room. The doors were open so she could dart back inside within seconds, but she so wanted to be able to sit outside and enjoy the cooler weather they didn't get often back in Texas. She might have agoraphobia, but she wasn't going down easily.

She painstakingly tapped out a text for Cade. She much preferred her full-sized keyboard, but she didn't feel like moving. She was here, it took too much mental effort to get out onto the small balcony as it was, so she wasn't going to mess with it at this point.

My doctor thinks you should come to a session with me.

Beth chewed on her thumbnail, waiting for Cade's response. It wasn't as if she thought he'd refuse to come, she was almost more scared that he *would* come.

Whenever it is, I'll be there.

She let out a breath. Beth knew he'd agree. She still wasn't completely sure about it, but she couldn't deny a part of her wanted nothing more than to throw herself in Cade's arms and have him hold her and keep her safe.

Whenever you can get here. There's no rush.

I can be there tomorrow if you need me.

Jesus. Just when she didn't think she could love the man more, he made her feel like an ooey-gooey marshmallow.

I have another session the day after tomorrow.

What time?

Whatever works for you.

I'll be there as early as visitors are allowed.

Beth put the phone down in her lap for a moment and looked up, trying not to cry as she had an epiphany about her relationship with Cade.

She hadn't run from him because of what he'd said...not in the way he probably thought. After she'd gone into his room, she'd realized he was right. Every single word out of his mouth was dead-on. She knew playing with the matches and candles was a slippery slope she might not be able to come back from. She'd traded one coping mechanism for another.

She wanted to be the kind of person Cade was proud to stand beside. She wanted to be there to support him, not have him be the one propping her up all the time. Knowing she wouldn't be able to if he was there holding her hand was what enabled her to make the painful break.

But suddenly the thought of seeing him again, and knowing he'd drop everything to fly halfway across the country for a simple therapy session, said everything it needed to.

Visitors are allowed at nine.

I'll be there at eight-thirty so I'm the first person through the door.

Beth could barely see the screen through the tears coursing down her face. God.

I love you, Beth. I'll be sure to wear one of the fancy pairs of underwear you ordered for me.

She smiled at that, thankful her man had a sense of humor.

Her man. She liked the sound of that.

Now if she could only make it through the session with Dr. Neal without blowing it.

CHAPTER 19

CADE SAT on the bench outside The Anxiety and Agoraphobia Treatment Center with his hands dangling between his legs and waited for it to open. It was eight-twenty, and he couldn't wait another moment to get there. He'd flown up the evening before and had only been able to sleep a couple of hours. Knowing he was so close to Beth but he couldn't get to her was killing him.

He needed to feel her safe in his arms. There were so many things he wanted to say, and the first would be an apology. He had no idea what she was going through. It was easy for him to say she was using him, but did he care? No. She could use him all she needed to.

A slender woman wearing a dark blue power suit walked up to the front door and stopped, looking down at him. "Cade Turner?"

Cade looked up in surprise. "Yes, that's me."

The woman turned to him and sat down on the bench, placing her dark brown briefcase on the ground next to her. She crossed her legs and held out a hand. "I'm Dr. Neal, Elizabeth's doctor."

Cade immediately reciprocated the gesture and gripped her hand. "It's good to meet you. Beth has nothing but good things to say about you."

"Then she's lying. There are times when she really doesn't like me at all, but it's all a part of the process. Thank you for coming today."

"There's nothing I wouldn't do for Beth. All she has to do is ask and it's hers." Cade didn't even fidget as the doctor looked him over for several moments.

Finally, she spoke. "I told her this already, and I think you should hear it too. I can't say it enough. It's possible she's never going to be completely cured. Many times, agoraphobia is a lifelong affliction. She'll get better and you'll think she's over it. Then there'll be a day where all she wants is to hide under the covers. You could be in the middle of an ordinary outing that she's done successfully hundreds of times and she'll have a setback. Being here isn't a cure, Cade."

"I don't think you get it," Cade articulated clearly, his ire showing through his modulated words. "I *love* her. She's the most amazing human being I've ever met. She's funny, smart as hell, compassionate, and I can't imagine my life without her in it. I don't want a perfect Beth. She's the way she is because of everything she's been through. I wish I could turn back the clock and make it so that asshole didn't get his hands on her, but I can't. All I can do is stand by her side now as she makes her way through the life she's got.

"As far as 'setbacks' go, I don't care. If she wants to hole up in our bed all day, I'll do what I can to be there with her. If she has a panic attack in the middle of the grocery store, I'll leave all our groceries right in the aisle and get her to a place where she feels safe. I need you to tell me what I can do to help her, but being by her side and supporting her isn't something you have to teach me. I'm already there."

"Good. And I agree. You should know that as much as it doesn't seem like it, Beth is one of the lucky ones. She's a highly functioning agoraphobic. Since it was triggered by a traumatic event it's easier to treat."

"What about the fire thing?" Cade asked, knowing what she told him in regards to it might not be what he wanted to hear.

Dr. Neal waved her hand in the air in dismissal. "I think that's the least of your worries." At Cade's look of disbelief, she continued, "Look, I know you're a fire-fighter and putting out fires is what you do for a living, but pyromania is an impulse-control disorder. That's not Beth's issue, feeling *out* of control is."

"Impulse-control disorder?"

"Sorry, yeah, it's where a person can't resist the impulsive desire to set fires. It's also the same disorder that causes kleptomania and gambling addictions. People with it usually know it's not right, but they literally can't stop themselves. Beth started experimenting with fire because it was something she had power over. It helped with her anxiety because it gave her something else to focus on, to control, other than what was stressing her out, but I firmly believe that by teaching her other coping techniques, the fire thing won't be an issue anymore."

When Cade didn't look placated, Dr. Neal asked, "What's your real concern, Cade? That she'll burn down your house? That you'll be embarrassed if your buddies know you're dating someone who likes to set fires? What?"

"No! God, I don't care about that. Okay, I did worry about that at first, but Beth—*Beth* is my biggest concern. What if she hurts herself? What if she starts a fire and gets trapped? If I can't get to her in time, she'll burn to death."

"Ah…a firefighter's biggest fear. Look, Cade, I can't promise that she won't get hurt, just as you can't promise her that *you* won't get hurt while on the job. Hell, you could get hurt lighting the grill in your backyard. The best I can offer you is to talk to her. Communication is really important with someone like Beth. Ask her how she's doing, ask what she's feeling, make sure she knows you're there to listen to her—and when she *does* talk to you, pay attention. Stop everything you're doing and really hear what she's saying."

Cade nodded and kept his eyes on the doctor, absorbing everything she was telling him.

"I honestly think the pyromania was a short-term thing. She was feeling out of control and the fires helped her get some of that back."

"There was a trash bag in her apartment full of matches and candles and stuff when I went to find her when she disappeared."

"Yeah, she told me about that. She'd already come to the conclusion that she needed to get that under control, which was a healthy decision. Not a lot of people in her shoes would've had the strength to do that. As strange as this will sound, I think the fire at her apartment complex was a good thing. It scared her enough to really see the road she was on was a slippery slope."

Cade sighed in relief and tried to sneak a peek at his watch. Eight forty-five.

Dr. Neal laughed, obviously noticing his not-so-subtle action. "Anxious are we?"

"You have no idea."

"One more thing before our meeting this morning."

Cade looked at her expectantly.

"There will be two other people joining our session. Beth doesn't know about them, but I honestly think she needs to see them."

"Will it hurt her? Because I don't want her—"

"I think the two of you will be just fine." Dr. Neal smiled hugely at Cade. "But to address your unimplied insult, I would never do something that would hurt any of my patients. Will she be surprised? Yes. Would she choose to see these people if I didn't invite them? I doubt it. But, Cade, it's my professional opinion that she *needs* to see them, to talk to them. If she's going to move forward, it has to be done."

Cade wasn't sure he'd like whatever the doctor had planned, but it didn't look as if he had a choice. He nodded once, grinding his teeth in frustration that he couldn't fight all Beth's demons for her. For now, it was enough that she'd asked him to come. That he'd be with her through whatever the doctor had planned.

"Come on," Dr. Neal said as she stood. "Let's go find your Beth. I know she's just as anxious to see you as you are to see her."

CHAPTER 20

BETH PICKED at the food on her tray in the small common area of the treatment facility. The fare was surprisingly good, but she didn't have an appetite. She was nervous and excited at the same time. The last time she'd seen Cade—it was hard to believe it was over a month ago—they'd both said some not-so-nice things, but she hadn't realized how much she would miss him until she'd been away from him. Texting was nice, but it wasn't the same as feeling his hand holding hers, keeping the world at bay.

Over the years since she'd been kidnapped, the computer had become her friend. It was reliable and did what she told it to do. She'd met hundreds of people online and would even call some of them friends...but she hadn't realized how lonely she was until Penelope and Cade came into her life.

It was one thing to see words on a screen and "hear" them in your head, but it was another altogether to feel the warm skin of someone else against yours. To hear them laugh, to watch them be worried for you.

Beth knew she'd never lose her love of computers, but she couldn't wait to see Cade again.

Dr. Neal stuck her head into the room and called out quietly, "Beth, you have a visitor."

Beth took a deep breath and nodded at the doctor. She picked up her tray and brought it to the corner, where she handed it to one of the ladies who worked in the kitchen, then shored up her courage and headed out of the room to see Cade.

Entering the visitor's room Dr. Neal had pointed to, Beth wasn't sure what to expect, but she shouldn't have worried.

As soon as she walked in, she was in Cade's embrace. He hauled her to him, wrapped both arms around her, and simply held her. They didn't have to say anything, and somehow Beth knew Cade felt the same sense of peace she did at finally being together again.

Finally, Cade pulled back and Beth looked into his eyes.

"I missed you," he murmured in the low, rumbly voice she loved so much.

"I'm sorry I—"

"Don't be sorry. I'm just so glad you're all right. Everything else can be worked out."

Wow, Beth hadn't been expecting that. Some sort of reprimand or something, but not immediate acceptance.

Obviously reading some of what she was thinking through the look on her face, Cade quickly said, "I was worried about you. Dr. Neal says that I should communicate with you as much as possible, so here goes. I might have been upset for a while that you skipped out of town, but Beth, I was more concerned about *you*. Everything I said that night came from right here..." Cade grabbed Beth's hand and laid it flat on his chest over his heart.

"I was so scared that you'd been trapped or hurt in that fire, I said some things that came out wrong. I love you. I love you so much I've been a huge asshole to all the guys at the station and Penelope is ready to disown me. I want you to get better so you can come home with me."

Home. The word settled into Beth's heart and the knot in her stomach loosened for what seemed the first time since she'd stepped foot inside the treatment center. "I want to be normal for you, Cade. And I'm deathly afraid I never will be."

"What the hell is normal, anyway?" Cade asked without missing a beat. "Are any of us normal? I run into burning buildings when everyone else is running out. I hear sirens and get excited. I haven't told you this yet, but I've named my truck Curly Sue."

She smiled a wan smile, but wasn't ready to be swayed yet. "You deserve more."

"More than what?"

"More than me," Beth told him.

"Come here, sit with me." Cade kept hold of her

hand and towed her over to the small loveseat in the room. He sat and pulled her so she was sitting on his lap.

"There is no one 'more than' you, sweetheart. I took one look at you all those months ago, standing in your apartment watching as we put out that oil fire, and I was a goner. You're the perfect package."

"I'm not perfect."

"No, you're not; neither am I. What I should've said is that you're the perfect package...for me. I feel like a better person when I'm around you. And this probably makes me sound like a douche, and Dr. Neal would have a field day with it, I'm sure—wait. Are these rooms monitored?"

Beth smiled a genuine smile for the first time. "If they are, I'll hack in and make sure the tape is erased. But for the record, I don't think you could say anything that would make you sound douchey."

"You needing me makes me feel complete." The words hung in the air for a moment before he continued. "I don't know what it is in my DNA that makes me want to be a hero. Maybe it's because of Penelope. She's my younger sister and I always wanted to protect her. She's as good a reason to blame for the way I am more than anything else." He grinned. "When she looked up at me when I told a funny joke, or when I pushed a boy down who was bothering her, I felt ten feet tall."

"I'm sure it's why I'm in the career I am. It feels good to help people. To be there when they need someone. But you...you make me feel like a knight in shining armor simply by letting me hold your hand. I don't think a relationship with a woman who didn't need me like you do would ever work out. I'd feel... superfluous or something. You think you're the one taking from me, but you're wrong. I get so much by standing by your side, helping you keep your demons at bay, you have no idea."

"So you could get the same feeling from helping anyone here at the treatment center? You'd be their hero too if they could hold your hand and have you keep their demons at bay while they took a walk around the grounds." Beth wanted to understand, but she couldn't deny his words soothed her soul and some of the worries she'd been carrying around.

"It's not the same, and I hope to God you know it. It's you, Beth. *You.* I hold people's hands all the time in wrecks, in hospitals, at fire scenes, but it's *your* hand I need to grab onto to feel complete. You make me want to be a better person. There's nothing, and I mean nothing, I like more than sitting with you, just like this."

"But you like being outside...you're athletic and have a ton of friends."

"*We* have a ton of friends, and you're right, I do like playing softball and hanging out with my buddies, but Beth, you have stuff you do that I can't as well."

"No I don't."

"Yes, you do. Your computer stuff. It'll always be over my head."

"But that's just for fun."

"Not if Tex has anything to say about it. Look, my point is that we don't have to spend every day, all day, connected at the hip. But at the end of the day, when I come home, you're the person I want to see and talk to. You're the person I think about telling funny things to while I'm at work. I love you, Beth. *You.*"

"Even though I'll probably always have panic attacks?"

"Yes. Will you love me if my hair recedes?"

Beth giggled. "Your hair isn't going to recede."

"I wouldn't bet on that, sweetheart. I think I have a bald relative or two in my family tree."

"Then yes, I'll love you even if you have to have a comb-over."

"If you'll take me as *I* am, I'll take you as *you* are."

Beth looked into Cade's eyes for a moment before collapsing on his chest and grabbing hold of him as hard as she could. "I love you, Cade Turner. More than you'll ever know."

"The feeling's mutual, sweetheart."

After a few minutes, Beth heard Cade ask, "What time is our meeting with Dr. Neal?"

"I think ten."

"So we have some time."

"Time? Yeah, I guess so."

"How private is this room?"

"Not *that* private," Beth told him with a blush.

"Beth, when we make love again, it won't be rushed, and it won't be in a visitors' room where who the hell knows what has happened in it or where anyone could walk in. We'll take our time and I'll show you how much you mean to me by relearning your body inch by inch. I only asked because I wanted to make out with you a little bit. We haven't been to second base in a while."

"Oh...okay."

Cade smiled and kissed her forehead. Then the tip of her nose, then her cheek as he made his way to her ear. Beth tilted her head, giving him more room to work. She felt his hot breath against her neck as he nipped and lightly sucked his way up. He took the lobe of her ear between his teeth and worked it gently as he nuzzled against her.

Finally, he let go and moved his lips up her ear. "I can't wait to feel your heat surrounding my cock. You have no idea how good it feels, how good *you* feel. But it's been way too long since I've felt your lips on mine. Kiss me, Beth?"

Ignoring the goosebumps that had spread down her arms at both his words and the feel of his length under her, Beth took Cade's head in her hands and gave him what he wanted. What they both wanted.

She crushed her lips to his and sighed when he immediately opened for her. Her tongue swept inside his mouth and he met it with his own. They writhed in each other's arms as the carnal kiss continued on and on. Cade tipped her back until he was holding her to him with one hand at her back and she was clasping him around his neck with both of hers. It wasn't until

Beth felt Cade's hand creep up the front of her shirt and pull down the cup of her bra that she realized where they were.

She pulled back, breathing hard, and stared up at Cade—and broke into tears.

Cade didn't say a word, merely pulled her upright into him again and held her against his chest as she cried.

"I thought I'd blown it!"

"Shhh, you didn't blow anything. I'm here. I'm not going anywhere."

"I haven't touched a match, candle, or lighter since I've been here." Her words were choked out between sobs.

"Good. You're so strong; you'll beat your demons, Beth. I know it."

They sat on the couch for a long time, sometimes talking, sometimes kissing, and other times just basking in the fact they were together again.

They were interrupted by Dr. Neal. "You ready for your session?"

"We'll be there after Beth freshens up."

"Okay, don't take too long, I've got a full calendar today."

Beth smiled up at Cade. "I think that was her way of telling us to stop making out and get our butts up to her office."

Cade ran his hand over Beth's hair lovingly. "You ready for this?"

"Yes. I think we both need to hear what she has to

say. She's been extremely helpful so far, and I want to make sure you know what you're getting into with me."

"What I'm getting into is having you in my arms every night. Loving you, laughing with you, and never knowing what package is going to show up at my doorstep next."

"Did you really wear one of the thongs I sent you?"

Cade stood up and helped Beth to her feet as well. "You'll just have to wait and find out for yourself."

"Spoilsport."

"Come on, I don't want to get on the doctor's bad side."

Beth tugged on Cade's hand before he could open the door and got serious. "If something happens up there today that you can't handle...it's okay. I'll understand."

Cade came back to Beth and settled his hands at the small of her back as he pulled her close. "Hear me now —*nothing* is going to scare me off. I see you, Beth. And I love what I see. We'll deal with those demons one at a time and day by day. Together. Okay?"

"Okay."

CHAPTER 21

BETH RELAXED against Cade and held tight to his hand as Dr. Neal continued to tell them both what to expect when Beth did finally go home. She'd thought the session was going to be super embarrassing, but as it turned out, Dr. Neal had only shared things that Cade already knew. She was feeling mellow, safe, and happy when the doctor calmly informed them that she'd invited someone else to their session.

Beth sat up at that, wondering who it could be. There were only a few people in her life who she really even talked to...her brother and parents, and her new friends in Texas. Had Dr. Neal invited some of Cade's firefighting or cop friends up to visit? She figured not; Cade would've told her they were here.

Before she could ponder who in the world her doctor felt should be invited to her session, Dr. Neal walked to the door and opened it.

At first, Beth was at a loss as to who the couple was

that entered the office. The woman looked to be around Cade's age, in her mid-thirties, and the man was tall, even taller than Cade. He had a long-healed scar on his face that made one side of his mouth droop down into a perpetual scowl.

Beth opened her mouth to ask the doctor who they were—when memories flooded her brain like a tsunami.

Suddenly Beth was back in California. She'd seen the woman's blue eyes filled with tears and looking at her in horror.

And the man...Beth hadn't really gotten a good look at him when everything had gone down, but she hadn't missed the way he'd tenderly taken care of the woman when they'd burst into the room.

From a long distance away, Beth heard Dr. Neal's voice introducing the couple, but she wouldn't forget them. Summer and Sam Reed. Of course, back then she'd been Summer Pack.

Without realizing what she was doing, Beth stood and backed away from the newcomers. She didn't want to see them, didn't want to remember what had happened.

Hearing nothing but the roar in her ears, Beth turned to flee, but there was nowhere to go. Summer and her husband were standing in the doorway and there were no other exits. Beth backed into a corner and dropped, grasping her knees and burying her head so she couldn't see the two people who could force her to relive what had happened to her.

Images flashed through her brain as if on fast-forward and repeat at the same time. Ben Hurst's laughing face, Summer's whimpers, the smell of Beth's flesh burning as a lit cigarette was pressed against it, the glint of a light off the knife…

Beth couldn't stop the keening noise that was coming out of her mouth. It was too much, she'd trusted Dr. Neal. She couldn't deal with this. Not at all.

Beth had no idea how long she'd been locked in her memories, but the first thing she noticed was that she was being held in a pair of arms against a warm, hard body. Her breaths were still coming too fast and she felt dizzy, but she could hear someone speaking into her ear.

Cade.

"You're all right. You're safe. I'm here. No one is going to hurt you. Slow down your breaths…that's it. Good. Do it again, take a deep breath, hold it. Good. Now let it out. Again."

"I-I need to get up."

"No, you don't. Just relax. When you're steadier you can. For now, concentrate on you."

"T-This is embarrassing."

"No, it's not."

Beth cracked her eyes open and saw Cade right there in front of her. "I just majorly freaked out, Cade."

"Naw, I wouldn't call that a freak-out. A flashback maybe."

Beth could see how worried he was about her, but

he'd done just what she needed, kept it light. His teasing felt good.

"Seven minutes," Dr. Neal said from across the room. "I'd say that was pretty good."

Beth looked at her in confusion, keeping her eyes away from the couple now sitting on the couch. "Seven minutes?"

"Yup," the doctor said as if she didn't have a care in the world. "You were out of it for only seven minutes. Remember the first time you tried to go outside when you first got here? I think you panicked for more like twenty."

Beth didn't know whether or be mortified or pleased with her progress. She went with pleased. "Thanks...I think."

Dr. Neal got serious, leaning forward in her chair, but not coming closer. "I know you think what I did was a dirty trick, but I believe you need this. You need to talk about what happened to you with someone who was there, who knows firsthand what you went through."

Beth felt her heart rate kick. Cade must've too, because he grasped her hand tighter in his and murmured, "Easy, sweetheart. You can do this."

Beth wasn't so sure, but for Cade, she'd try. "Okay."

Dr. Neal busied herself getting two chairs set up in front of the couch. Cade nuzzled Beth's ear and whispered, "If it gets to be too much, just say the word and we'll take a break, okay?"

She looked at the amazing man in her arms. She

had no idea how she'd gotten so lucky, but she swore then and there to always make sure he knew how much she loved him and how much he did for her. She didn't think he was a douche for admitting he liked it when she leaned on him. She understood that feeling helpful was a bone-deep need for him, and she'd gladly make sure that he got whatever he needed.

Nodding, she awkwardly got to her feet, stumbling as her head spun. Cade put an arm around her waist, steadying her. He led them to one of the chairs and instead of sitting next to her, once again pulled her onto his lap. Beth blushed, it wasn't exactly the position she wanted to talk to Summer and her husband in, but it was obvious by the tight hold Cade had on her, she wasn't going anywhere.

Beth finally looked up into the face of the woman who'd been the target of the madman's rage so long ago. Deciding to take the upper hand, Beth said in a shaky voice, "Hi. It's good to officially meet you. I'm Beth."

Summer smiled gently and responded in a friendly, even voice, "You don't know how good it is to meet you too. As you know, I'm Summer, and this is my husband, Sam. He was one of the Navy SEALs who found us that day."

Beth would've thought Summer was meeting any ol' person at any ol' get together, if it wasn't for the whiteness around her knuckles as she held on to her husband's hand. That small sign that she wasn't as relaxed as she portrayed went a long way toward making Beth feel better.

"And before we go any further, I just want you to know how sorry I am. I know you were just in the wrong place at the wrong time and nothing that happened to you was your fault. I would've done anything to have taken your place, it wasn't—"

Beth spoke at the same time as the gorgeous man at Summer's side did.

"It wasn't your fault."

"Sunshine, don't," Sam said in a soft voice as he put his free hand on her knee.

They all smiled weakly at each other before Summer continued, "I've been through therapy. Intellectually, I know what he did wasn't my fault. I didn't want that to happen to you, or me, but it did. But emotionally I have a harder time with it. You know?"

"Yeah, I know," Beth told the distraught woman honestly.

"Okay, now that introductions are out of the way… does anyone have any issue with me leading the conversation for the next thirty minutes or so?"

Beth sighed in relief. Dr. Neal wasn't a pushover. She'd make you own up to whatever you were feeling, but she was a damn good psychiatrist and knew when to push and when to back off. Beth was glad she was there to help her get through this meeting with the one woman she'd never thought she'd see again.

An hour later, Beth sighed in relief as Dr. Neal

announced that she thought they'd made a lot of progress.

Reliving what had happened hadn't been fun, but hearing from Summer how it felt to watch what was happening to her was eye-opening. She hadn't thought about how it would've felt to be Summer, and to have been helpless to do anything while Hurst had been hurting Beth. It gave her a whole new perspective to the entire incident.

It wasn't a miracle cure, the fear of being surrounded by strangers and being snatched out of thin air was still there, but it was somehow...dulled. Summer's husband and his team had gotten there just in time. Beth didn't remember a lot of her rescue, only a lot of confusion and being held in strong arms as they'd made their way off the mountain.

They headed to the door and Summer put her hand on Sam's arm. "Can I have a minute with Beth?"

Beth recognized the look in the SEAL's eye as he gazed down at his wife. She'd seen it that morning in Cade's eyes. Adoration. "Of course. I'll be right down the hall if you need me."

Summer leaned up and kissed her husband. "Thanks."

Cade mimicked Summer's actions and kissed Beth. He drew back and stared into her eyes for a moment, as if he was making sure she was really okay before following the SEAL down the hall.

"Thanks for agreeing to come today, Summer," Dr. Neal said. "You both are amazing women, and I'm as pleased as I could be with both of you. Take your time. I'll keep your men busy."

Summer grinned as Dr. Neal followed the two masculine men down the hall and turned to Beth.

"I'm really sorry for being sprung on you today. I thought you knew we'd be here."

"Dr. Neal seems to like surprises," Beth told Summer without malice.

"Obviously. I wanted to say something that isn't really related to us and what we went through."

Beth's eyebrows went up. Not that she was complaining, she felt she'd been through the wringer over the last sixty minutes. A nap was looking more and more like it would be in her immediate future. But she was intrigued about what Summer could possibly have to say that wasn't related to Ben Hurst and their kidnapping. "Go ahead."

"You should take the job that Tex has been pleading with you to take."

"What?" It was so out of left field, Beth had a hard time wrapping her brain around what Summer meant.

"Long story short…all right? Tex used to be a SEAL. He's friends with my husband and the entire team. He had to retire because he was injured, but he works behind the scenes to help out not only my husband's team, but several other military groups—and probably others that I don't want to know about. He's the one who orchestrated this meeting today."

"I thought—"

"I know, you thought your doctor did. Well, she

received an email from 'me' asking to meet you...even though I had no idea where you were and what you were up to."

"Tex."

Summer nodded. "He likes you. We don't talk to him as much as we'd like, but he came clean and let me know what he did. Of course, he then had to explain how he'd connected with you...it makes my head hurt, but he mentioned something about firefighters, the Middle East, an Army Princess and backdoors."

Beth smiled. Yup, that about summed up how she knew Tex.

Summer continued, "He told us that you were probably smarter than he was when it comes to hacking and computer shit. And let me tell you something, that's freaking amazing, because Tex is hands-down the most talented man I've ever known when it comes to the Internet. If he says you're smarter than he is, that's one hell of an endorsement."

"He said he could get me a job if I wanted it."

"I know. That brings me full circle back to what I wanted to talk to you about. Take it."

"But, I'm not sure—"

"Seriously, take it. Beth, you might be dealing with stuff up here," she pointed to her own head and went on, "but that has nothing to do with who you are inside." Summer put her hand on her heart to emphasize her point. "If working with computers makes you happy, that's what you should do. If you want to be a professional puzzle-putter-together, then do that. But

I've seen Tex at work. He has saved lives, including yours and mine that day."

At Beth's gasp, Summer narrowed her eyes. "You didn't know?"

Beth shook her head.

"He tracked your cell phone. Hurst got rid of it, but not before Tex got a bead on where he was headed with you. If not for him, Sam and the others might not have found us in time."

Beth couldn't believe it. At no time since they'd been talking had Tex ever mentioned *that* little tidbit. She'd just thought he was Pen's friend. Wait until she got ahold of her and explained how much Tex was intertwined in all of their lives. It was as if he was a real-live Kevin Bacon...the six degrees of separation were completely uncanny. Beth wondered briefly who else the man knew.

But his interference with both her and Summer's lives made sense. Tex was the kind of man to inspire loyalty in those around him. Hell, Beth had lashed out at another hacker one night when he'd made fun of a piece of code Tex had written and shared in a chat room on the Dark Web. She'd only talked to the man online a couple of times after he'd tried to hack into her computer, but it was enough to know and trust him.

"I'll talk to Cade about it."

"Good. One more thing..."

Beth saw Summer hesitating. "Yeah?"

"Can I give you a hug? I've wanted to for so long."

Beth opened her arms immediately and took a step forward. She and Summer were around the same height, so it was easy to bury her head between her shoulder and neck and hang on tight.

Being able to connect with the one person who'd been to hell and back with her was one of the most satisfying and heartbreaking things she'd ever been though in her entire life. After several moments, they pulled apart and gazed at each other.

"I've cried over what happened more than anyone will ever know, but you should know right now, I have no desire to cry," Summer said. "I'm just so happy to be here with you, you have no idea."

"I think I have *some* idea," Beth joked.

"Do you think, if you're up to it…you might want to get together again?" Summer hurried on. "Wherever you want. I can come to Texas, or here, or wherever."

"I'd like that. Very much."

Summer sighed in relief. "Okay. Good. Maybe you can drag Penelope along with you?"

Beth once again knew she had some things to talk to her friend about. Why Summer would want to get together with Pen was beyond her, but she was too tired to figure it all out now. "Sure."

"Thank you for being so damn tough that day, Beth. I have no idea what Hurst would've done if you hadn't been."

The knot in Beth's throat that had disappeared came back. She'd never thought of it that way before. If she'd have died, what would've happened to Summer?

Hurst would've started in on her without a doubt. It put a whole different spin on it. "You're welcome." The words were inadequate, but they were the best she could come up with at the moment.

"Are you ready to go, Sunshine?" Sam had come up behind them and stood off to the side waiting for his wife. "We can either drive back to Pittsburgh today, which I'm leaning toward because I'm afraid to leave April with Tex and Melody too long. He'll either teach her how to hack into our iPads to watch cartoons or Melody will decide to kidnap her, what with her pregnancy hormones being all out of control these days. Or we can stay the night here and take off in the morning."

Summer laughed and snaked her arm around Sam's. "As much as I'm a little frightened of what Tex might teach our daughter...I think I'd love to have you all to myself for the night."

The gleam in Sam's eyes was easy to see, and Beth felt a small prick of jealousy slide through her. She wanted that with Cade. She knew they had some work to do to get there, but she was more determined than ever to get there.

"It was really nice meeting both of you," Beth said, leaning into Cade's side as he came up beside her.

"You too. Take care of yourself, and if you ever need anything, please know you'll have me and my entire team at your back," Sam told her, sincerity clear in his tone.

Beth wasn't sure what to say about that, other than a short, "Thanks."

"I'm exhausted," Beth said into Cade's shirt after Summer and Sam disappeared from sight.

"Why don't you take a nap? I'll come back later."

Beth looked up without releasing him. "I don't want you to go." She bit her lip as Cade studied her.

"Then I won't. Come on."

Beth didn't know where they were going, but ultimately it didn't matter. Cade was here with her, he could've walked her into a closet and she wouldn't have protested.

It wasn't a closet, but the TV room he led her to. He'd obviously seen it as they'd passed by on their way to the session earlier that morning.

He settled into the corner of the couch and held out an arm. Beth immediately curled into him and sighed in contentment.

"I love you, Cade."

"I love you too, sweetheart. Close your eyes. Get some sleep."

"You know others use this room too, right?"

"Yeah, as long as they don't run screaming in and out, I have a feeling you'll sleep right through it."

"Don't rule out the screaming. This *is* a treatment facility, Cade."

He chuckled under his breath. "So noted." Cade kissed her forehead. "Close your eyes. I'll keep you safe."

"I know you will. I've never had one doubt of that since we've met."

Dr. Neal looked into the room a while later and

smiled, seeing Beth and Cade sound asleep. Beth might not be quite ready to go home yet, but she'd made giant strides forward that morning. Cade had been everything the doctor wished all her patients had: a loving, supportive person to stand by their side, no matter what.

And seeing Cade help her come out of her panic attack during their session had been educational and satisfying. These two would be fine. Beth was going to be one of the lucky ones. She'd make it through this, and with love, a bit of medication and continued therapy, she'd be able to live a long, happy life.

CHAPTER 22

BETH TOOK a deep breath as the front door of Cade's house shut behind them. It'd been a long day, made much easier by the cocktail of drugs Dr. Neal had prescribed for her. After some trial and error, she'd started taking Effexor, which treated the social anxiety she felt when she went outside, and Klonopin, which helped reduce the panic attacks.

For the trip home, Beth had taken a Xanax to get her through the ordeal of flying. Cade had also gotten them first-class tickets, so they had more room and weren't stuck in the back of the plane. It was that, along with a hundred other things he'd done for her over the last few weeks, that made Beth fall in love with him all over again.

They'd spoken every night on the phone, talking about nothing important. Cade had joked about the guys and the trouble they were getting into. Apparently Driftwood had met a woman on shift one night, and was having a hard time getting her to agree to go out with him. It wasn't often the man struck out, and he'd apparently made it his goal in life to get the woman to "fall in line."

Beth had giggled at that, telling Cade, "Fall in line? He's going to crash and burn."

Cade put his hand on the small of Beth's back and followed her into his living room. "Have a seat, sweetheart. I'll get you something to drink."

Beth nodded and settled on the sofa as she watched Cade putter about in his kitchen. It was late, and she was tired, but she wanted to make sure Cade knew how much she appreciated his traveling with her. She'd been willing to try it on her own, but he wouldn't even think about letting her fly from Philadelphia to San Antonio without him.

On one of her last evenings at the treatment facility, Dr. Neal, David, and Beth had gone out to a fast-food restaurant for dinner. It wasn't a long trip, but it was enough to give Beth the boost she needed to feel like she just might be making progress.

Trips to Walmart would probably always be off the table, since she'd been snatched from their parking lot —even seeing the sign sometimes triggered an attack— but knowing she could possibly do with Cade some of the things that most normal couples did made her feel much more optimistic about her future with him. She hadn't thought about the Memorial Stair Climb in a while, but that was definitely going on her list of things she wanted to do...eventually.

Cade came back to the living room and put a glass of orange juice, without pulp, on the coffee table for her. He put his own glass of water down and pulled her into his arms. "How are you holding up?"

"I'm okay. I feel a little out of it because of the Xanax, but it'll wear off by the morning."

"I'm proud of you. You did great today."

Beth shrugged. "I'm glad they had those family bathrooms."

Cade chuckled. "I can just imagine what people would've thought if I'd followed you into the women's restroom. As it was, I think they probably thought we were having a quickie in there."

Beth laughed and nodded. "I just...I felt like everyone was staring at me."

Cade kissed the top of her head. "They were... because you're beautiful."

Beth rolled her eyes and shook her head in exasperation. "Thank you for coming for me."

"Any day, anytime. How was your visit with David?"

"Good." Beth yawned and settled deeper into Cade. "He came by this morning and we said our goodbye's. He wants to come down and visit later this year."

"No problem. I'm sure he's worried about you and would like to see you. I'd like to spend more than fifteen minutes with him too. I don't think he's completely forgiven me yet, but I really liked him and we had a good conversation."

"What did you talk about?"

"Oh, this and that."

Taking the cue that Cade really didn't want to discuss it, she let it go. "I also got a text from Summer today."

"You did?" Cade asked in surprise.

"Uh-huh. I think Tex must've given her my cell phone number. She said she was happy to have met me and she extended an open invitation to come to Riverton, out in California, to visit her anytime."

"Ummmm."

"I'm not sure I'm ready to go back yet."

"Whenever you are, I'll be right by your side. We can swing over to see your parents, as well as meet up with Summer."

Beth was still exhausted and felt like her head was swimming in a fog, but she sat up and straddled Cade's lap. "Have I told you today how much I love you?"

"Nope."

"I love you."

"I know."

Beth smiled down at Cade. "Brat." Without giving him a chance to say anything back, she leaned down and kissed him, melting into his chest as they lazily explored and caressed each other.

Beth pulled back and rested her head on his shoulder, sighing in contentment as she felt his arms go around her back and hold her to him. "There's nowhere I feel safer than right here in your arms."

"Good. Because while you were gone, I moved all your stuff that wasn't destroyed by water damage over here."

Beth's head came up at that. "Um...what? When were you going to tell me that little piece of news?"

Cade shrugged and flushed guiltily. "I just did. Besides, your place smelled like smoke, and probably is full of mold now. The landlord was letting people out of their leases because of the mess, so I took him up on his offer."

Beth didn't have the energy or desire to get pissed at him. The Xanax was probably *also* helping her with that. "Okay."

"Okay?"

"Uh-huh. I feel safe with you...it doesn't matter if you're at my place or I'm here. So as long as moving my stuff means you want me to live here with you, I'm good with it."

"I want you to live here with me."

Beth yawned again and put her head back down. "Great."

Cade chuckled and stood, easily lifting Beth in his arms. "Come on, sleepyhead, you need to get some sleep."

"Don't expect me to always be like this," Beth warned.

"What? Compliant, warm, and snuggly in my arms?"

"Exactly. When the Xanax wears off, I'll be back to my snarky self."

"Good. I like you like that too."

Beth was asleep before her head hit the pillow and didn't remember Cade getting her out of her clothes and into one of his Station 7 T-shirts. She didn't recall turning into him and throwing an arm and a leg around his body when he climbed in next to her. And she definitely didn't have any idea how tightly Cade held her to him as she slept.

CHAPTER 23

It was amazing the difference a week made. Beth had lost her customer service job when she'd fled to Pennsylvania, but she'd taken Tex up on his offer to work with him and the government, and was neck-deep in research about some guy who lived and worked in the Waco area. She had no idea who Tex was getting the information for, but she had enough respect for him that she wasn't going to ask. Besides, she was getting a ridiculous amount of money for doing what she loved; it was definitely a win-win situation.

The guys from Station 7 had all come over the other night to welcome her home and to make sure she knew they were happy she and Cade were together. Cruz, Quint, and Daxton had also shown up with their girlfriends. It was great to see Mackenzie again, as she was hilarious and took a lot of the attention off Beth and everything that had happened. The guys spent an inordinate amount of time laughing at her when she rambled on about whatever topic came up.

Quint's girlfriend, Corrie, was blind, but Beth wouldn't have been able to tell if she hadn't known beforehand from Penelope. She was the least helpless "disabled" person Beth had ever met, and was her new idol. If Corrie could get around with little to no assistance, then so could she, darn it.

Cruz, the FBI agent, looked content to hang out on the large armchair with his girlfriend, Mickie, sitting on his lap. She was gorgeous and curvy, with short black hair, and the two looked totally in love with each other. Beth hadn't had many girlfriends in her life, but she hoped she'd be able to meet up again with these women at some point. Their men looked to be as possessive and head-over-heels in love with them as Cade seemed to be with her. It would be nice to get another woman's perspective on some things every now and then.

It was late and the house was quiet. Cade had gone to bed hours ago while she'd been in the midst of her "computer thing," as he called it. It was now two in the morning and Beth's eyes felt crossed from looking at the computer screen for so long without a break. She was tired, but wired at the same time, probably because her body was still getting used to the medicine she was taking to control the agoraphobia.

Smiling to herself, Beth put aside her laptop and made her way up the stairs to the master bedroom. She eased open the door and felt her smile get bigger. Cade was sound asleep, almost spread eagle on their bed. He'd kicked the comforter off, not wearing a stitch of clothing.

He'd taken to sleeping in the nude once she'd moved in with him. He'd told her that it was simply easier to not have to worry about his clothes getting in the way when she did come to bed each night. The first night, Beth hadn't wanted to disturb him and had slept on the couch. He'd woken up to find the space next to him empty and came downstairs and carried her back to their bed, telling her that it was important to him that she always crawled into bed, no matter what time it was.

Ever since that night, she'd carefully eased onto the mattress at his side, trying not to disturb him, but every time he'd woken up. Some nights he'd make sweet love to her, and others he'd simply gather her into his arms and hold her close until she fell asleep. Beth didn't know which she liked better.

But tonight, she wasn't feeling in the mood to cuddle, or to go to sleep right away. In all their love-making sessions, Beth hadn't ever gone down on him, and tonight was her night. He was the most unselfish lover she'd ever had—which wasn't saying much, since he was only the second man she'd ever slept with of her own free will, but she'd been doing some research online and she was ready to see if the tips and tricks she'd picked up were useful or not.

Without a sound, Beth peeled off her tank top and pushed her leggings down her legs. Deciding the best way to go about this was from below, she climbed onto the mattress very carefully from the foot of the bed, easing her way toward Cade slowly and steadily. He made her job easier because his legs were already spread, so Beth lay between them and tried to steady her breathing.

She leaned down and inhaled, loving how Cade always smelled like...Cade. She would recognize him anywhere. Knowing he'd most likely wake up the second she touched him, as he wasn't a heavy sleeper, Beth got down to business.

She wrapped her hand lightly around his cock, put just the tip in her mouth and sucked gently. When he didn't move, she got braver and began to lick all around the mushroom head, making sure to pay special attention to the underside, where all the videos online said men were the most sensitive. He hardened in her grasp and she smiled, loving that she could arouse him so quickly.

She could tell the second Cade fully woke and realized what she was doing. One hand came to rest lightly on the back of her head and the other curled into a fist at his side.

"Lord, Beth..."

She didn't stop to talk, simply continued with her ministrations. Feeling bold, she scooted up onto her knees and took as much of him into her mouth as she could. She felt him tap the back of her throat and pulled back. Taking a deep breath, she went down on him again, this time relaxing her throat enough that she felt him push past her gag reflex. She swallowed once, exaggerating the motion, and she felt him twitch.

Beth was loving the sounds coming from Cade and continued to give him what she hoped was the best blow job he'd ever received in his life. She alternated between using her hand to squeeze and pump him, and taking him as far into her mouth, and throat, as she could manage.

Deciding to tease, she moved her mouth to his balls as her hand continued to stroke, taking one into her mouth and sucking hard. Knowing she'd hit pay dirt— by the expletives that came out of Cade's mouth and the way his hips pumped upward—she concentrated her efforts there until she could feel his pre-come dripping out of the slit at the top of his cock.

Wanting to feel him lose control more than she wanted almost anything, Beth moved back up to his throbbing tip and licked him clean. She looked up at his face and said, "I love you," in a quiet voice, then dropped her head back to him, worshiping his body.

It wasn't long before Cade told her, "Beth, I can't hold on, come up here."

She ignored him, pleased as she could be that she'd brought him to the edge so quickly, and sped up both her hand and her head. Tasting his muskiness as he got closer and closer to the edge, Beth took him as deep as she could and swallowed twice in succession, while at the same time humming. That did the trick.

"Beth!" was all he got out before he exploded in her mouth.

She pulled back just enough so she could breathe and swallowed as fast as she could, trying to make sure she didn't miss even one drop. He continued to twitch in her grasp as she milked his cock until he'd finished coming.

Letting him pop out of her mouth, she kissed the crease where his leg met his torso and gently caressed him, loving the feel of his soft dick in her hand almost as much as when he was aroused. It was intimate, and heady, knowing she'd satisfied him.

Before Beth was done basking in the glow of pleasing her man, Cade took her by the biceps and pulled her up. He rolled over, trapping her beneath him, and took her mouth in a hot, carnal kiss. She would've pulled away, tell him she'd go and wash her mouth out before he had to kiss her, but he didn't give her a chance.

A couple of minutes later, when they were both breathing hard, Cade pulled back. "Lord, woman. That was the most amazing wake-up I've ever had."

"Oh? I'm sorry, I didn't mean to wake you up."

"Brat."

"I love you, Cade. You've done so much for me and I feel like all I ever do is take from you. Thank you for giving me that tonight. For letting me take you all the way."

"You're welcome. Now, lay back and let me say thank you properly."

"You don't—"

Her words cut off with a squeak as Cade changed

his mind and rolled, pulled her over him until she was straddling his chest. Beth looked down and saw the wicked smile on his face. "I know I don't have to, believe me, this is no hardship. Get up here and let me make you feel good, sweetheart."

Without a word, and with Cade's guiding hands, Beth moved into position over him. She grabbed onto the headboard and held on for dear life as Cade proceeded to rock her world...not once, but twice.

* * *

A couple of hours later, Beth barely stirred as Cade's alarm went off and he climbed out of bed. She vaguely heard the shower come on as he got ready for his shift. He came back into the bedroom and sat next to her on the mattress and brushed a lock of hair off her forehead in a loving caress.

"I don't know how you can get up this early," Beth complained sleepily.

"I don't stay up until the wee hours of the morning on the computer like some people," Cade told her with a smile.

"It's unnatural that you're a morning person."

They'd had the argument several times over the last week, and he always smiled at her, letting her have the last word.

"I'm working a twelve today; I'll be back around eight-thirty tonight."

"Be safe."

"I will. I'll let you know when I'm on my way home. Want me to pick up anything?"

Beth closed her eyes and snuggled farther into the blankets. "Uh-uh. I'm good."

"Okay, I'll let you get back to sleep. Text me when you get up. I'll miss you."

"Miss you too."

Beth was asleep as soon as the words left her mouth and didn't feel the gentle kiss Cade left on her lips and forehead before he stood and left the room and headed off to the station for his shift.

She woke up a few hours later, feeling wide awake, which was typical. When she crashed, she crashed hard, but once she woke up, that was it. She was awake.

Beth stretched and thought about what she was going to do with her day. She needed to finish her research for Tex, then see if she couldn't track down the ISP address for the sicko pervert she'd found the other night who was trying to find kids to buy on the Internet. Who the hell bought children on the Dark Web? A perverted asshole, that's who. Beth had no doubt what he wanted to do with the little girls and boys once he had them.

She'd eat a big lunch, and then see if Cade was hungry when he got home. When he worked twelve-hour shifts, sometimes the squad got to eat at the station and other times they wouldn't, depending on when—and how many—calls for assistance came in.

As Beth lay in bed, remembering the feel of Cade's

body against hers as they'd drifted off to sleep the night before, she heard an odd noise.

Because inside was where she felt the most comfortable, she'd memorized the "normal" sounds the house made. The air conditioner kicking on and off, the icemaker dropping ice, even the far-off sound of the garbage truck as it rumbled by every Thursday. But this wasn't a sound she'd heard before—and that alone made her immediately tense.

Hopping out of bed before she'd really even thought about it, Beth grabbed the Station 7 T-shirt she'd been wearing before she'd come to bed the night before. She had it over her head and her sweats on before the sound came again.

Beth tilted her head and her brow wrinkled as she tried to determine what it was and where it might be coming from. Before she'd figured it out, male voices interrupted the serenity of the morning.

"Shut up, you asshole, do you want the entire neighborhood to hear you?"

"Jesus, Frank. There's no one here. Guy's truck is gone and the nearest house isn't close enough to see us or care about what we're doing."

"Well, shut up anyway. You might as well make a billboard that says 'burglars here, call the police' with the way you're stomping around."

Beth froze in her tracks. The voices were downstairs...but she figured at some point the intruders would make their way up the stairs to try to find more valuables.

A thousand thoughts swirled through her head and she had a hard time deciding what she should do. She fought against the panic attack desperately trying to force its way out of her body. Cade's home was her sanctuary, where she was safe. But bad guys had infiltrated her cocoon. If she wasn't safe here, was there anywhere she *could* feel safe?

Yanking her thoughts away from the dark feelings that threatened to overwhelm her and send her into a monster panic attack, Beth tried to figure out where she could hide, but looking around frantically, she realized there weren't any good spots to hunker down undetected in the bedroom.

Their bed had drawers underneath it, so she couldn't duck under there to try to avoid the thugs finding her. She tiptoed quickly to the closet and looked in. Cade had brought her clothes over, but she didn't have a lot of nice clothes that had to be hung up, mostly comfortable, hang-around-the-house clothes that were safely put away in drawers. The closet was a bust. Cade's shirts and pants hanging neatly in there wouldn't conceal her in any way.

Beth thought about the bathroom and immediately dismissed it. The clear shower door wouldn't conceal her like a plastic shower curtain might.

Feeling her breathing pick up at what she knew she had to do, Beth still didn't hesitate. She reluctantly turned to the window in the room.

The bedroom was on the second floor, but the first thing Cade had shown her when she'd moved in was

that in case of a fire—he *was* a firefighter, after all—
they could climb out the dormer window and make
their way to the side of the house, where a large tree
stood. He'd demonstrated how easy it was to grab hold
of one of the branches that extended a bit too close to
the house and shimmy down to safety.

She'd asked him why he didn't have a safety ladder,
and he'd looked at her in confusion. She'd laughed at
his explanation at the time, that he could get out of the
house faster by shimming down the tree than bothering with a ladder. But right now she could've totally
used one.

The thought of leaving the house where she'd
thought she was safe was daunting at best. Maybe she
could just surrender to the men downstairs and they'd
take what they wanted and leave her alone.

"Fuckin' A, Frank. Check out the girlfriend. I'd tap
that in a heartbeat."

Beth figured they'd found the picture Cade had
framed and put on the table in the hallway. She was
snuggled up next to him on the couch, smiling at something he'd said. Penelope had snapped the picture just
as he was looking down at her, and the look of love on
his face was clear.

"No way in hell, Jimmy, would you ever get a
chance to tap a chick like that."

"Well, duh, but who said anything about giving her
a choice?"

As the evil laughter rolled up the stairs, Beth's decision was made. No way was she going to give anyone

the chance to rape and torture her again. No fucking way. Not when she had a chance to prevent it.

She tiptoed to the window, knowing that sometimes when Cade walked around in their room she could hear his footsteps downstairs. Beth held her breath as she unlocked the window and prayed it wouldn't stick. It didn't. Like everything else, Cade kept the windows in perfect working order, just to be safe.

She hated what she was about to do—and had no idea if she'd even be able to do it—but she didn't have a choice. She thought about grabbing a couple of Xanax pills, but knew she didn't have the extra fifteen seconds it would take. She was on her own. It was put up or shut up time.

Peeking outside, making sure no one was around—as if someone would be waiting on the roof to grab her—Beth eased one leg out, then the other. When she was standing with both feet firmly on the shingles, she closed the window quickly but quietly. The last thing she wanted was to be caught on the roof with no escape. It took her a moment to drop her hand from the side of the house. It seemed as though as long as she was touching the bricks, she had a connection to it and would be safe...but hearing something break from inside made a lie out of that tenuous thought.

As if in a trance, Beth hurried over to the tree, which seemed to be twice as big as it was when Cade showed her what to do in an emergency. Knowing she was breathing too hard and too quickly, but not able to do a damn thing about it, she reached out for the limb and carefully began the climb downward.

Before she knew it, Beth was on the ground—and she froze.

On the ground. Oh God…she hadn't taken her meds that morning and she could totally tell the difference. She probably should've taken the time to grab the Xanax. Instead of feeling mellow and able to roll with the punches, she felt panic crawl up her throat and stick there.

The world spun around her as she tried to slow her breathing. She wasn't safe inside but she certainly wasn't safe *outside* either. Where should she go? In her panic, she hadn't even thought to grab her cell phone, or to pick up Cade's landline and call nine-one-one before she'd fled.

Stupid stupid stupid! Now no one knew she was in trouble—just like California.

Before she had a full-blown panic attack, Beth tried to remember what Dr. Neal had told her. She concentrated on her safe place and tried to think.

The men inside had no idea she was there, otherwise they would've come upstairs immediately. If she could find a place to hide, she'd be fine. They'd take what they wanted and leave. Then she could go back inside and call Cade, or maybe his friend Quint instead. He worked for the San Antonio Police Department; he'd come and help her.

Beth took a few hesitant steps forward, frantically trying to decide where the best place to hide was, when one of the men suddenly opened the front door of the house and looked right at her. She'd obviously walked far enough forward that he could see her.

The burglar had Cade's laptop and some other odds and ends in his hands, and was making a trip to the beaten-up, black, nondescript car parked in the driveway. The tree she'd climbed down was to the side of the house, but Beth was standing in plain view of the front.

"Hey!"

It was all Beth gave the man time to say before she spun and sprinted for the trees at the back of Cade's house.

He'd told her it was over a mile to the nearest neighbor's house, but it was mid-morning on a weekday; most people were probably at work. No one would be home to let her in or help.

Beth wasn't in the best shape. She knew losing herself in the trees was her best bet at escaping—if she could only get there before the men caught up to her. She remembered the story of Corrie climbing a tree to hide from the men who were after her. If Corrie could do it blind, surely Beth could too.

"Frank! There was someone in the house, she saw me! Come on, we have to get her!"

Beth barely heard the words as she ran toward the relative safety of the woods. Reeling at a pain in her foot, she looked down as she ran. Dammit. She hadn't even put on a pair of shoes, and just realized it after stepping on one of the frickin' burrs Texas was known for. The damn weeds were everywhere and hurt like hell.

She didn't even slow down, and blocked out the pain from the insidious burrs that seemed to pop up out of nowhere and imbed themselves into the sensitive soles of her feet. Finally reaching the trees, Beth kept her straightforward course until she looked back and couldn't see the house anymore. Then she made an abrupt right turn, trying to get as far away from the men as she could before they broke through the trees and saw her.

The robbers weren't trying to be quiet as they gave chase, yelling threats and warning about what they were going to do to her when they caught her. Knowing she'd lose in any kind of physical altercation, Beth tried to find a place to hunker down and hide until the men gave up. With any luck, they'd think she'd made it to one of the nearby houses and flee.

There were no trees appropriate for climbing and hiding in, so that plan was out. But finally Beth saw something that she thought might work. Knowing she was about to hyperventilate and needed to stop anyway, she threw herself into the ditch and grabbed the nearby logs and dead leaves, frantically trying to cover herself from head to toe with the forest litter. It wasn't ideal, but she didn't have any other choice at the moment.

Not letting herself think about how vulnerable she was, and how scared, Beth tried to concentrate on slowing her breathing. She'd never stay hidden long if she kept huffing and puffing the way she was. It was extremely hard to imagine her safe place when all that kept flitting over her eyelids was the memory of Hurst holding her down and hurting her. The images were vivid, the current situation bringing them to the forefront of her mind.

Beth heard the men as they came closer and closer to her hiding place and almost whimpered out loud before biting her lip hard enough to draw blood.

"Bitch has to be here somewhere, she couldn't just disappear into thin air."

"Well, where the hell is she then? Do you see her anywhere? And where the fuck did she come from anyway?"

"She must've been in the house."

"I thought you staked it out, Frank! You said the fire guy lived alone."

"He did...at least he did the last time I followed him home."

She heard a loud smack and one of the men grunted. "Well, he obviously moved in the girlfriend at some point, didn't he?"

Beth breathed as shallowly as possible so as not to make the leaves concealing her rustle and give away her location.

"Come on, the bitch is probably well on her way to the neighbor's by now. Let's get the hell out of here."

The two men's voices faded, but Beth didn't dare move. She hardly dared to breathe. She had no way of knowing if they'd really left, or if they were just pretending to so she'd come out and they could get their hands on her.

Beth closed her eyes and pictured her safe place, just as Dr. Neal had taught her. If she concentrated hard enough, she could almost picture herself there.

Refusing to let any thoughts of another day and another place seep into her safe place, Beth did her best not to lose it.

CHAPTER 24

"SLEDGE, HOW'S BETH DOING?" Crash asked between calls while they relaxed in the TV room at Station 7.

"Better. The other day we actually ate dinner out on the patio. That's a huge step for her."

"That's great," Crash enthused, genuinely pleased. "And I can tell you're much happier, you son of a bitch."

The others laughed and Driftwood joined in. "Yeah, she must be taking verrrrry good care of you."

Cade threw a pillow at his friend's head. "We take good care of each other," he returned easily, not embarrassed in the least that his friends knew he was getting some on a regular basis.

Later, Cade texted Beth for the second time that day. He hadn't heard a response to his first text and wanted to touch base with her.

I miss you. How has your day been?

After twenty minutes with no response, Cade was

concerned. She usually responded immediately to his texts. He thumbed in another message.

Beth? All okay there?

He waited another ten minutes, but as the emergency tones once again pealed throughout the station, he didn't have a chance to worry about it further as he jumped into his bunker gear and into the truck.

Returning an hour and a half later, after getting a fire under control that had started in the laundry room of an elderly lady's home, Cade checked his phone and saw that Beth still hadn't responded.

Extremely worried now, knowing instinctively something had to be wrong—there was no way Beth would ignore his communications for that long—Cade headed for the fire chief's office. He needed to get home. Now.

After getting permission to end his shift early, Cade drove as fast as he dared, Penelope hanging on for dear life as he took the turns that led to his neighborhood. She'd seen him heading for his truck and had jumped in without asking. She'd called both Hayden at the sheriff's office and Quint at the SAPD, to ask that they meet them at Cade's house as they headed down the road. Just in case.

Quint had made her hang on for a moment, then came back on the line and said that there had been no nine-one-one call from his house or neighborhood.

That didn't reassure Cade in the least. He couldn't get the picture of Beth hurt and bleeding out of his head. She could've slipped in the shower and hit her head and was lying unconscious in the bathroom. Maybe she cut herself while making something to eat. God forbid she'd had a setback with the fire thing and she was trapped in his burning house.

The horrifying situations Beth could've found herself in that would make her unable to get to the phone raced through his head.

He pulled into his driveway and saw that Quint had beat them there. Cade cut the engine, jumped out of his truck and ran toward his front door, which was standing open. Quint caught him before he could enter.

"The door was open when I got here, Cade. I need to check the house. Stay here."

"The hell I will. What if it was Corrie in there?" Cade knew it was a low blow, but he couldn't just stand around if Beth was inside hurting.

"Then I'd want to make sure I didn't put her in more danger by rushing in without thinking or figuring out what was going on first," Quint retorted without missing a beat.

Cade sighed, and wanting to hurry the entire situation, impatiently gestured to the door. "Fine, check it out. Hurry. Please."

Quint nodded and gritted his teeth in determination as he unholstered his weapon and held it at the ready as he eased inside the house.

Cade waited with ill-concealed impatience for Quint to reappear. He paced outside the door, imagining the worst.

"Cade…look," Pen said, pointing at the ground.

He looked to where his sister was gesturing and saw footprints in the dry, dusty ground near the side of the house. His brow wrinkled and he took a step toward them just as Hayden arrived. "Quint inside?" Her words were no-nonsense and to the point.

"Yes. Look at this," Cade said, pointing at the set of footprints. There were small ones, but also larger ones. All of them were spaced widely apart, as if the three people had been running. "Those have to be Beth's."

"No offense, but would she be outside?" Hayden asked.

"Maybe," Penelope answered for her brother. "The meds she's on have done a lot of good and she's been working on spending time outside of the house."

At Hayden's look of disbelief, Cade picked up the conversation. "She wouldn't be out here for an afternoon stroll." He looked up at the large tree. "I showed her once how she could climb out of our bedroom window and get down this tree if the house was ever on fire and the other exits were blocked."

Quint appeared back at the front door. "Inside is clear, although there's no sign of Beth. I hate to be the one to break it to you, but it looks like you've been robbed, Cade. You'll have to come inside and see what's missing."

"That's it. Jesus. Someone broke in while she was inside, she escaped out the window and ran into the trees. Remember how fascinated she was with Corrie's story? I'm sure she remembered how she was able to get away from her kidnappers by running into the woods and climbing a tree. That has to be what she did." Cade refused to believe someone had kidnapped her again, and no other scenario made sense. If someone had broken into his house while she'd been inside, it would've brought back memories of being kidnapped. She'd probably bolted, using the tree as a ladder to get out of the house. Cade had started walking before he'd finished speaking, Hayden, Penelope, and Quint hurrying to keep up.

They followed the footprints as far as they could, until the dust ended and the grass began, and then headed into the woods, hoping against hope they'd find Beth waiting for them.

"Beth! Are you here?" Penelope called out.

"Let's split up. Cade, you and Hayden go that way, and me and Penelope will go in this direction," Quint said in a quiet voice. "We'll find her."

Without taking the time to agree or acknowledge his friend's words, Cade headed east, calling himself all sorts of names for not being there to protect Beth as he'd promised.

He could hear Penelope and Quint calling Beth's name as they headed away from them. Hayden also chimed in, yelling for Beth as the two of them combed the dense woods for any sign of her.

"Make sure you look up as well as down," Hayden cautioned. "It was amazingly effective when Corrie did it."

The two split up about ten feet or so and combed

both the ground and the trees, occasionally calling Beth's name.

Cade heard Hayden shout something, but didn't understand what it was. He looked over at her and saw her running ahead. Immediately, he followed, knowing Hayden wouldn't be running pell-mell through the woods if she hadn't found something important.

It took a moment, but Cade picked up his pace when he saw for himself what Hayden had obviously seen. Beth. A very disheveled Beth, but she was alive.

They made more noise than a herd of elephants, but Cade didn't even really notice. All his attention was on the woman he was afraid he'd never see alive again. He and Hayden reached Beth at the same time and Cade put his hand on the middle of her back, relieved to feel her quick breaths.

Beth was standing barefoot in the middle of a grouping of three trees, with her arms around one of the trunks as if she were hugging it. Cade felt as though *he* was the one having the panic attack this time, and he looked at Beth in confusion as she turned to them with a huge smile on her face.

A grin was the last thing he'd expected to see. In all the time he'd known Beth, he'd never seen her looking happy when she was outside. She never really looked unhappy, but concerned and focused was more the emotions that radiated from her. But joy was the emotion written all over her face at the moment.

She was covered in dirt, his Station 7 T-shirt she liked to pilfer was smeared with debris, and Cade

279

could see some dead leaves sticking stubbornly to it. She had a small stick stuck in her hair as well as more leaves. Her sweats were hanging extremely low on her frame, almost mooning them as they stood there.

But it was the smile that was most out of place.

"Cade." Beth breathed the word.

He could hear the relief in the one syllable as if it came from deep within her. He took a step closer, wrapping his arm around her waist. "Are you all right?"

"Surprisingly, yeah. I think I am."

He brought his other hand up to her face and brushed his knuckles down her cheek. She hadn't let go of her death grip on the tree, but was following him closely with her eyes. At his touch, she sighed and he could feel her melt a little into his hand.

"What happened?" Hayden asked, looking around as if the bad guys would pop up from behind a tree at any moment.

Penelope and Quint joined the trio. Penelope ran up to Beth and hugged her awkwardly—she still hadn't let go of the tree and Cade's arm was still around her waist —and exclaimed, "Thank God! We were so worried about you!"

"What happened?" Quint asked Hayden.

"Not sure, she hasn't had a chance to tell us."

"You're safe now, you can let go of the tree," Cade told Beth, putting his free hand on her forearm, ready to take hold of her hand as soon as she let go of the trunk.

"It's the weirdest thing, Cade," Beth told him

without letting go of the tree. "There I was, scared out of my mind, hiding under a bunch of leaves, knowing if I dared come out, the men would be there waiting to get me...and I realized...I was outside. By myself. No one knew where I was—and I was okay. I was afraid, and panic was right there—is *still* right there—but I'd done it. Without my lighter. Without any drugs. Without you or Pen holding my hand. Me. All by myself."

Cade got it—and he was so proud of her. "I've told you all along how strong you are, Beth. On one hand, I'm sorry this happened to you, but on the other, I'm thrilled that it's made you see what the rest of us have known all along."

They grinned crazily at each other for a moment before Cade told her in a low voice, "If you wouldn't mind though, *I'm* a bit freaked out. Would you mind if you took hold of me instead of that tree? I could use a hug."

It was as if his words broke her fragile hold on her emotions. Beth let go and turned to Cade. He caught her in his embrace and sighed in relief.

The last thirty minutes had been absolute hell. Not knowing where she was, what had happened, or if she was all right, had eaten at him. It reminded him way too much of the days after she'd fled to Pennsylvania. Beth's arms went around his waist and the knot that had been in his belly loosened for the first time.

"You're shaking," Beth told him without lifting her head.

"Adrenaline dump," Cade explained, not giving a shit that the others were still standing there witnessing him tremble.

"Can you at least give us the short version of what went on?" Hayden demanded for the third time, clearly losing some of her patience.

Now that Beth was safe in Cade's arms, she could talk about the events that had led to her being in the woods without any issues. "I was still in bed when I heard someone in the house. They were talking about robbing it and how they'd been watching Cade. They saw the picture you took of us, Pen, and made comments about wanting to 'do me.' I realized if they knew I was there they would probably hurt me. There wasn't any good place to hide, so I went out the window and down the tree. I was going to hide somewhere outside when one of them came out and saw me standing there, trying not to freak out. I ran into the woods and hid. They couldn't find me and decided to leave. Now you guys are here."

"How long ago did this happen?" Quint's voice was no-nonsense as he asked the question.

"What time is it now?"

"One-thirty."

"Wow, um, maybe around ten?"

"You've been out here for three hours?" Cade asked incredulously.

"Probably more like three and a half," Beth told him, wanting that extra thirty minutes tacked on there. It seemed important to include it in the count, considering how well she'd done.

"I love you," Cade told her in a soft voice, hugging her to him again.

"We need to get back to the house," Quint told the group. "Cade, you have to see what was taken, and I need to coordinate the backup officers that have probably arrived by now. They'll be looking for us, and we need to get a description of the men so we can be on the lookout for them."

Beth took a step backward and winced, the tiny burrs in her feet making themselves known, now that she wasn't alone and panicking.

"What is it?" Cade asked urgently, looking on the edge of panic himself.

Beth lifted one leg and showed him. "Have I ever told you how much I hate these damn things?"

Cade didn't hesitate. He bent and picked Beth up as if she wasn't only a few inches shorter than him. "Hang on."

Beth didn't complain as they headed back to the house—those suckers *hurt*. She felt herself settled even more when Penelope rested her hand on her leg as they walked. Being surrounded by the two people who knew her best made being outside all that much easier.

* * *

Beth sat very still with her teeth clenched as Crash worked on her feet with a pair of tweezers. Pen had called the fire chief to let him know what was going on and that Beth was safe. Quint radioed for medical assistance when he'd seen the extent of the damage to her feet, and now it seemed like all of Cade's friends were there.

She winced and tried really hard not to flinch away from the man sitting at the other end of the couch as he plucked the burrs out of her flesh one by one.

"Damn, that hurts," Beth said in a voice laced with pain.

"Yeah, these things suck," Crash commiserated. "Of course, I've never had over a hundred stuck in my skin at the same time. You're just an overachiever."

Beth appreciated his attempt at levity. She turned her eyes to Cade standing on the other side of the room, telling Quint what he thought was missing. Beth had told him the names of the men who'd been in the house, Frank and Jimmy, and had given a rudimentary description of Jimmy and the car. There was now a BOLO, Be on the Lookout, for the men and their vehicle. If there was any chance of catching them, as soon as possible after it happened was the best time.

Now that Beth was inside, even though the house had been breached, she felt calmer…grounded. Cade had gotten her meds as soon as they'd returned and she could feel herself relaxing even more as they made their way through her bloodstream.

Wincing as another one of the burrs popped out of her skin, Beth tried to distract herself from what Crash was doing.

"So…Crash…how'd you get your nickname?"

As if he knew what she was doing, Crash humored her. "My first day on the job there were four car wrecks. We'd get back from one and immediately be called for another. The other guys decided it was my fault, and christened me Crash."

"What's your real name?"

Crash looked up at her and raised one eyebrow. "I'm not sure I want to tell you."

"Why not?" Beth asked, almost offended.

"I know how you are with that computer. You'll probably sign me up for some weird service like singing telegrams or something."

Beth laughed. "Crash, if I wanted to mess with you, first, I don't need you to tell me your name in order to do it. I could find it within minutes. And second, I'm much more creative than that. Give me some credit."

Crash leaned back toward her feet and continued plucking the insidious burrs out of her soles. "That's probably true. It's Dean. But no one calls me that."

"No one?"

"Nope."

"Ever?"

Crash looked back up at her in annoyance at her persistence. "No, not ever."

"So when you're in bed with a woman, she calls out, 'Oh, Crash, harder. Yes, Crash, right there.' That's weird and a little creepy." Beth laughed at the incredulous look Cade's friend and fellow firefighter was giving her. "Seriously, it's weird. Trust me on this. When you find a woman who truly interests you, don't introduce yourself as Crash. Say, 'Hi, my name is Dean, it's good to meet you.' I think things will go a lot better for you if you do."

"Are you seriously trying to help me with my love life?"

"Yup."

Crash smirked and tried to look at her sternly, but totally failed.

Changing the subject, Crash told her, "It looks like I'm almost done here. You're going to want to stay off these for a while, they're going to be sore. You also need to keep the antibiotic good and smeared on them for at least twenty-four hours, to make sure they don't get any more infected. Running around in the dirt while they were bleeding didn't do them any good. If they continue to look red, you need to go to a doctor. Hear me?"

Beth wanted to keep on the subject of Crash and his love life, but understanding the moment was gone, she sighed in relief, knowing the torture of having the burrs removed was done. She smiled in contentment when she felt Cade's hand on the back of her neck.

"I'll watch her and get her in if needed. Thanks, Crash."

"You're welcome. All done with Quint?"

Cade nodded.

"Do you think they'll catch them?" Beth asked, holding on to Cade's hand.

"Hopefully. Quint said you'll need to identify them if they do. He can bring a picture lineup to the house."

"Okay, I'll do my best. I'm not sure I'll be able to pick them out though," Beth said, worry lacing her voice. "I was...stressed...and didn't really get as good of a look at the one guy as I should've. I didn't really see the second one at all."

Cade kissed the side of her head. "No worries, sweetheart."

"What if they come back?"

Cade pulled back a bit and looked Beth in the eyes. "You're safe here, Beth. I know I haven't done a very good job of making sure of that, but I've already called and made an appointment with an alarm company. I should've done it before, but I got complacent. This is your home now. I want you to feel absolutely safe. I'm pissed those guys got in and made you feel afraid for even one second."

Seeing his friends about to get into a deep conversation, Crash stood up. "I'll just get my stuff together. Remember, the fire chief said you didn't need to come back in today, Sledge."

"Thank him for me."

"Will do."

"Crash?" Beth asked before he left.

"Yeah?"

"I was serious about the name thing. And you never

know when you'll run into the woman meant to be yours. So keep your wits about you. Yeah?"

"I know you are, and I'll keep it under advisement." He brought his fingers up to his head as if to tip an imaginary hat. "Keep off those feet."

"Yes, sir."

Crash smiled at her and headed to the front door.

"What was that all about?" Cade asked, confused.

"Nothing." Beth waved off the question and got back to his earlier statement about the alarm. "Cade, I *do* feel safe here. The first thing you did was teach me how to get out of the house just in case, and that's what saved me. They were talking about what they'd do to me if I was here…I didn't have any place to hide. So you teaching me about the tree saved me from that."

Obviously not believing her, Cade replied, "I'm very thankful you got out of the house, but I'm still pissed you had to do it in the first place. I'll be here when the alarm is installed in two days, I don't want you feeling weird having strangers in the house. But this is a top-of-the-line model. It can be connected to our tablets and laptops so it can be accessed and monitored from anywhere. They'll teach you how to activate the alarm and—"

"Cade, I'm a hacker. I think I can figure out the mechanics of the alarm, especially once they put the software on my laptop. Thank God they didn't have time to grab it when they were scooping up other stuff. In fact, I'll probably tinker with the alarm and make it even better once they're gone."

"Oh, yeah…I forgot."

"You forgot I was a hacker?"

"Yeah."

"I love you."

"Um…thanks. I love you back."

Seeing his confusion over her enthusiastic response to him forgetting about her computer skills, Beth rushed to explain. "Thanks for seeing the good in me past all my issues. I know I'm not a peach to live with. As Dr. Neal said, I'll probably always be nervous out in public. I'm getting better, even I can see that, and I might even be able to make it to that softball game sooner or later, but trips to Disney will never be something I can stomach. Maybe even Walmart. I haven't even tried to tackle that one yet."

"And you don't need to. There are plenty of other places we can shop."

"I know, but that's not the point. The point is that you make me feel safe. I figured it out while I was in Pennsylvania. Not my apartment. Not your house. Not the lighter and fire, not even my computer. You."

"But you were alone today and I wasn't here with you."

"But you *were* there," Beth tried to explain. "While I was hiding and trying not to hyperventilate I thought about my 'safe place.' It's what Dr. Neal taught me. When I get stressed out and uncertain, I'm supposed to visualize my safe place. For some it's the beach. For others it's a lake or some other physical place that holds good memories for them. For me? It's in your arms. All I had to do was close my eyes and imagine your arms around me and I felt safe. I swear I could almost feel the heat of your body surrounding me and your heartbeat against my cheek as you held me while I was hiding. I knew you'd come. The tree was a poor substitute for your body, but it allowed me to hold on until you came and found me."

Cade pulled Beth into his arms, not even thinking about his sister and friends still wandering around his house. He opened his mouth to speak, but Beth beat him to it.

"I'm sorry about the fire thing. I never got a chance to apologize. It was stupid, and if I'd hurt someone else with one of the fires I'd set, I would've felt horrible about it. I know why you reacted like you did and you were perfectly justified. I swear I won't go there again. Ever."

"You won't need to. I've got your back, Beth. Always."

"Are you guys good here?"

They looked up and saw Hayden gazing down at them. She had a weird look on her face, and Beth couldn't read it. She almost looked sad...and that was an emotion Beth hadn't ever seen on the tough deputy's face in all the time she'd known her. She was always the bad-ass, show-no-emotion cop.

"We're good," Cade answered matter-of-factly.

"Okay, then I'll let Quint do his thing. I'm glad you're all right, Beth. I swear to God I don't know what it is with trees and women saving themselves, but I'm glad you had the fortitude to get out of the house and to safety. I'll see you later, Sledge."

After she'd turned around and left, Beth turned to Cade. "Is she going to be okay?"

He looked at the door Hayden had disappeared through. "Yeah. She's Hayden. She's as tough as steel, nothing bothers her. I suppose running in the woods behind my house reminded her a bit of when Corrie saved herself." He shrugged.

"Did Hayden seem sad to you?"

"Hayden's never sad."

"Cade. She seemed unhappy," Beth repeated more firmly.

"Okay, I believe you. But right now I'm more concerned about you. I'm thinking you need a shower…and maybe a nap."

Beth smiled up at the man she loved more than anything else in the world. "Yeah, I think you're right. But I don't think I should be left alone."

"It's a good thing I have some free time and can chaperone you then."

It was longer than either of them wanted before everyone left. But as soon as they did, Cade carried Beth up the stairs into their bedroom. After a hot shower, which ended up being a whole lot shorter than Beth had expected, Cade hastily dried them both off and helped her into the bedroom. The covers were already thrown back from when she'd exited the bed earlier that morning in a hurry.

"I need you, Beth." Cade's words were heartfelt and desperate. "But I don't want to hurt you."

"You won't. I'm ready for you. I need you inside me."

Cade had done his best to get Beth wet while they were in the shower, and now he eased inside her, sighed in relief at how ready for him she was. He pushed all the way until his cock was completely surrounded by her wet heat and balanced himself on his hands as he looked down on the best thing that had ever happened to him.

"I love you, Elizabeth Parkins. I love you just the way you are…warts and all."

He felt her spasm against his hard length and held her eyes as he drew back and pushed back inside her.

"I love you too, even though I don't have any warts," she teased. "Thank you for coming home early to find me."

"I'll do my best to always be there when you need me." Cade came up on his haunches, not losing his connection with her in the process. He shifted her hips higher onto his lap. His hands were now free to roam her body as he kept his thrusts slow and steady, building her up higher and higher.

Neither spoke as he continued to love her. Cade used his hands to caress her breasts and pinch both of her nipples as he ground himself against her. She moaned and hitched her legs higher on his thighs, and he felt her heels digging into his ass. He kept his pace steady even as Beth writhed under him.

Feeling his sac draw up in readiness for his own orgasm, Cade moved one hand to where they were joined. He found the small bundle of nerves peeking out from under its protective hood and, using her own wetness to lubricate his thumb, rubbed it hard. She almost broke away from his grasp as she bucked under him, surging up as her orgasm hit.

Cade watched, gritting his teeth as Beth lost herself in the pleasure he was giving her. She was absolutely beautiful. He drew out her orgasm by continuing to stroke her sensitive clit. He felt her hips jerk and she groaned as she had another small orgasm. Finally, as she began to settle, Cade put both hands by her shoulders and leaned over her, forcing her legs wider as he changed positions. He waited until her eyes opened and she looked up at him.

"You are beautiful."

She was still breathing hard, but she gasped out, "Fuck me, Cade."

Her permission was what he'd been waiting for. He pulled back and slammed into her, sliding easily through the wetness generated by her orgasms. He did it again. Then again, not slowing down. It was fucking at its finest, and he couldn't remember ever being more turned on.

Cade couldn't keep eye contact with Beth anymore and threw his head back as he felt the come boiling up from his balls. Her hands pinching his nipples were the impetus he needed to throw him over the ledge.

"Jesus fuuuuuck," he groaned out as he buried

himself to the hilt inside her and came. It was a couple of moments before he realized he was shaking. Beth had wrung him out, and he'd never felt better in his entire life.

Easing himself down, but careful to take most of his weight on his elbows, Cade kissed Beth, hard. He devoured her mouth even as he felt her inner muscles clenching around him, trying to prolong his pleasure. Her hands were on his back, clutching him to her.

Cade drew back an inch, just enough to look her in the eyes. "The next time you need to imagine your safe place, this is what I want you to see. Remember the feel of me inside you, remember how protected you are right here in our bed."

Tears gathered in her eyes, alarming Cade. His Beth wasn't a crier. She hadn't cried today, and if that didn't make her cry, he wasn't sure what was causing it now. "Oh shit, don't do that. I didn't mean to upset you."

She sniffed and controlled her tears. "You didn't upset me. This *is* my safe place. With you. Under you. With you in me, on me. I love you, Cade."

Cade eased his upper body to the side, trying to stay connected to her. They both huffed out a disappointed breath when his softening flesh slipped out of her soaked sheath.

"I hate losing you," Beth said drowsily.

"That's my least favorite part of making love to you," Cade agreed.

"You didn't use a condom," Beth noted.

"Nope."

Beth chuckled. "What if I'm not on the pill?"

"Then I guess we'd better get married so you don't have my child out of wedlock."

Beth pushed up to look at Cade in surprise. She wasn't able to read his tone. "Um...I *am* on the pill, Cade."

"Darn." He smiled gently at her. "Beth, I love you. I want to marry you. I know this has been fast, and we've got some stuff to work through, but you should probably know, I talked to David when I was in Pennsylvania."

"What? When?"

"Before you were discharged. I wanted his approval to ask you to marry me."

Beth's brow wrinkled in confusion. "You asked David? Why not my dad?"

"Honestly? I knew your brother would be the harder sell. He loves you. He wants what's best for you. Oh, I'm sure your dad does too, but you're David's little sister. He's protected you his entire life and he'll always have your back. He's the one I wanted to make sure was okay with us getting hitched."

Beth flopped her head back to the pillow dramatically. "I can't believe this. How did we go from having the best sex ever, to talking about contraception, to you...wait, did you just propose?"

"What would your answer be if I said yes, that's exactly what I just did?"

"I'd say you're crazy." Beth must've seen the focused

look on his face, because she whispered, "You're serious."

"Don't move." Cade untangled his limbs from hers and scooted to the side of the bed before heading out of their room, bare-ass naked. He returned a minute later and pulled Beth to a sitting position in the middle of the bed. He lowered himself in front of her, spreading his legs, putting one on either side of her hips, ignoring the fact that he was naked and open to her in every way.

He held out a diamond ring between them, noticing vaguely how shiny it looked in the light of day.

"Elizabeth Parkins. I love you. You are the strongest, most stubborn, delicious, snarky woman I've ever met, and I want to spend the rest of my life making sure you're happy, safe, comfortable, and protected. I'll move heaven and earth to give you what you need. I'm sure we'll fight. We'll have to work on meshing our schedules since you like to stay up all night like a vampire and I like to actually sleep during those night-time hours like a normal person."

He smiled so she'd know he was kidding. The blank look on her face was freaking him out a little bit, but he hurried to complete the proposal he'd spent so much time trying to perfect.

"I'm going to make mistakes—'cause I'm a guy, and it's what we do—but I'll love you forever. I promise never to force you to do anything you don't want to do, and I'll be by your side, cheering you on when you need it and carrying you when you can't make it on your own. Will you marry me?"

Beth looked at the man sitting before her. On the surface he looked calm, cool, and collected, but with a second glance she could see how worried he was. His jaw was clenched and when she put one hand on his knee next to her hip, she could feel his muscles jerk under her touch.

She looked down at the beautiful ring he was holding up between them. It was platinum with a large princess-cut diamond front and center. On each side of the diamond was a smaller square ruby. He hurried to explain his choice of ring.

"The diamond is because it's traditional. The rubies are fire. One for me, and one for you. I hope to God you don't need the flames to help you feel safe anymore, but I wanted to give you two to carry with you wherever you go, so you know I'll fight your demons for you from here on out."

"Yes."

Cade didn't say a word, simply stared at her.

Beth licked her lips. "Did you hear me?"

"You'll marry me?"

"Of course. You're my safe place. How can I get through my panic attacks without making you mine officially?"

Cade lunged for Beth and pulled her to him, lying back until she was straddling him. "I love you. God, you have no idea."

"I have a little idea," Beth said with a smile, shifting

over him, feeling his hardening length under her. Feeling the evidence of their previous lovemaking smearing over his hardness as she shifted, reminded her of the other conversation they needed to continue.

"As I said, I'm on the pill, Cade. I went on it after I was abducted. I was so messed up, the last thing I wanted was to accidentally get pregnant."

Correctly identifying the question behind Cade's confused look, Beth quickly went on. "You're the first person I've been with since it happened, but I think deep down I was afraid that if I'd been raped once, it could happen again. My paranoia and all of that. So I wanted to be sure that if it did, I wouldn't have to worry about a child."

"When, and if, we decide to have kids, we'll have the discussion together, okay? When you're ready. We've got time. But I have to say…I'm fucking thrilled I get to mark you as mine every time we make love now," Cade said in a husky voice.

Beth rolled her eyes and brought a hand down between their bodies to caress him. "You're a Neanderthal."

"When it comes to you, yup. When I said I'd protect you, Beth. I meant in all things. Protecting your womb from being fertilized before you're ready is just one of those things. If you want me to wear a condom, I will."

"I like this," Beth told him honestly, releasing him long enough to scoop up some of their come from between her legs and using it to lubricate his hard length.

"Fuck, that is so sexy."

"Maybe not so much when we want to have a quickie though. Running down my leg or soaking my panties isn't very comfortable."

"I have to admit, I've never really thought about it before," Cade said, arching into her touch as she continued to caress him.

"Not something many guys think about. Besides, if you have sex with a condom, it's not an issue."

Cade flipped Beth to her back without warning, startling a girly shriek from her mouth. "Give me your left hand."

She did, and watched as Cade slid the beautiful ring down her finger until it rested at the base. "Fucking gorgeous. Fire and Ice." He slid down her body, making room for himself between her legs and holding her open to his gaze.

"Cade! What are you—"

Beth didn't finish her sentence before his mouth was on her. It was obvious he loved their combined taste, because he spent an inordinate amount of time licking, sucking, and cleaning her. When she was on the verge of another orgasm, Cade lay back. "Climb on, Beth. Fuck me."

She immediately did as he asked, not caring that he had an unfettered view of her body as she rose over him. She took hold of him and guided him to where she needed him the most. Beth sank down to the hilt and they both groaned.

She leaned backward and arched her back, pushing

her breasts up into the air, and rested her hands on his upper thighs, smiling as she rode him, knowing he could see every inch of her. She felt truly happy for the first time in a long time. Memories of Ben Hurst and what he'd done to her were fading quickly, and she had more confidence in herself after being able to go outside alone. She wasn't going to worry about the break-in. Cade and his friends would take care of it —and her.

"Beth Turner. I like the sound of that."

"Oh shit, sweetheart," Cade swore, sitting up quickly, holding Beth in place as he changed position. She was now sitting on his lap, and while she didn't have the leverage to pump up and down on him because of his tight hold, she could still squirm and pull at his cock with her inner muscles. Even though he'd recently come, Beth felt Cade jerk inside her as he exploded.

She quickly snaked a hand between them and flicked at her clit roughly, and with only a few hard passes, she joined him, moaning at how good he felt inside her as she orgasmed.

They held each other for long moments afterward, panting and replete.

"I love you, Cade. So much."

"Back at'cha future Mrs. Beth Turner. Back at'cha."

EPILOGUE

HAYDEN CLOSED her apartment door behind her with a sigh. She dropped her keys on the table next to the door and headed down the hall to her room. The small two-bedroom apartment was sparse. She had some pictures of her parents in the main room, there were a few paintings on the walls, but there weren't any of the typical girly things to be seen anywhere in the main part of her space.

No frilly pillows, no flowers on the kitchen counter. The apartment didn't smell like any frou-frou air freshener. If someone looked in her kitchen, they'd find a lot of pre-packaged meals, canned soup, and not much in the refrigerator except condiments and maybe some string cheese.

Hayden ignored everything; her only thought was for a nice hot shower. Opening the door, she was already stripping off her uniform. The sheriff's deputy badge she wore was taken off and dropped on her dresser; the bulletproof vest was un-Velcroed and dropped on the floor. The utility belt she wore around her waist was unbuckled and placed on the carpet by the shower, where she left it without a thought.

She unbuttoned and unzipped her brown uniform pants and leaned into the shower stall and turned it on. Hayden blinked back her tears and hurried to strip off her clothes, leaving them in a pile on the tile before stepping over the tub and into the spray of hot water.

She huddled under the water, letting it pound against her shoulders as her head drooped.

It'd been a hell of a day. As many days went, it was interspersed with bouts of extreme adrenaline-inducing fear and excitement, and hours of boredom and routine police work. But it was thinking about the love between her friends and their women that had done Hayden in.

It was an amazing thing. The love Dax and Mack, Cruz and Mickie, Quint and Corrie, Wes and Laine, and now Cade and Beth had for each other was true. If she wasn't so cynical, she would've said they were all soul mates who had somehow found each other in the big bad world. Oh, she'd read about it in the romance books she secretly devoured, but hadn't thought it actually existed. She thought it was something that dried-up, sexually frustrated, frumpy romance writers dreamed up in their lonely heads.

How wrong she'd been. Hell, the romance authors who wrote her favorite stories were most likely having sex way more than she was. They had to get their inspiration from somewhere, right?

Hayden shakily brought her hands up to her hair and smoothed it back as the hot water continued to beat down on her. That kind of love had eluded Hayden her entire life. As a kid, a teenager, a college student, and even as an adult. She'd had her fill of boyfriends, even some she could've loved...if they'd given her half a chance. But not once had *she* evoked that kind of emotion from another human being.

She'd eavesdropped a bit tonight on Beth and Cade and their obvious love, despite the fact the challenges they'd faced in the past, and that they'd certainly face in the future, were overwhelming. It was apparent that Cade didn't care one whit about Beth's illness. To him, it wasn't a big deal. She was amazing and perfect.

Hayden thought back to when they'd found Corrie after she'd been kidnapped and everyone realized she'd climbed a huge tree to hide from the assholes after her. Quint had turned to look at Hayden as she was about to climb up that tree and said, "Be careful." Hayden had gotten a glimpse of what it might be like to have a man worry about her.

But then Quint had continued. He'd said, "Be careful, she means the world to me."

She should've known Quint wasn't telling *her* to be careful, because he'd been worried about Corrie, and not her. She was Deputy Sheriff Hayden Yates, no one worried about her.

Hayden took a deep breath and quickly washed her

hair, and then poured some body gel over her shower poof and scrubbed her body. She rinsed and turned off the water. She grabbed a towel and briskly ran it over herself, hanging it back on the rack when she was done. Standing naked at the sink, she brushed her teeth and swished some mouthwash before spitting it into the basin.

She strode out of the bathroom with large strides, which had been called manly on more than one occasion, and threw back the comforter on her bed. The main space in her apartment might not have a speck of girly in it, but her bedroom was a different story. It was the one place where she always felt as though she could be herself. The sheets were one-thousand count and luxurious against her naked body. Her comforter was pink and flowery and was almost obnoxiously feminine. Her room was her safe place, and she needed that right now.

Hayden snuggled down and held her childhood stuffed animal tight to her chest. It was a pink elephant that had seen better days. The fur had been worn off long ago and the stuffing had been replaced several times. Ellie the Elephant's trunk had been sewed back on awkwardly more than once. Hayden had never shown anyone her prized possession, knowing it wouldn't fit their perception of her. Tough. Competent. Tomboy.

She choked back a sob and buried her head in Ellie's soft body, thinking back on everything that had happened over the last several months. Seeing the way

Cade gazed at Beth and didn't see someone who was afraid of walking outside, but instead saw the amazing woman she was inside. And seeing Quint and his obvious love for Corrie, his relief when she was safe and the looks on their faces as they'd held each other tight after Hayden had helped her out of the tree...

Hayden's sad, lonely words rang out in the empty room, with no one to hear them but her.

"Just once, I'd like someone to be afraid of losing *me*."

* * *

Be sure to get the next book in the Badge of Honor: Texas Heroes Series, Hayden's story, in *Justice for Boone*. AVAILABLE NOW!

And if you're interested in reading about Summer and Mozart and to see what happened to Elizabeth in California, pick up *Protecting Summer*!

Would you like Susan's Book Protecting Caroline for FREE?
Click HERE

JOIN my Newsletter and find out about sales, free

books, contests and new releases before anyone else!!
Click HERE

Want to know when my books go on sale? Follow me
on Bookbub HERE!

Justice for Boone
Badge of Honor: Texas Heroes, Book 6

Sheriff's Deputy Hayden Yates has worked hard to gain
the respect and admiration of her fellow law
enforcement officers. She's succeeded so well, in fact,
that she's become just one of the guys. As her friends
slowly begin to meet their soul mates, Hayden longs to
be seen as a desirable woman, and not the tomboy she's
always been.

No slouch when it comes to attracting the opposite sex,
cowboy Boone Hatcher might want to give it a rest for
a while, especially after his last girlfriend accuses him
of domestic abuse. Deputy Yates sees right through his
ex's ruse—and Boone sees right through Deputy Yates.
Hayden might seem all business, but her need for
justice comes from a heart that beats with pure
passion.

A few dates turn into something more, and as the
couple's relationship deepens, so do the threats from
his ex. It's up to Hayden to convince Boone the danger

is real...before jealous antics escalate to deadly obsession.

** *Justice for Boone* is the 6th book in the Badge of Honor: Texas Heroes Series. Each book is a stand-alone, with no cliffhanger endings.

Also by Susan Stoker

Badge of Honor: Texas Heroes Series

Justice for Mackenzie
Justice for Mickie
Justice for Corrie
Justice for Laine (novella)
Shelter for Elizabeth
Justice for Boone
Shelter for Adeline
Shelter for Sophie
Justice for Erin
Justice for Milena
Shelter for Blythe
Justice for Hope
Shelter for Quinn
Shelter for Koren
Shelter for Penelope

Delta Team Two Series

Shielding Gillian
Shielding Kinley (Aug 2020)
Shielding Aspen (Oct 2020)
Shielding Riley (Jan 2021)
Shielding Devyn (May 2021)
Shielding Ember (Sept 2021)
Shielding Sierra (TBA)

Delta Force Heroes Series

Rescuing Rayne
Rescuing Aimee (novella)
Rescuing Emily
Rescuing Harley
Marrying Emily (novella)
Rescuing Kassie
Rescuing Bryn
Rescuing Casey
Rescuing Sadie (novella)
Rescuing Wendy
Rescuing Mary
Rescuing Macie (novella)

SEAL of Protection: Legacy Series

Securing Caite
Securing Brenae (novella)
Securing Sidney
Securing Piper
Securing Zoey
Securing Avery (May 2020)
Securing Kalee (Sept 2020)
Securing Jane (Feb 2021)

SEAL Team Hawaii Series

Finding Elodie (Apr 2021)
Finding Lexie (Aug 2021)
Finding Kenna (Oct 2021)
Finding Monica (TBA)
Finding Carly (TBA)
Finding Ashlyn (TBA)

Ace Security Series

Claiming Grace
Claiming Alexis
Claiming Bailey
Claiming Felicity
Claiming Sarah

Mountain Mercenaries Series

Defending Allye
Defending Chloe
Defending Morgan
Defending Harlow
Defending Everly
Defending Zara
Defending Raven (June 2020)

Silverstone Series

Trusting Skylar (Dec 2020)
Trusting Taylor (Mar 2021)
Trusting Molly (July 2021)
Trusting Cassidy (Dec 2021

SEAL of Protection Series

Protecting Caroline
Protecting Alabama
Protecting Fiona
Marrying Caroline (novella)
Protecting Summer
Protecting Cheyenne
Protecting Jessyka

Protecting Julie (novella)
Protecting Melody
Protecting the Future
Protecting Kiera (novella)
Protecting Alabama's Kids (novella)
Protecting Dakota

Stand Alone
The Guardian Mist
Nature's Rift
A Princess for Cale
A Moment in Time- A Collection of Short Stories
Lambert's Lady

Special Operations Fan Fiction
http://www.AcesPress.com

Beyond Reality Series
Outback Hearts
Flaming Hearts
Frozen Hearts

Writing as Annie George:
Stepbrother Virgin (erotic novella)

ABOUT THE AUTHOR

New York Times, USA Today and *Wall Street Journal* Bestselling Author Susan Stoker has a heart as big as the state of Texas where she lives, but this all American girl has also spent the last fourteen years living in Missouri, California, Colorado, and Indiana. She's married to a retired Army man who now gets to follow *her* around the country.

She debuted her first series in 2014 and quickly followed that up with the SEAL of Protection Series, which solidified her love of writing and creating stories readers can get lost in.

If you enjoyed this book, or any book, please consider leaving a review. It's appreciated by authors more than you'll know.

www.stokeraces.com

susan@stokeraces.com

Made in the USA
Monee, IL
06 April 2022

94214326R00177